Mountain Melodies

By

Elizabeth

Wilmoth Solazzo

To
Best
Enjoy
Elizabeth
Solazzo
8/31/99

Cover art

by

Carolyn Teague

With Special Thanks

Also by Elizabeth Wilmoth Solazzo

Saxapahaw - Once a Mill Village, stories

Chasing the Wind, collection of short stores

Saxapahaw Girl, collection of personal essays

A Little Book of Stories, collection of personal essays

Dedication Page

To My Family above all

A special thank you to my 'Story Sisters', Doris, Jan, Sally and Brenda for their recommendations and encouragement.

Other writing friends from the Burlington Writers Club were also instrumental in editing and proofreading.

To my early readers, much, much thanks. Doris Caruso, Nikki King, Patsy Rohrer, Andrea Nider-Schlau and Peter Schlau - all errors that remain are entirely my own.

KATIE
November 1999

Chapter 1

D r. Katie Cook turned her dusty red jeep off Highway 25E and roared up the ridge, her four wheel drive taking the hills and curves without effort. It was a warm autumn day, with leaves swirling in the light breeze, sunshine blazing through the thinning trees lining the side of the dirt and gravel road. She slowed and lowered her window to take in the fresh mountain air, a sharp scent of wood smoke lingering in the air, probably from an early morning wood fire. She heard the crunch of leaves and gravel under her tires. One switchback after another brought her higher up the ridge. She didn't usually make house calls but Lovey was a special patient.

Lovey Lephew lived alone in a mostly log cabin built on rich bottom land down by the Clinch river. She had been born in the last hour of the last year of the nineteenth century and would celebrate her 100th birthday soon. Admiration for her strong spirit had nurtured a fast friendship between Katie and the old midwife. Katie checked in on her often. Mainly just to visit and hear some of her wild stories. The old woman had been a close friend to Katie's own grandmother, now long gone.

Newly licensed to practice medicine, Katie moved to Tazewell, Tennessee from Chapel Hill, North Carolina and hung a shingle outside an old medical office along Main Street. There hadn't been a licensed doctor in town for many years and most residents drove the thirty miles to Morristown for medical care or even to Knoxville, almost an hour away. Katie was determined to change that and had smiled and chatted her way through many dry chicken dinners at community pot lucks and church suppers throughout the long summer. The process seemed helpful in rounding up patients. After six months the practice was growing but was still slow enough to allow an occasional afternoon away.

This small mountain community didn't readily accept strangers and she struggled to make friends even with her deep family roots here. Her grandparents, Buddy and Betty Wolfe, were once well-known residents in Tazewell when they lived at the base of Clinch Mountain and her granddaddy preached at Raven Ridge Church. Katie had spent quiet summers roaming the hills and valleys and exploring old caves hidden inside the mountains. She felt more alive here and always dreamed she would return.

Each time she drove up the ridge, she noticed more open spaces with grassy green lawns replacing the forest. New brick houses sprouted like alfalfa grass after a spring rain. Despite that, the landscape was striking in its remoteness.

Near the top of the ridge, she slowed at the Riley farm and made a sharp turn past her small rented home onto a single dirt lane named Lower Caney Valley Road. It would take her back down to the Clinch river. Bumping over a small planked bridge covering the shallow creek, she saw jersey cows standing in the swollen water of a creek-bed that ran along the road. She zipped around an old graveyard on the hill, with neglected tombs leaning like dominos. A canopy of red, orange and golden leaves hung above her, dappling the sunlight as she descended further into the cove.

Muddy tracks led off the road to nooks and crannies where hidden homes nestled in the rocky terrain. Houses were few along this stretch of road and the trees were giants, undisturbed since the logging boom of the early 1920's. Shifting into low gear, Katie let the jeep roll forward.

Lovely Olia Lephew, called Lovey by most, lived alone in a log home built of chestnut wood. It was strong and weathered like its occupant. Katie parked the jeep at the side of the house, stepped out and walked the short distance to the water's edge. River water rushed against its banks, high from recent rains, offering a thump and bounce of melodies from its steady flow. The water had stopped just short of flooding the yard.

Majestic oak and birch trees shaded part of the fast-flowing muddy river. A small motor boat appeared from a nearby cove and raced by, leaving the sharp smell of gasoline in its wake. Katie watched as it moored across the river and two men hopped out and climbed the steep bank. There was nothing over there but woods and an old family cemetery but people hiked there. Katie knew most folks on the ridge now but didn't recognize these two.

Lovey came up behind her, carrying a shotgun, as the men reappeared and started down the bank. The small woman raised the gun, sighted it toward the opposite river bank and let loose with a quick volley of shots. Both women watched as the boys jumped in their boat, cut the rope and fired up the engine. Miss Lovey hooted as the boat came to life. "I can take care of myself, Katie. Always have and always will."

She walked back toward her cabin and Katie stared after her, speechless. She felt weak in the knees and her ears were ringing. As the smoke cleared, she followed.

Chapter 2

Katie and Lovey shared an old settee in the small front room of the log cabin as if nothing had happened. The sofa had elaborately carved legs and arms, as well as a scrolled back with a cushioned seat. Katie worried she might break this fragile piece of antique furniture but Lovey always brought Katie to sit here. The furniture was antique but felt solid. Neither of them spoke and the room was quiet, with just the whisper of a low fire burning in the fireplace. Embroidered pillows leaned in the corner of the sofa to one side of Katie. One wall above the fireplace held a gallery of photographs, some in color but most in black and white, in a wild mixture of frames. Lovey often took down pictures of her grown daughters and their families, and one daughter who had died young, but today there was no sound as they waited for the local sheriff to arrive.

Katie had insisted she call although her friend didn't think it was necessary at all. She hadn't even had a house phone until recently. As they waited for the sheriff's arrival, Lovey served cake and coffee. An apple stack cake, light and tasty along with strong black coffee, cleared Katie's mind and settled her nerves, at least enough so her hands no longer shook. Finishing the snack, she stood and walked to the window.

"It'll take him a spell to get out here, Katie. But those hoodlums won't be back anytime soon." She chuckled. "Did you see how they scurried down that hill?"

Katie turned back to the old woman. She was a tough old bird. Where did that kind of grit come from?

A black and white patrol car sped into the lane and parked behind Katie's jeep. She watched as a tall, trim man with broad shoulders exited the car and walked to the door. She met him there before he knocked. "Please, come in," she said, opening the door wide and stepping back.

He offered a hand. "Sheriff Bobby Lane, miss."

Katie took his hand and then the card he offered. He came inside the room as she studied the card. He brought the outdoor scent of fresh pine in with him, along with a clean soapy smell. He was clean shaven, had a strong chin and his head was covered with a riot of dark brown curls. His hand shake was firm and his height commanded attention.

"Hey there, Miss Lovey. What have you done now?" He went to her where she sat on the sofa and squatted to her level before he offered a friendly hand.

"You know I can take care of myself, Bobby. I shot at some trespassers across the river and they scattered like cats caught stealing fresh cream off a bucket of milk." She cackled. "I've seen them come and go a few times, likely up to no good. My mama's buried over there on the top of that hill. Nobody should be over there."

The sheriff hid a smile with his cough as he stood. "You were within your rights, ma'am. But we've had some problems with drugs growing in the county and some of these people can be dangerous."

"Pooh. No worse than in my day. But I think I scared my young friend here. Have you met the new doc in town? She opened a medical clinic on Main Street."

He turned to meet her gaze. "No, I haven't met her but I've heard we have a new clinic. The Sheriff's office is at the south end of Broad Street, less than a block around the corner from you."

"I rent a small house at the top of the hill and Lovey allows me to hike around her place. Photographing old crumbling structures is a hobby. Stone fences fascinate me and I always wonder about the people who built them."

"You must be the tenant at the old Riley homeplace? You seem familiar to me, though. Not sure why."

"My father brought me here every summer to visit his parents and show me the real USA, as he always said. I loved it here."

"Maybe our paths crossed sometime or the other."

Deep dark eyes moved up and down her athletic frame and he all but nodded his approval at her muscular legs. She regretted the running shorts she had put on when she left the clinic. They offered a better view of her long legs than she usually allowed. His wide mouth curved into a confident smile. Was he one of those guys who thought every woman he met would fall all over him.

He smiled at her and she felt a little skip of breath. Wow, he was a good-looking man. And immediately she looked at those big capable hands and spotted a gold band. All the good ones were taken already.

"And you make house calls too?"

She raised her gaze from his hand to find him staring at her with a question in those dark brown eyes with a circle of gold surrounding them.

Katie looked back to the sofa, over to the fireplace, the pictures on the wall, and around the room. Anywhere but into that handsome smile. "No, not really. Miss Lovey and I are friends. We sit by the river or here at the hearth and she tells me the stories of her life and the history of Claiborne County." She was chattering and wondered if her face had betrayed her with a blush. It felt warm.

He looked back to the old woman with warm affection and Katie was relieved to escape that penetrating gaze. She took a shallow breath and stepped across the room, putting distance between them.

"I bet you do have some interesting stories to tell, Miss Lovey."

Lovey smiled back at the young man, preening at his attention. "There are stories from these old hills that might raise the hair on your head, son. Come on by sometime and I'll spin a few yarns for you." She moved to stand up. "Now, can I get you some coffee and cake?"

Sheriff Lane pulled out a little notebook and began to write up a report of the incident. "No, keep your seat. No cake today. This visit's official. I'll get a boat and go over to see what those fellows are up to. Probably just some local boys who have a small crop of pot growing. It's become a real problem here with so much vegetation to cover for the marijuana plants.

He took descriptions of the men and Lovey described the boat in detail. "It was a runabout, about 22 feet long, white with blue trim, powered by an outboard motor."

Katie walked the sheriff out to his car. The sun was still high in the sky and it was warm by the lane. "Thanks for coming. Do you think she's safe here alone?"

"I wouldn't worry about Miss Lovey. She really can take care of herself and I'm shocked if these are local boys. People around here know to steer clear of her."

Katie watched as he drove away, thinking how nice it would be to find someone like him to come home to at night after what she dreamed soon would be long days of work in the clinic. She watched the dust settle from his car on the dirt lane and then went back inside. Although Miss Lovey had been calm and cool while firing her weapon and talking to the sheriff, Katie worried she might show some adverse effects from all of the excitement. She brought her medical bag in and convinced her friend to allow a quick check of her vitals. Her blood pressure was a bit higher than usual but still in a normal range. It amazed Katie that the woman took no prescription medicine at her age. She had grown to care about her quite a bit.

"I should go if I'm to get a hike in. Promise you'll take it easy this afternoon."

"I ain't got nothing pushing. I'll sit here, put my feet up and dream about the past until supper. Does that suit you, young lady doctor?" She giggled like a little girl.

Standing over her, Katie patted her hand. "Yes ma'am. Perfectly."

"But I could tell you some things about that young sheriff before you go if you want." Her teasing expression promised mischief as she leaned back and closed her eyes.

Katie felt her face flush. Had her interest been that transparent? She screwed up her face and cocked her head to the side. "He's married. That's all I need to know." But she did sit back down on the old settee.

Deep laughter sang out like music in the warm room. "Things ain't always what they seem, Katie girl."

LOVEY
Spring 1918

Chapter 3

Lovey Lephew gazed at the greening of the distant ridges, blinking slowly in the early morning light like a black bear coming out of its winter hibernation. The spring awakening made her young heart ache with joy at the stark beauty of her mountains. She loved the isolated valley of her home with her granny who had mostly raised her while her own mum worked for other families. She had no prospects for much of a future here.

Granny said she dreamed too much. At seventeen, it was well past time to find a man and set up housekeeping. Slashing rain and flash floods had nurtured the dormant plants now coming alive around their cabin. The rains had forced Lovey to stay inside the past week but today the morning offered a promise of sunshine behind lingering dark clouds sweeping across the sky. New buds on the dogwood trees and the green stems of daffodils pushing through the mud along the path announced that spring had arrived in the Appalachian Mountains. Spring brought hope. To the poor dirt farmers who called this area home, it couldn't arrive early enough. Many neighbors up and down Raven Ridge had struggled to survive the bitter winter with the root vegetables in the cellar and whatever meager stores were packed away in the smokehouse.

Lovey felt the sun grow warmer on her back, penetrating her frayed gray sweater, as she made her way down the sloping path to fill two tin buckets from the natural spring. Snow melt from higher land trickled along the rocks by the path as it flowed downward into a clear pool to join cold spring water raging from the gap in the split rock near the bottom of the hill. The loud cascade falling into the river below competed with a chorus of blackbirds. In the clear morning air, she heard Ned Singleton's cow bawling to be milked from a mile down the ridge.

Water flowed strong and steady this morning. She lowered the first bucket under the gap and filled it. Shifting to set it on the bank and retrieve the other, one foot slipped sideways in the mud, and she fell on her backside. As she tried to stand, she instead slid down the steep bank on her rump, bouncing high into the air as her body turned before flying backwards into the Clinch River below. Squeals echoed in the crisp morning air before she went under the murky water. The iciness of the river on this March morning quickly stole her breath as she struggled against the onslaught of roaring rapids that had appeared mild from the hilltop. She was sucked under. When her face next broke the surface, she began to stroke out with her skinny arms, a sliver of alarm rising in her throat.

The shore was close and the river not very deep here but her arms thrashed against the cold water. She tried to swim back to shore but the bubbling rapids stopped any advancement. She took a ragged breath, each moment ticking slowly away as she swam hard without results. Panic rose as the swirling water twisted her body in circles like a ragdoll.

The roar of the water filled her head as she was pulled under the rushing river water for the third time. Pushing to the top of the dark water and back into the sunlight, her mind briefly cleared. Gulping air, she forced her body to go limp against the force of the rapids, and floated free into calmer water. The strong current carried her down river where she finally was able to swim to shore, her arms like rubber, her shallow breath frosting the air.

"Ugh…" she muttered, dragging herself out of the river, her fear fresh as the cold wind made her shiver. She dashed away the water running down her cold, red face and kicked at the soft ground. She brushed at the scratches on her legs where dots of blood bubbled.

"Hello?" she called, swinging her head back to search the top of the riverbank. "Anyone there?" Of course not. Only she and Granny lived on this section of the ridge and it was still early morning. She would have to pull herself up the steep hill covered with scraggly pines, downriver from the path where she had started.

Where was Prince Charming when you needed him? Standing for a moment with hands on hips, she gauged the best places to plant each foot to allow her to crawl up the bank. She was trembling. Icy cold water dripped from her sweater and skirt and she had to keep moving before she froze. She cautiously placed one foot forward, digging her boot into the mud before reaching for the next foothold, grabbing onto any small scrub or young tree she found to pull herself up and forward.

As her head topped the steep bank, and her foot searched for a final toehold, a large black dog ran from the nearby brush, barking. Her left foot started to slide below her and she dug her fingers into the ground, praying she could maintain her position. "Get back, go on," she screamed, hoping the animal was tame, despite his show of teeth.

She barely managed to hold her ground as the dog walked back and forth above her, growling, guarding his space. Fortunately, a man soon followed on the heels of the dog and rushed to help, leaning forward and reaching out to her over the high bank.

"Take my hand," he yelled, his words almost lost in the roar of the water from below and the frantic barking of the dog.

Lovey let go of the thin twig she held to and reached for the solid hand he offered. The man planted his feet and pulled her over the edge, where they both tumbled onto the ground before standing. Lovey was breathing hard, stringy hair hanging limply in her face and muddy clothing clinging to her slender body, but she straightened to her full height on quivering legs. Relief washed over her at being back on high ground. Wringing out her skirt, she tied it between shaking legs, ready to make a dash to the house. "Can you call off this mutt? He about pushed me back in the dang river."

"Bear, sit," the man commanded, and the dog immediately stopped barking, backed away and sat on his haunches, but still watched Lovey with narrowed eyelids.

"You all right?" he asked, offering her a rough blanket from the pack he had thrown on the ground. "Bear don't mean you no harm. He's just a young pup I picked up for my mama and I got to train him yet."

Lovey felt like a drowned muskrat. "I'll live but no thanks to that dog of yourn. If he ain't full growed yet – I don't want to see him when he is." She used a corner of the green blanket to rub at her face and hair before wrapping it around her shoulders. The addition of the blanket warmed her and she stared at the large furry dog where he sat obediently but alert at the feet of his owner. She looked at the stranger and wondered who he was as the remaining river water drained from her eyes. "I usually don't take a swim this time of year but it looks as if I'm none the worse for wear. Just cold."

Her breath was coming easier and her legs felt stronger under her. Her gaze narrowed as she studied the man. He was older than she – maybe forty - and not anyone she recognized from the ridge. His eyes were blue jets of mystery under a low-slung hat that sheltered his angular face.

As her body began to shake, he urged her home. "You better get inside and get out of those wet clothes. Here, take this blanket," he said, sweeping it more firmly around her shoulders. "Is that your cabin I passed at the top of the rise?"

"It is," she said. She ducked her head, blinking against those intense blue eyes that watched her. Her voice became softer. "I'm beholden to you for helping me, sir." She reached a slender hand forward but quickly pulled back as the warmth of his touch caused a tingle to race through her cold body. She turned to run for home, the rough wool blanket flying out behind her like a cape in the early morning mist.

Chapter 4

The next week, Lovey walked along the trail that followed the river bank, taking a jar of soup to the Widow Winstead, across the ridge. The old woman was a medicine woman of sorts who used herbs and potions to minister to the mountaineers. Talk around the ridge was a bad case of croup had laid her low and she was suffering something awful. People had claimed for years she was a witch because of her ability to heal with herbal medicine but Lovey figured she must not be other-worldly if she couldn't rid herself of this common little sickness.

Lovey had other motives for the visit. She meant to question the woman about the Epperson family, especially that John Epperson she had met at the river. The Eppersons lived on the opposite ridge – but they were never mentioned in her household. They lived at the top of the rise where Lovey would turn into the woods toward Granny's place in a hollow down by the river. It was time she knew what had caused this feud between the families.

Lovey's heart beat lightly as she skipped down the ridge. Warm sunshine peeked from behind the clouds. A good omen? She planted each foot firmly in the dried mud, as she came closer to the riverbank, remembering her recent splash in the water. She had pert near drowned in that icy river water and she didn't intend to fall in again. Shivering at the memory, she thought she might have dreamed the handsome stranger were it not for the physical evidence of the army issue blanket now folded across the bottom of her single bed and the all too real presence of the man at her father's home this past weekend.

Last week she had worked on her father's large farm alongside half siblings to get the fields ready for a new crop of 'baccer. Ocee Daniels had gone on to marry and have a mess of children after suffering rejection from Lovey's mum. Lovey's caring but somewhat distant relationship with her father didn't prevent the friendship and love she felt for his family.

Family and neighbors had finished the week of hard labor with a gathering to celebrate the beginning of the growing season. Delicious food and music and dance for all. It was a welcome break from their hard work, although the women helped in the fields as well as preparing the food and serving the men. That didn't seem fair somehow and Lovey wondered if she even wanted a husband at all.

There was a longing in her for something more. She didn't mind hard work but she dreamed of a tender lover to sweep her off her feet, like the fairy tales she had heard. Her laughter echoed across the open fields as she thought of herself as Cinderella, dressed up high and mighty and attending a ball. Her laughter caused a pair of mourning doves to take flight, their wings whistling as they flew south.

Trudging around the next bend at the little white church in the fork of the road, she stopped to catch her labored breath. She hoped Granny would attend the church service this week. The church had censured her daughter, Naomi when she refused marriage with Lovey's father and Granny still harbored some hard feelings. But Lovey liked to go to see her friends and neighbors.

She wore a blue flowered cotton dress this morning, with ribbons attached down the front and around the waist, cinched tight to accentuate her narrow frame. A warm, tightly crocheted shawl covered her boney shoulders and fended off the slight chill still in the air.

Lovey wanted to study nursing at Lincoln College, like a girl she knew from down in the valley but the Taylors were well to do so Jewell was afforded the opportunity to leave the farm for a year or two of school. Most mountain girls were like Lovey, desperately needed at home to help farm the land so as to eke out a living for the family. Granny owned half of Clinch Mountain but only worked a little crop of tobacco for some ready cash because she and Lovey couldn't handle more work.

Her land had come down through ancestors who first settled here after leaving Scotland behind many generations ago. She would never part with it. Granny also claimed a family line of French aristocrats who had to change their name and start anew. The land was too mountainous for much crop production but a joy to gaze upon. Granny Lephew was a proud woman who held tight to her land despite its hills and valleys and worked the kitchen garden like a man. Melinda Lephew was respected in the community.

Lately she had accepted a bit of help from Harold Davis who had quietly pursued Melinda in recent years. Lovey giggled at the thought of her Granny being romanced but reckoned Granny was still young enough for a beau at 56.

Her eyes blinked in the sudden brightness of the sun sailing from behind a fluffy cloud, only to watch it disappear as the quickly moving clouds once again blocked the light. Lovey gazed skyward, fascinated by the changing shapes of clouds, remembering a childhood game she played with her best friend Betty Jean. They had laid on the warm green grass of a newly mowed meadow in late summer, naming objects they saw in the clouds. Her friend accused Lovey of seeing things she couldn't possibly see, but she had merely laughed with secret pride at the mystical shapes she envisioned where hardly anything existed. Her granny said she might have the second sight that allowed her to see and know of events before others. Lovey didn't think she had any such gift as that but admitted she had some wild imaginings sometimes.

The squawk of a blue jay snapped her out of her fantasies. Granny would be anxious for her return after the incident in the river last week, but she lingered by the church, appreciating the faint shades of green that dotted the hillside above her, promising new life.

She started to climb the opposite ridge, her high-top boots dusty from the dirt road. She had accepted that her life was here with Granny and her mother, and maybe one day a husband and children, although that seemed less likely with each passing year. Her face creased with a smile as she skipped around the mountain this morning as light in spirit as if carried by fairies. It must be the spring weather creating her strange mood. Or maybe the chance to see John Epperson had brought this light step.

Lovey was of an age when most girls were married, as Granny reminded her often. Boys and men came to call regularly but Lovey hadn't seen anyone she wanted for keeps. During the long evenings of winter in front of the fire as they had pieced quilt-tops together, Lovey had dreamt of her future, with Granny telling her to keep her head out of the clouds. "You need to consider that young Autumn Wilmoth's proposal of marriage," Granny said. "You could do a lot worse, you know."

She hadn't refused but she hadn't agreed, either. Lovey didn't need to think about it, though. She knew the answer would be no, despite the pressure from Granny and her mother, Naomi, to make a good match.

She thought of Frank and Jim Hayes, who had acted fools over her for years, when everyone knew they were much too young for courting. That hadn't stopped the silly twins competing for a seat beside her at Raven Ridge Baptist Church on Sundays. She could hear Jim to this day, saying, "Here, Miss Lovey. I've saved you a seat on the back row." Then he flashed a sunny smile to convince her.

It was hard to believe he was gone, felled by a large chestnut tree that came down the wrong way last month on Lone Mountain. He had worked for the Weaver Logging Company which seemed determined to chop down every tree standing in the county. Jim would never experience this unspoiled mountainside again and Lovey felt desperate to drink in its beauty to make up for his lost life at just sixteen. But she refused to settle.

Lovey was determined to hold out for love and excitement for someone who also lived in these hills she loved. She knew she wanted something more from her life. Sometimes she wanted to leave this lonely valley behind and explore a different world that she knew existed beyond this narrow sliver of land that her mother and grandmother settled for much too easily.

She felt her face grow warm when she thought back to the mysterious man whose bold gaze had followed her around the picnic last Sunday at her father's home. Yet, he was much too old for her. Leaning lazily against a tree, one foot propped flat on the trunk behind him, his sultry gaze followed her every movement across the openness of the valley land as she helped her cousins lay out the food on a patchwork quilt that covered a wagon bed.

His crooked smile made her heart leap and she felt her pulse quicken as he coolly asked, "Have you recovered from your dip in the river?"

"I suppose I'm none the worse off – despite your horse of a dog," she snapped back. "What kind of dog is he to grow so big?"

"He's a Great Dane mixed with husky. The Great Dane part gives him his height." He put a hand on the dog's head, as he sat by the man's side, obedient.

"Oh," she replied, despite being unsure what else to say, she lingered, not ready to move away from him either. She reached out, allowing the dog to sniff her hand.

Finally, she smiled and forced herself to go back to the women to help with the cleanup but her breath got caught in her throat and she found it difficult to talk to the neighbors as he watched her. She didn't need to look since she felt his stare on her and knew her face glowed pink in the fading afternoon light. Later she learned he was a widower with grown children but there was no denying the sparks they both felt as the evening light grew dim and the lighthearted afternoon ended on a high note of song as Mr. Welch played his fiddle.

Chapter 5

E vie Winstead was sitting on the porch as if she'd been waiting for Lovey, the sun full on her face. "Welcome, girl. What have you brought me there?"

"Soup - Granny made it for you. I told her you had a bad case of the croup." Lovey put the jar on a little table and sat down in a straight-backed cane bottom chair beside the slight wisp of a woman.

A pleasant smile lit the woman's face and made her look younger despite the croak in her voice. "Tell Melindy I'm much obliged. This sun's helping sweat the croup out of me, I reckon, along with a dose of warm whiskey each night before bed. That rot the Wilder boys make will either kill you or cure you, I always say."

Lovey twitched in her chair, impatient to ask questions but knowing it was too soon. She gazed through slit eyelids at the old woman, who was staring out to the big sycamore trees that lined the path by her cabin.

Nobody knew the woman's age. Her face was unlined despite years of hard work in this unforgiving landscape and that made it difficult to guess her age. Some said she had buried a husband during the 'war between the states'. Legend told a tale of a deep undying love for the beautiful, young Evie Winstead that brought him back to her side, a deserter fighting for the south, only to be captured and killed by the Yankees who had set up camp over on Lone Mountain.

Lovey supposed this was the very cabin where the young lover had returned to so long ago. Miss Evie had lived here alone as long as anyone could recall. She wore faded pants and a soft flannel shirt some said belonged to her long dead husband and she chewed tobacco, aiming and hitting the spittoon from ten feet away. She worked her farm by herself and could shoot as straight as any man on the mountain.

Lovey cleared her throat and stared at the massive trunks of the old trees with their still mostly bare limbs making them appear naked. They would soon be dressed in lush greenery that would provide welcome shade during the hot summer to come.

"You want to know about John Epperson, I expect." Miss Evie spoke first and Lovey turned back to the woman.

"Yes, ma'am," she admitted, her face growing warm under the intense examination.

"He's a grown man, experienced in secrets to the heart of a woman, Lovey. He's a right good man if he has made a few mistakes in life. He was once a close friend to your Uncle Roscoe." The older woman went back to rocking and Lovey felt released from a spell when she turned her penetrating gaze away.

"What does Granny hold against him, though? She won't speak of the Epperson family at all. She just says they are no friends of hers. What does that mean?"

"I expect you'll have to ask her about that. It's not my place to say."

Lovey waited a while more but knew the old woman had said her piece and would not add more. She took her leave.

***

The sun was high in the sky as Lovey left the widow's place, grinning like a fox chasing a chicken. She had learned that John Epperson came home to see about his ailing mother, and Mrs. Winstead had seen him go down the mountain in the early morning light. Walking slowly, Lovey hoped she might meet him on the road but gave up when she reached the fork and turned toward home.

The tall evergreens stretching over the mountain reminded her of uniformed soldiers marching off to war without their winter coats of snow to warm them. The beauty of her mountain brought tears to her eyes. The trees bent in unison against a sudden gust of wind but quickly righted themselves in the next lull. Her desire to leave home alongside the fear of being away from these familiar hills confused her. She spotted a long formation of geese flying north and wondered if she would ever experience that kind of freedom.

Chapter 6

A cool spring rain fell in large drops against Lovey's face as she
raced the last steps to their secret cave. Five weeks had passed
since John had helped her out of the river and she was in love beyond all
reason. The rain didn't dampen her mood. The weather had been
unusually warm this spring as the ridge grew colorful with red bleeding
heart and white dogwood blooms competing with pink coneflowers
growing wild across the hills.

She was slightly damp as she pushed back the large evergreen
branches almost covering the opening and stepped into the dark, dank
hole in the side of Clinch Mountain. John was there already, dry and
anxious as she rushed into his arMiss In the dim light, she enjoyed his
wet kisses and pressed against him, fitting her body to his, her eyes wide
open as she watched him. He moaned and pushed her away from him.

"You're killing me, Lovey." He paced in the small space.

Lovey followed him and reached to hug herself to his back.
"What is it, John? Being with you brings me a joy I've never felt
before."

John turned, took her small hand in his, and led her to the large
bale of hay he had recently added against the side of the rocky wall
where he had carved their names last week. He sat beside her. "I feel the
same but let's slow down — I want to do the right thing here."

She pulled her gaze away from the intense blue that engulfed her when she looked into his eyes. She tried to cool herself now and think of other things.

"How's your mum, John?"

"She's pitiful and sad, still mourning my sister, Delores."

"At least your visit makes the loss more bearable." Lovey couldn't imagine the heartache the woman must feel, losing her daughter so unexpectedly, in childbirth, just because the girl's husband had stubbornly refused to take her to the hospital in Knoxville.

"I've done all I can, though. I have to get back up north soon. There's no work for me here except logging and I want no part of that."

"You'll break your mother's heart," Lovey said calmly, allowing her back to go limp against the rock wall. She crossed her legs at the ankle and turned to face him, her voice soft, not betraying the panic she felt heaving in her chest. Please don't leave me, she wanted to beg, but didn't.

"My mother and I have a complicated relationship and I'm afraid I've often disappointed her. She'll forgive me." He smiled. "She always has."

"I won't be very happy either," Lovey said, her bold words catching in her throat. She couldn't meet his gaze and turned away, noticing the rain had passed as quickly as it had come. Sunlight was shining through the opening of the cave.

Lovey turned, wide eyed, as John dropped to his knees in front of her and brought a hand up to brush it against the bare skin above her elbow, tracing circles with a rough thumb on the inside of her arm. "When I go, Lovey, I want you to come with me, to be my wife. Will you?"

Lovey's light blue eyes sparkled as she nodded, tears pooling, as she reminded herself to breathe again. She brushed aside the moisture, knowing this was right, although it wouldn't be easy to convince their families they belonged together. Despite what he said about his mother, Lovey hadn't received any warm gestures from Mrs. Epperson and suspected his family disliked his pursuit of her as much as Granny did. The difference in age had been mentioned but she knew there was more. Granny would only say he was a dishonorable man and she didn't trust him.

"How, when," she asked? Her face was warm in the closeness of his embrace and the dampness of the cave.

"We'll elope. We'll go to the justice of the peace in Tazewell late next week, and take the train back to Michigan, leaving word behind of our marriage."

Lovey's heart swelled at the idea of a romantic elopement. She had dreaded talking to Granny about this love she felt for John. Besides, she was much too bothered by his sweet kisses to wait any longer to became a real woman.

Chapter 7

"B"e careful of folks that try to turn a pretty girl's head," her grandmother warned early the next week. "You don't want to be tied to an older man like that John Epperson. He's already put one woman in the ground and left his mother to raise his orphan children without a backward glance." Lovey knew Granny had seen the moony eyes that passed between she and John. Lovey wanted to confess her planned elopement, but was quiet, fearful of what Granny might do to stop her. She nodded without a word.

Each activity was bittersweet as she milked the single cow and fed the small batch of chickens, and collected the fresh eggs in the long apron she wore over her old cotton dress. Time spent with her mother and grandmother over the past week-end had been especially bittersweet since she didn't know when she would return home.

As the night sky lightened with the first streaks of daybreak, Lovey rose from the sleepless night she had spent alone in her narrow bed. She was all a flutter. She had watched Granny watch her with a frown darkening her wise old face. She had held her tongue all week as she and Granny completed their chores around the small farm, trying to hide her excitement. Now it threatened to boil over like a hot pot left on the stove.

She quickly pulled her nicest dress over her head and pressed her shaking hands together before she buttoned the lacy collar with fumbling fingers. Breath still caught in her throat when she thought of how quickly she had agreed to marry John Epperson. He had a job at the Hudson Motor company in Michigan and promised to cherish her. Life with this handsome stranger was her destiny.

Carefully folding two dresses, one made up in bright blue and the other dark brown, in the same simple pattern, Lovey added them to the cloth bag holding her few belongings. She had the little rag doll she had slept with tucked into the bottom, along with the intricate crocheted shawl her grandmother had made for her two winters past. John would buy her new dresses in Pontiac. And a heavy coat. They planned to meet at the edge of the river at the bottom of the ridge. Lovey moved quietly in the cool early morning hours. She left a note on the kitchen table and tiptoed out the back door without making a sound.

Once outside, she stood and gazed at the small log cabin where she had lived all of her days. Dark shadows from the long row of cedars, which stood tall and sturdy, sheltering the house from strong winds, fell across the porch as the sun broke through the sky at the edge of the ridge rising behind the house. A small stream here meandered down the hill in front of the house, and joining the roaring river at the bottom of the ridge. She loved these hills of her birth but intended to grab all she could in life.

Lovey's mother used to say there was a wandering streak in the family. They had tried to protect her from that – especially after her Uncle Roscoe left home and ended up killed by a bullet to the head in a small Texas town. He was buried there far from home. She set her jaw, turned her back on all that was familiar and quickly hiked to the bottom of the ridge. She paced in the dim light, straining her eyes for a glimpse of John.

The water rushed in ripples under the river bridge, crashing over white stones rubbed smooth by the constant motion of the tumbling water. Lovey turned to watch the river, mesmerized by the soothing sound of the rushing water. Her skin tingled. She loved her mother and grandmother but was weary of the lonely days on the little farm. She craved adventure. She whirled around at the snap of a branch.

She was shocked to see it was her father who stepped from the woods, his jaw set. "Your granny told me this was your plan, Lovey, but I didn't believe her. Let's go home now, child."

KATIE
November 1999

Chapter 8

Back at work on Thursday, Katie stayed busy for most of the day. Offering open hours for flu shots two afternoons this week had brought new patients into the clinic, although mostly young parents and children. Despite the many public service announcements, older people tended to avoid flu shots, as suspicious of the vaccine as they were of strangers. She wondered sometimes why Lovey had accepted her so soon. And boy, had she been accepted. Her scalp still tingled from the stories she had heard yesterday.

The afternoon spent with Lovey echoed like an old black and white movie as Katie looked at charts and gave shots. The hilltop where Lovey had blasted warning shots at boys barely out of their teens was only five miles away but seemed like another world altogether.

Tazewell, the sleepy little town here at the base of Clinch Mountain, was a throwback to the middle of the century. It offered a few small shops along Main Street. There was the Tazewell General Store, a family institution of more than 85 years, anchoring the corner at Main and Broad. A Family Dollar had strung up on the east end of Main Street across from Elliott's Menswear. After several empty store fronts from failed businesses, Mitchell's Pharmacy was on the west end, with a lunch counter for coffee, sodas and sandwiches. Katie and her young nurse, Misty, often got their lunch there. Jenny's Grill and Tastee Freeze, one street over, was where Katie ate her dinner alone in a corner booth most evenings.

Lovey's words from yesterday still rang in her ears. The gossip after Sheriff Lane left had been delicious. Katie wasn't what to believe of the far-fetched tales Lovey told of life on the mountain. The woman could sure tell a story.

"Bobby Lane was the catch of the county," she had explained as the sheriff's car headed down the ridge. "Now he is again. Married once but his pretty bride took off and left him last year – leaving all the old maids swarming him like honeybees. Once bitten, twice shy."

Katie wasn't sure she understood. "Left him? Where did she go?"

"Chicago, I hear tell. A local girl who learned too late that marriage and motherhood wasn't what she expected it would be. It happens sometimes."

"Motherhood? The sheriff has a child too?"

"A boy. Women can do anything now - not like in the old days when I struggled just to put food on the table for my family."

The wood fire had died down and Katie felt a chill run through her body as Miss Lovey stood and flung a fresh log on the smoking embers. "Maybe she'll come back. He must love her since he's still wearing a wedding ring." Katie rubbed her bare ring finger. "How old is his son?"

"Five or six, I think. Cute little fellow with sad brown eyes who misses his mother something terrible. I see them at church. Hey, there's where you can come for patients. There's plenty of old people sitting in those pews to lure down to your clinic."

Katie laughed at the invitation as she stood to leave.

***

Katie and Misty closed the clinic at 6:00 and now Katie sat on a hard bench at Jenny's Grill, waiting for her take-out burger and fries, rehashing her interaction with the sheriff yesterday. Eating in the car on her way home would enable her to finish a short hike before sunset.

Laughter from a large group in the back corner caught her attention. Little boys giggled as the waitress brought their food. On closer examination, she noticed the sheriff was part of the group. The sight of him caused Katie's face to blush pink. He sat facing the large room just past the entryway, so he couldn't see Katie staring at his broad back. His shoulders looked even larger and inviting in a loose forest green pullover sweater. The tumble of chestnut curls was replicated in the small child beside him as they leaned close to one another.

Katie stepped to the counter to pay and collect her dinner as her name was called. Walking to the exit with her bag of food, she offered a small wave when the Sheriff turned, his gaze boring into her with sharp appraisal. Face flaming red now, she hurried outside to her jeep and slid in. Cracking open her window to catch her breath and breathe in the cold evening air rolling in from the mountain, she cranked the jeep.

Chapter 9

Katie shifted into reverse, but Sheriff Lane came out of the diner and waved her down before she left the parking lot. Puzzled, she pulled back into the space she had just vacated and opened the window wider.

He stepped closer and leaned over to speak to her, one large hand leaning against the roof of her jeep. "Hope I'm not keeping you but I wanted to give you an update on the men you saw across the river." His casual clothing seemed out of place with his official tone.

Katie killed the ignition and shifted against the soft leather seat, glad the coolness of the evening mountain air covered the blush in her hot cheeks. "No need, really. I was just a bystander."

"You live close enough to know. We discovered a huge drug operation when we went back out there. Besides busting up an old barn filled with tables and what looked to be a meth lab, there was quite a field of healthy pot. Now we're waiting on some community volunteers to help with the controlled burn we'll do."

"That's cool. I didn't know law enforcement did that." She smiled at the thought of everyone getting high from such an event.

Bobby smiled as if following her train of thought. He crouched his long legs to lean closer to the open window. His lazy brown eyes with gold flecks appraising her caused a deep pull in the depths of her stomach. She was staring but couldn't seem to look away.

"Just exercise caution. Your house at the top of the road might be far enough away but I wouldn't hike around the riverbank in the next few weeks."

Katie blinked. "Are they dangerous?"

"Could be. No telling what they'll do when they see their crop's wasted. Some of these groups are out of Ohio and Indiana and even Chicago and can be rough characters."

"What about Miss Lephew?"

"I'll go talk to her tomorrow. Maybe I can convince her to stay with a friend in town for a while until I can catch this gang – or at least whoever is their local connection."

Katie turned to him with a chuckle. "How well do you know Miss Lovey?"

The lines that appeared with his smile lit his face and caused a sparkle to light his eyes. Katie thought he didn't look near as fierce as he had with his sheriff face in place. "You're probably right about Lovey. She's not one to be pushed around. At least she's an excellent shot with that old gun."

"I saw that. She's one feisty lady but it sounds like she's lived a hard life if the stories she tells are true. Fascinating family. Surely, we aren't in any real danger in this quiet community, though."

"Maybe not but crime is crime wherever you are. They'll be sniffing around for a while and they may be more entrenched in the community than I know. I plan to find out."

Katie felt a flicker of fear. Tazewell was a small town in the middle of nowhere, not at all like Durham or Chapel Hill, where she had grown up and gone to school. Although she had always felt safe and protected, she was aware of the crimes and active drug scene at home. Her parents would have a fit if they learned any of this.

"You go on home, Dr. Cook. Sorry. I didn't mean to scare you – or keep you so long your food got cold."

Katie waved his comment aside. The sun was setting behind him, turning his hair to a golden mop. She no longer felt hungry and didn't regret her lack of exercise for a minute.

"I better get inside. The boys want to celebrate their soccer win with some of Jenny's famous brownie sundaes."

"Wow, that sounds good. I'll have to try it sometime if I can get in more hikes than I have lately."

After a flick of those sexy eyes up and down her body, he raised his eyebrows. "Women – always worried over their bodies. I'd say you're in pretty good shape."

She blushed at the compliment and her mind raced for something interesting to add but it had suddenly gone blank. He didn't help by remaining silent and grinning at her obvious fluster. Was he flirting with her?

"Maybe I can convince Lovey to come stay with me for a few days?" she finally blurted out. "I enjoy her company and she wouldn't be back there by herself at night, totally cut off without a phone or anything besides her gun. What do you think?"

"That's a great plan. I'll give her your invitation if that's ok. I'll be out there first thing in the morning." He tapped her roof and nodded at her as he turned to go inside.

Katie watched him as he walked away. She pulled a cold fry from the top of her bag to nibble on as she drove home alone to a cold, dark house.

LOVEY
Spring 1918

Chapter 10

Lovey snatched her arm free from her father's hand and walked ahead of him on the path, her pace fast and angry. John wasn't coming. She and her father were half way home, climbing the path she had so recently descended with unrestrained joy. She turned to question him again, finding his story unbelievable. "Why are you here? What did you say to John?"

Ocie Daniel was a man of few words and took his time to answer, hitching his bibbed overalls higher and readjusting the strap of her cloth bag over his shoulder. "It just ain't right, Lovey. John Epperson's too old for you to take up with and he knows it." Her father stepped closer, prodding her on toward home as if he were herding cattle into the barn at dusk. He lowered his eyes, avoiding her angry gaze.

Lovey climbed a few more steps before she whirled on him again - this man who had lived on the fringes of her life. The slope of the path gave her height over the slight build of her father and her anger gave her unexpected force. "But what did you say to convince him to go? I know he loves me."

"He agreed we should work this out as a family."

She threw up her hands and her sparkling blue eyes snapped daggers. "We're not a family. You've never tried to tell me what to do before. Why start now?"

"I don't have nothing against John Epperson myself. But your Granny has a terrible grudge against his family and him especially and he agreed stopping the elopement was probably for the best – for now anyhow."

"What right do you have in this? Why do you care who I marry?" Lovey demanded, her hands coming to rest on slim hips, elbows bent sharply.

"I did it for your Granny, I reckon. But I care about you, Lovey - you're my girl – my own flesh and blood. Reckon I love you too and don't want you running off like this."

Lovey was touched by his simple words as she stood in the path, her shoes making grooves in the rich black dirt, blocking his way forward. He blocked her way down the path as well. The sun had risen higher in the cloudless blue sky and the air was warm and still, or perhaps her breathing was too ragged to hear even a breeze. This day's promise had fallen far short of her expectations.

"John told me what happened between him and Uncle Roscoe but Granny can't blame him for the death of her precious son. It was Roscoe's decision to go to Texas after losing his girlfriend to John."

"I think your Granny might have a bit more of the story to share."

Lovey had begged for details but no longer cared. "It doesn't matter now," she said. "Granny doesn't know what I want in my life any more than you do." Tears of frustration ran down her checks. She was disappointed in John most of all. How could he so easily be dissuaded from their plans? Why wasn't he fighting for her?

Ocee looked away as he spoke, seeming to ponder the fog still laying low over the top of the mountain that rose high to the left side of the ridge they climbed. "You know the Lephews and the Eppersons have bad blood between them, Lovey. Why would you let yourself be led into a marriage with an Epperson?" Ocee met her gaze again and stepped toward her on the path but she didn't move. She stared him down where they stood.

"I love him, Daddy. It's that simple." Lovey allowed her tears to fall without trying to stop them, her ache raw and hurtful. "And I thought he loved me too." She covered her mouth with one hand and squeezed her eyes shut.

Ocee reached out for Lovey and she allowed herself to fall into his arMiss He patted her on the back with a rough hand. "Oh, he does, honey, he loves you dearly. He didn't want to leave. He made me promise to explain that he would delay his trip north by only one day to wait by the river tomorrow morning in case you still want him after hearing your Granny out."

"He did?" Lovey's face brightened at the words, her tears drying quickly. She stepped back to look at her father.

"Yes, but he agreed that you should hear Granny's side of the feud before you marry him. And he's right. It's the least you can do for her, Lovey." Her father released her and paced on the path, obviously uncomfortable with the situation he had been placed in.

"She better have something more to say than I've heard before or I'll be gone for good tomorrow." Lovey's chin came up in a defiant tilt. She felt her father's awkwardness and briefly felt sorry for him before she allowed her anger to grow strong again. How dare her people try to stop her. She would do as she pleased and they needed to understand that.

"All right, let's go. I'm ready to hear Granny out and get on with this." Lovey turned and rushed up the hill, her father left to follow on the steep path.

Chapter 11

G ranny waited by the door. Lovey's father nodded to them both and took his leave while Granny held the door wide. Now that she was home, Lovey's anger had cooled some. She pulled off her sweater, threw down her bag, and followed her grandmother to the front room, reserved for company and important conversations.

The slipper chair in the far corner allowed for distance and Lovey sat up straight there, crossing her arms around her thin body, toes tapping. She watched from the corner of her eye as Granny sank into the settee like an old sow falling in mud. Shivers crawled up and down the girl's naked arms and her heart bumped against her chest.

"This is my fault for not telling all this before but it pains me so to speak of it, Lovey. And I had no idea this had gone so far. Mrs. Epperson herself come to call yesterday and told me Rubin had let it slip that his brother was leaving town with you today. I had to stop you, child."

"Why?" The one word exploded from her mouth, more harsh than she meant.

"John Epperson killed your Uncle Roscoe." Granny's words faded around a sob.

Lovey's mouth tightened. "Granny, he did no such thing. You're exaggerating. I've heard the whole story from John."

"He may as well have pulled the trigger himself. Roscoe was never the same after Ellen broke his heart by taking up with John." Spittle flew from her mouth as if the name tasted like dirt on her tongue. "Life in Texas was supposed to make him wealthy enough to win her back but it cost him his life instead." Granny's lips puckered.

"John told me it was Ellen who was sweet on him. He didn't mean for it to happen the way it did." Lovey's clear blue eyes pleaded. She leaned forward. "If you really knew John, you would know he's a gentle soul who wouldn't hurt any living thing."

"It was their betrayal and his shame that pushed Roscoe out into the world and made him roam so far away. That's enough reason for hate to fill my heart." The old woman closed her eyes and shook her head, unwilling to hear Lovey.

"You can't blame him for the fickleness of a silly young girl, Granny. Ellen decided she wanted him instead of Roscoe. Your grudge is unfair."

Granny had stopped crying and Lovey saw the set of her chin as the woman gazed out the front window at the rising sun chasing fog off the mountaintop. They would never agree on John. "Roscoe was shy around girls and took John with him to talk to Ellen. They all knew one another from school and met up with a group of friends for church and such." Granny reached out to a polished side table for the only photo she had of her dead son. She held it close. "Roscoe was sure of Ellen. He was about to go to her daddy and ask for her hand when Ellen come up in the family way. It was John's child and they got married right quick."

Lovey came out of her chair and moved to sit by her granny. Family legend claimed that Granny had gone a little crazy over Roscoe's death. She reckoned the woman needed someone to blame for the loss of her only son but that didn't mean Lovey had to feel the same way. She took her granny's hand and patted it. "It'll be alright. I'm always here for you."

Lovey imagined John as the dashing young man that her granny described, along with her uncle. Any girl would find him exciting. Young people often made mistakes and people were hurt without malice. All Lovey knew was that John lit up her life.

"Uncle Roscoe was handsome, wasn't he, Granny?" Lovey took the picture, her anger burned out. Tarnish had collected on the silver frame and Lovey pulled the hem of her skirt up to polish it.

Granny smiled. "He was so perfect in every way, child. I wished you had knowed him."

"Me too. You miss him something terrible, don't you, even after so many years?

"If John hadn't been so sneaky things could have turned out different. Instead, Roscoe and Ellen are gone and that John Epperson is still running around Raven Ridge like he owns it, even taking up with my own granddaughter behind my back."

"I'm sorry, Granny. We don't mean to hurt you, but I love him and this side of the story hasn't changed that." It hurt Lovey to say the words and she saw Granny flinch. She wished it could be different but she would follow her own path.

Chapter 12

By late morning the following day the couple stood outside the preacher's home. She had come to meet John by the river this morning and was happy to find him there waiting for her, tall and handsome.

Lovey felt dusty from the long walk and wished she could freshen herself before the ceremony but knew she still had a long train ride through the night before she would be at home. Her first true home as a married woman. She took a moment to catch her breath and admired the bluebells that had erupted into a profusion of bright color against the white picket fence surrounding Preacher Coffee's home. Her hand fit snugly into John's larger one and his fingers curled around hers. She was warm in her Sunday dress - the best she owned – and couldn't say if the sun contributed to her warmth or if it was only the rashness of her actions that made her sweat. But her steps didn't falter as they crossed the porch and John knocked smartly against the door with his knuckles. Preacher Coffee opened the door himself and led them inside.

"So you want to marry, do you?" he chattered like a school girl as he arranged them in the front parlor and took out his little black book. "It's the month for it. Seems in the spring and early summer I get a stream of young'uns out of these hills wanting to tie the knot." He buttoned his threadbare jacket, smoothed his scraggly gray beard against his chin and smiled at them. "We'll do the service and then the paperwork and fees. It'll be $2.00 total. "Mrs. Coffee, we need you in here."

John nodded his agreement over the figure and the preacher began as soon as his wife joined them to witness.

"Do you take this man to love, honor and obey, girl? If so, answer, 'I do'."

Lovey's head buzzed with the words of warning her grandmother had offered but she was determined to go ahead with this match. She had waited late to marry but she knew her own mind and was ready to make a family. She tightened her grip on the small bunch of white peonies she had picked along the route from home and answered in a strong voice. "I do."

"What about you sir, you promise to love, honor and cherish this little lady here, for all the days of your life?" The preacher looked expectantly at John and back to Lovey. "You've got yourself a pretty one here, looks like."

"I do," John responded, grinning widely.

"All right then, sign these papers and you'll be all legal." He scurried behind his desk. "Oh, you can kiss the bride. I almost forgot that part."

Lovey melted into her husband's embrace, ignoring the silliness of the preacher and only feeling John's strong arms come around her. Her heart fluttered with delight and hope for a wonderful future as Mrs. John Epperson.

Chapter 13

Hours passed and Lovey sat stiffly awake, trying to relax and accept her hasty actions of the day. She didn't regret her elopement but was mournful of the hurt she had caused her family. The silence in the car and the gentle sway of the passenger train should have put her into an easy slumber. Instead, she thought of those she had left behind. Granny would miss her most. It was they who spent their hours together, while Mum worked in town. It was they who labored in the garden, fed the livestock and handled the farm chores. Lovey assuaged her guilt with the knowledge that Harold had become closer to Granny with his courting and would likely help her with the little farm and perhaps even convince the old woman to finally marry him.

Lovey tried to imagine the adventure waiting for her in Michigan but couldn't. Prickles of excitement crawled up and down her arms Pleased at her courage in breaking out of the stale pattern of her life in the hills, she glanced at John. His head rested against her shoulder. His eyes were closed and his breath was deep and even. Sleep had taken him.

Instead of talking with her new husband, she took in her surroundings. There were frequent stops all through the long night, with a lighted station building squatting alone at most. Her head nodded briefly, but rose when the train slowed to another stop. She refused to miss anything. She listened to John's gentle breathing.

The night had brought a chill and it seemed to grow colder with each passing hour that they moved north. She pulled her crocheted shawl tighter around herself and pressed closer into John for his body heat.

Watching throughout the night, she saw tired children snuggled against their mothers for comfort. Families exited the train during quick stops and she imagined their lives in these little towns stretched across the country like tiny insects in a huge ant colony. As the sky lightened she saw open lands that lay flat for miles. John awoke and kissed her shyly on the neck, glancing around as if to assure himself others were still sleeping. He suggested they get off the train at the next stop and buy some breakfast. "They have milk and bread and ham that will hold us until we arrive in Pontiac this afternoon. There's a woman who runs it with her mother and I usually stop in. They call me the hillbilly."

Lovey smiled and nodded as she lowered her lashes at the desire in John's eyes. She saw a hunger for more than food and it reflected her own desire. She was ready to seal their quick words in front of the preacher yesterday and she longed for them to reach their destination.

She felt the heaviness of John's arm around her shoulder and his fingers caressing her arm, adding heat to her body. "There's a beautiful little stream at the back of the station that reminds me of the Nolichucky River back home." The love in his gaze made her feel she was dancing in the morning light and her breath caught as his hand moved higher to caress the bare skin of her neck with callused fingers that tickled her pale skin.

Others around them were awakening and the day was beginning. John took her hand and held it tightly in his. When the train pulled into the station, he quickly pulled her to her feet, allowing only enough time for her to pull her satchel along, and just as the train came to a full stop, they exited. Lovey rushed to match his long stride. She felt a tinge of pleasure as his arm came around her waist and he slowed to her pace. He did the talking as they entered the small station with its café in the back, a huge potbellied black stove in the center the only source of heat against the morning chill, with passengers hurrying through. John introduced her to Molly and her mother, Rose, ducking his head a bit as they accused him of robbing the cradle.

"John, you did pick a pretty one, didn't you then?" Molly stood still, staring at Lovey until the young girl's face turned red at the scrutiny.

"Do you want ham, John? And what about the missus?" asked Rose, using a huge fork to turn thick slabs of country ham on the flat grill behind her. "Eggs too?"

"Just pack up a sack for us, will you Rose?" He handed her some coins. "We're going to stretch our legs outside."

John showed Lovey to the small room at the back containing private toilets. "Never mind Molly, Lovey; she's jealous of your youth and sour over her life stuck here in the middle of nowhere with her mother."

"Are you sure that's all, John? She looked at you like she could eat you up." Lovey felt hesitant in this place filled with strangers.

John tipped her chin up and kissed her full on the lips, backing her against the door of the ladies' room. "When you finish, meet me outside the back door here," he instructed, opening the outside door at the end of the hallway and stepping out into the dim light of a Midwestern morning.

Lovey stepped into the room marked for ladies and tried to freshen up the best she could. The water in the china bowl on the dresser was frozen over and she had to use the metal dipper to break the thin layer of ice. She splashed a bit of the icy water on her flushed face after quickly peeing in a china commode like she had never seen. She stared in the ornate framed mirror and combed her hair with a fine-toothed comb from her bag and then fluffed her wrinkled skirt the best she could after the heat of yesterday's walk to the preacher and the sleepless night on the train. Feeling the cold of the room seep into her bones, she hurried out to meet John, as anxious to be together as he.

Closing the door, still carrying the quilted satchel, she stood for a moment with one hand on the knob behind her, looking for her new husband in the gloomy light. Did he want what she thought he might?

As Lovey took in the frosted ground and the nearby cove of trees, she heard the rush of water running against its banks. John stepped from behind a tree and waved for her to join him. Her stiff fingers let go of the clutch they had on the cold doorknob and she stepped ahead, taking his hand and trusting John to lead the way. They moved closer to the water, and he took her in his arms, leaning against a tree bordering the stream. His hot kiss had her heart pounding and her nipples pulsing against the scratchy fabric of her dress in mere seconds. Kisses were all they had allowed themselves as they roamed the banks of the Clinch River and over the hills of Raven Ridge these last weeks of their courtship. Now she knew they could go farther and her heart skipped with anticipation.

"Lovey girl, you are so beautiful," John whispered in her ear, pushing her curly hair off her long neck. She had heard these endearments before but now his large hand lowered to her breast, briefly brushing her nipple before hurriedly moving under her dress to caress her bare upper thigh. His movements took her breath and she only wanted to please him in return. She moaned over the flutters he brought to her belly and raised her arms to fully embrace him, open to his every desire, not feeling the coldness against her backside as he bunched up her dress. He found an opening in her assorted undergarments and lodged himself there for a moment before pushing with a quick thrust. The train whistle blew, covering Lovey's sharp cry, and reminding the newlyweds where they were. John held her face in one hand, gazing deeply into blue eyes, as his other hand lifted her bottom and he pushed deeply into her, thrusting several times before he withdrew, quickly refastening his trousers. "Sorry, Lovey, it'll be better next time, I promise."

Lovey's breath still came sharply in her chest as she began to rearrange her clothing, finally feeling the coolness against her naked skin. "Okay," she whispered hoarsely. Was that it then?

John reached to rearrange a stray curl of her hair behind her ear and hugged her tightly to him as they heard the second whistle from the train. He took her hand, and they raced back through the station. "Thanks, Rose," he yelled, grabbing the brown paper bag with their food inside.

The couple was barely in their seat as the train chugged out of the station, and Lovey wondered about the tingles in her body, unanswered and aching. What had this devil done to her?

Chapter 14

Lovey and John exited the train a few hours later, this time in a city filled with scurrying men and women and large buildings. Pontiac was the capital of the automotive industry and the railroad ran through the downtown center. They exited on Woodward Avenue and John pulled Lovey along with him, his long stride threatening to leave her behind in the crowd. Many passengers exited along with them.

"Southerners are pouring in to work in the automotive factories." John spoke over his shoulder, her hand held tight in his as he guided her forward. The street was clogged with rushing people. The largest crowd she had ever seen was at Raven Ridge church when Preacher Taylor came around on the circuit to preach there. Most of the ridge folks attended then, except for a few heathens who didn't reckon they needed religion.

They turned onto Saginaw Street. Big flakes of white fluffy snow fell on them and quickly melted, leaving them damp, as they hurried down the sidewalk. Lovey recalled a surprise snowstorm one time at Easter on the ridge but that was unusual. She laughed aloud. The quick pace invigorated her and the snow caused her to feel like a fairytale girl. Maybe she had fallen into one of those little glass globes holding a winter scene with snow that fell when you shook it. Mrs. Hobbs had brought her one back from New York City once and she had gazed into it all winter, dreaming of a magical life to come. She pulled on John's hand to slow him as they rounded a corner onto Auburn Street.

John slowed and turned to her, laughing at her wide eyes. "Are you all right?"

"I reckon so but how much farther is it?" Despite the cold and discomfort, she never wanted this special day to end but was anxious to be at her new home with John.

"Not far, darling," he answered, his strong arm encircling her small waist for support. "Remember, I just have one large room in a boarding house, but you'll like the other wives."

Joy warmed her against the sudden gust of wind that swirled a heavier snow into her face. She loved John's tenderness. Didn't he know she was used to doing without?

John guided her past another tall three-story brick building that she would later learn were called tenement houses and they rushed inside. The building's interior was only slightly less cold than the temperature outside.

They took the stairs to the third level. There John set down their small bags and pulled a large metal key from his coat pocket to unlock the stout mahogany door. He put a hand on her arm to stop her and stole a quick kiss. When he broke the kiss, his blue eyes sparkled. "Let me carry you across the threshold of my home, such as it is, Lovey."

She blushed as John swept her into his strong arms and stepped inside. She ignored the cry of a child down the hall, quickly followed by the bellow of a deep voice in complaint. John set her on her feet on the other side of the door and reached his big hands up to cradle her face before pulling her against his body for a deeper kiss. She felt a wave of dizziness. She was glad for his strong arms to hold her to this physical space and keep her from floating away into a silly fairytale. As the kiss grew intense he kicked the door shut with one boot shod foot and her heart jumped with the anticipation of the true beginning of her married life.

Chapter 15

The days melted one into the other as Lovey and John settled into married life. Lovey enjoyed setting up a home and taking care of her husband. After nights of sweet kisses and nightly embraces Lovey soon suspected she was with child. She noticed an ache in her breasts and a new roundness to her belly by January. The other women in the tenement house recognized the signs and predicted the birth first. They quickly told the naïve Lovey what to expect.

"The honeymoon's over now," proclaimed Nerva, a sharp tongued slender woman who hailed from Kentucky and constantly complained about her life. She spoke with conviction while nursing her latest child in a string of girls, a bright eyed six-month-old with red cheeks and a constant runny nose.

"Don't discourage the girl," said Alice, a friendly woman not much older than Lovey who seemed wise beyond her years. She turned to smile at her young friend now, as she finished pulling in a load of freshly washed diapers from the clothesline that stretched from her window to another across the alley. She had two little boys, only a year apart, both still in diapers. She called them her Irish twins, and seemed happy despite the hard work of her daily life. "I can't wait to have another baby. I told Orville I need a little girl to soften up these little roughnecks." She carried the load of clean diapers to the table to fold, shooing the little men ahead of her.

"Have a few more and see how you're treated then, Alice. But at least you have boys and fathers are more pleased with sons." Nerva's lips pinched shut as she cradled her sleeping baby girl.

"But John and I are in love and I've never felt so cherished."

"I remember those first months together and how sweet that time alone was. Don't you, Nervie?" Alice picked up the neat stack of diapers to put them away, smiling over her memories as she patted Nerva on the shoulder.

"Maybe, but it never lasts long enough?"

Lovey stayed quiet, delighted at the quiver of life she felt inside, as she allowed the conversation to flow around her. These women didn't understand what she and John had together. They held one another long into the night and shared their dreaMiss John wanted to return to the river valley in Tennessee after he earned enough to buy some land. Lovey had longed to leave the hills behind but had already become homesick for her kinfolk. People here called them hillbillies and thought they were dumb because they talked slow. And she hated the northern winter. Snow quickly grew dirty here instead of remaining untouched across rolling hills like a dollop of white frosting.

Dreaming of home brought contentment. Lovey was reminded of the letter she had received from Granny. "What's done is done," the large block print had read. Her family might still have misgivings but she knew John was a fine man and they would see that one day too.

KATIE
November 1999

Chapter 16

The next week an early snowstorm blew in on Tuesday afternoon, making Katie appreciate her jeep as she drove home from the clinic on the mountain road under a darkening sky. Snow swirled around the hilltop. The local weather girl had predicted only a light dusting from the expected storm. Recently installed snow tires held firm as the gears of her vehicle whined on the slick, steep roads. Miss Lovey had agreed to come stay with her – for the week at least – and waited at the lighted window as she brought the jeep to a stop and scurried inside. A pot of pinto beans bubbling on the stove and hot cornbread fresh out of the oven welcomed her. The woman made simple food much like Katie's grandmother had cooked.

A few hours later the women were snug in bed. The fire was banked low with the gas furnace blowing hard when Katie was awakened from a deep sleep. She rolled over and grabbed the phone before it could ring a second time.

"Yes," she answered, her voice a whisper in the night, imagining the coffee she smelled in the dim room.

"It's Bobby Lane, Dr. Cook. I'm out on Route 33 at the scene of a car accident and I need to bring the young couple to your clinic. Can you come in?"

"Of course," she responded, with more confidence than she felt, wondering how much more snow lay on the ground. But that was why she had the jeep, she reminded herself as she dressed in warm jeans, a long sleeve t-shirt, and a heavy blue sweater along with thick socks and boots.

Tiptoeing from her room, she stopped cold. Lovey stood at the kitchen stove, in a long white flannel nightgown and a crocheted shawl wrapped around her shoulders. Coffee perked in the pot and she was placing sizzling country ham between biscuits. "I made some breakfast for you, girl."

Katie gaped at her. She reached for her thermos and filled it, realizing she had indeed smelled coffee instead of dreaming about it. This wasn't the first time the older woman had known things before Katie did but it still surprised her.

"So you know I need to go to the clinic?"

"I know you're needed somewhere tonight. And your strength might be sorely tested before daybreak, but remember, women are made strong so we can do whatever is needed of us. It was a night just like this when I lost my oldest girl birthing the prettiest little boy I ever did see. I miss them both to this day."

Katie hugged Lovey to her. "I'm sorry to hear that. That had to be so hard I'm not sure how you survived it. Will you tell me about it one day soon?"

"Maybe. But that kind of sorrow isn't easy to share – even after so many years." She turned back to pack the biscuits in a brown paper bag and handed it to Katie, her strong jaw rigid. "Go on now. You're needed."

"Thank you, Lovey. Stay warm and I'll check in when I can."

"Don't worry none about me. I love snow and always say, 'snowflakes are kisses from heaven' and magic can happen when those kisses float down to earth."

Slipping on her coat and hat, Katie turned back from the door as she pulled on her leather gloves. "I'm glad you're here, Lovey."

Chapter 17

Katie drove down the mountain as fast as she dared. The clinic lot was empty. Opening the door, she turned on lights as she walked through the building and bumped up the thermostat. Only then did it occur to her to wonder why the sheriff was bringing the accident victims to her when he should have called for an ambulance to come from Knoxville.

A horn beeped as a large SUV with the police lights strobing, raced into the lot. Katie threw open the door, headlights blinding her as the Sheriff carried Jill Greene, with her husband, Rick, following close behind, his hand hanging by his side. She ushered them into her largest exam room.

"We slid on some ice and crashed into a snow bank at the turn coming down Lone Mountain," Rick explained. "With no cell service, I started out on foot. Before I got far, Sheriff Lane came by and brought us the rest of the way into town."

"Looks like you have a broken hand, Rick. And Jill is unconscious? Sheriff, can you call for an ambulance while I check on her. We'll do what we can here while we wait." She pulled on sterile gloves as the sheriff lay Jill on the table.

"I called but the road to Knoxville's blocked by downed power lines. That's why I called you. Rick has a busted hand but it's Jill who needs your attention."

"She's been out cold since we crashed." Rick said, hovering by his wife as Katie pinched open the young woman's eyelids, shining her light into the large pupils. "It was my fault. I was driving too fast but she had me scared because her contractions were coming so fast. This is our third baby and the doctor warned us not to wait." A blush crept up his neck and face. "We always wanted a big family but this one surprised us. She couldn't get pregnant when we first started trying but now she's as fertile as a rabbit. All I have to do is look at her good."

The man was almost hyperventilating and had a dried stream of blood crawling down the side of his face from a small cut on his forehead. Katie watched for signs of real distress from him but thought he would be ok if she just let him talk it out. His anxiety was making her nervous though.

Sheriff Lane clapped the other man on the back and chuckled. It sounded hollow in the room. "Yeah, we hear you, Rick. You and Jill never could keep your hands off one another, even back in school." The comment brought a smile to Katie's lips as she took a deep breath and noticed Rick's blush spreading deeper but the crack had relaxed him. Had that been the sheriff's intent?

"Well, that too, maybe," Rick admitted with a husky voice. He stood by his wife and brushed her wet hair off her face. Katie stood on the other side. The blood vessels in her forehead were visible under the pale skin but her breathing was deep and steady. There was a lump on her head the size of a robin's egg but no other visible injuries. Blood pressure and heart rate all looked good. Probably just a concussion that knocked her unconscious. At least Katie hoped that was all.

"I think she's ok, guys. Sheriff, there's a splint in the next room if you want to take Rick and get him patched up. And maybe bandage his forehead too. He might need stitches but that can wait until I've finished checking Jill."

Katie turned back to the table. "Jill, talk to me." She leaned over the petite woman with an extended belly and lightly tapped her pale cheeks. "Please," she whispered in the quiet room. The woman's abdomen visibly tightened with what looked like a painful contraction but she made no sound. Another contraction followed. Katie did a quick vaginal exam and found the patient was already fully dilated. She threw the gloves in the trashcan in the corner and reached for her coffee on the desk. A quick sip steadied her but when she set it down too hard, she grabbed at it before it tipped over.

The doctor had studied a rotation of L&D but had never actually delivered a baby. It might be best to keep that to herself. Katie gulped air and quickly ran through the steps for a healthy birth. It could still be hours – and especially without the mother's help.

She had met the Greens once and if this was the woman's third child, maybe they wouldn't need much help from her. The baby's heartbeat sounded strong but there was no ultrasound machine or fetal monitor here. Katie gathered and stacked supplies on a rolling cart for an emergency delivery, praying the EMT's would arrive first.

The men came back and Rick again rushed to his wife's side. His hand was wrapped and the bloody cut on his head was cleaned and bandaged. Katie met the gaze of the sheriff, noting the silent question reflected in his chocolate colored eyes. She shook her head and whispered as he stepped close. "I've never done this."

"That should make it interesting." His smothered guffaw took the sting from his comment. "Is the ink even dry on your medical license yet?"

"Shh…" she said. "No need to announce it."

They both hoped she was up for the task ahead. Her movements were quick and confident as she readied her table with stirrups and spoke calmly to Rick Greene.

"Rick, I'm sure your wife's fine but this baby is ready to come most anytime. I'll need help to get it here. Do you know if it's a girl or boy?" It didn't matter but she was hoping to distract him – and maybe herself - with questions.

"It's a boy, Doctor. We have two girls at home already. He leaned over his wife, grazing her cheek with the back of his free hand, watching for some sign of wakening. "Are you sure they're alright, doctor? The baby's not due till December."

"I believe so. She took a hard lick to the head here – probably from hitting the windshield." Rick stepped back as Katie moved to the side of the exam table and once again checked the woman's pulse.

"We both did when we hit the ditch." Rick reached up to touch the bandage on his own head as if just remembering it was there.

"She has a nice sized hematoma but she's not bleeding. Mostly I think her body is under stress from the active labor and the accident so her brain has shut down, kinda like it's protecting her from what's happening. She'll wake when she's ready."

"But what about the baby? Can you deliver it?"

"It's not ideal but can be done. More equipment would help."

"Can I help?"

"Sheriff, have you delivered babies before?" Katie frowned as she studied him, trying to breathe evenly and control her rising panic. The sparkle in his eyes helped.

He grinned at her, his eyes crinkling. "None that were human but I don't think it's much different. I watched my son, Matthew, be born, and I cut the cord."

"I did that too," added Rick. "I can do that." He had stumbled back to stand near Jill's head, crooning to his wife as he brushed her bare arm.

She handed them both blue gloves pulled from a box on the wall. The large man with the badge popped on the gloves and clasped his large hands together as his eyes bore into her as if he could see right inside to the depths of her soul.

"I thought you were going to call me Bobby, doctor. Didn't we agree on that the other night?" Glad she wasn't a criminal under that intense stare, she broke eye contact and turned to Rick.

"Ok, Rick. I might need your help too." Katie arched an eyebrow, hoping to learn he was more experienced than she was. "Especially if Jill wakes up startled.

Katie pulled up a stool and peeked under the sheet she had used to cover Jill and saw that the baby was already crowning. She gently guided the head as it turned. "It's coming."

Both men joined her at the bottom of the table and looked on, mouths open and speechless. She delivered the head and quickly cleared the airway as Rick moved back to his wife's side.

"You're doing great, baby. Our little fellow's coming." His voice, filled with excitement, might not be as soothing as he thought but at least he was busy with something.

With the next contraction, Katie held the head, and Bobby leaned in and cradled the little boy as he slipped from the birth canal. The sheriff caught the tiny baby in a warm blanket and stepped back with him, giving Katie room at the bottom of the table as if they had this routine memorized.

She waited for the next contraction of muscles to help deliver the afterbirth and moved fast to clear away the waste and clean everything up. Nervous giggles erupted from Rick as he leaned close to the sheriff, and reached for his child.

"Keep him warm," she called to the men. "Bobby, want to check on the road conditions to see if they've improved. We could really use an ambulance about now."

"Is she ok?"

Checking on Jill's vitals again, Katie was happy to see she was still steady with all of her readings normal. "Yes, but I would rather the EMT's finish up with the baby if they get here soon."

Bobby put an arm around her and hugged her to his tight hard chest. "Good job," he whispered close in her ear, his hot breath causing a shudder to pass through her body. "Your secret's safe with me."

"Go on, get out of here." She pushed him away but laughed at his foolishness. She had seen a different side to the serious sheriff tonight. Maybe he had been a little stressed out too and was feeling the same relief she was. She took a deep breath as she started cleaning up the mess of gauze and blue under-pads that had slipped to the floor. Delivery could have gone a lot worse.

The baby was small but had whimpered and turned pink as she rubbed his chest. Now he was quiet as he watched his father. His eyes were charcoal. She prayed Jill would be alright too. Wouldn't she be shocked to wake and find she had slept through the birth of her baby. Color had returned to her face and she didn't appear to be in any pain. As the sky lightened over the snowy hill outside the clinic, they heard the siren of the ambulance, which had finally gotten through the blocked road.

LOVEY
August 1919

Chapter 18

As Lovey grew large with child and the days slowly grew longer and warmer, the couple's relationship did change, although she didn't understand why. As the summer days passed, John began stopping after work for a beer with the men on his shift. Even on the weekends several men from the tenement house on Auburn Street often found some task to take them away from their women. It was no secret they could be found at the corner bar on Lafayette Street.

Lovey spent long days alone, awaiting the birth of her child. She secretly hoped for a girl. She was beginning to feel disappointment with John, whom she had pinned such high hopes on to give her a life rich with love and excitement far away from the life she had known in the hills of home. Instead, she spent lonely afternoons with the other women, who shared stories of their life, perhaps trying to help her feel John's actions were to be expected, although she had hoped for much more from him.

"It's the way of men, Lovey." Alice told her and Nerva agreed as she pulled her youngest into her arms to rock while the women talked around the scratched metal table in her apartment on this warm summer afternoon. Lovey didn't tell the women that John had forgotten their first anniversary last month.

Nerva's apartment consisted of two rooms, their large open room filled to capacity with beds for the children. Nerva and Ted had three girls in school already and a toddling girl but Nerva said Ted still dreamed of a boy to carry on the family name and wanted to keep trying until they had one. Nerva was keeping her distance but seemed resigned to having more children – regardless of their ability to care for them. Lovey watched her and wondered about her life and if she found any happiness here with Ted and her brood of daughters.

"They work hard at the plant and need to blow off some steam," Alice explained, parting her two little ones who started to fight over a toy at her feet. "It doesn't have anything to do with their love for us and their families," she added quietly, smiling serenely.

"What's got you so forgiving today, Alice?" Nerva stood and walked to the bed to lay her little one down, and then rejoined the other two women where they sat drinking coffee. Her raven hair had escaped its neat bun and she reached to secure it as she smiled at Alice. "I thought you hated it when the men went out drinking."

Alice's grin widened. "I do. But I'm happy today and don't want to think about anything unpleasant." She leaned forward across the table. "I think I'm pregnant."

Nerva crowed. "Better you than me. I'm still nursing Janie because it'll keep me from having another one so soon. At least I hope so."

Lovey took her friend's hand. "I'm so happy, Alice. Our babies can be playmates."

Alice reached out a hand to touch the ripple that ran across Lovey's belly. "I'm so excited."

"I say good luck to you both and leave me out of it. My hands are full as it is and I'm sometimes glad when Ted comes home too drunk to do anything but sleep."

Lovey blushed, hiding a smile behind her hand, and Alice laughed at the admission. "Laugh if you want, young ladies, but just wait until you have more little ones under foot," Nerva said, a sad smile crossing her face. "I wouldn't worry over the men drinking a bit, Lovey, and whatever you do, don't nag him. That'll only cause more trouble."

Alice moved her hand from Lovey's belly and put an arm around her shoulders and squeezed. "Nerva's right. It's okay as long as they come home."

"If you say so," Lovey answered, although reluctantly. She planned to find a way to bring John home to her and the baby. She craved so much more for all of them. She stretched backwards in the hard kitchen chair, allowing her belly to push forward ahead of her, still feeling dissatisfied with the way of husbands. She hoped her friends were wrong when they said this was all there was. She watched the sunny day come to a close outside the window and wished for the days of courtship she and John had shared on the ridge. She remembered the greening of her mountains and felt a physical ache in her heart to see those hills again.

Chapter 19

Cold, dark winter days continued to linger late into the spring of 1921. A cold wind blew off the lake despite the calendar that announced spring. Lovey rose early each day and baked biscuits and stirred together the milk gravy John loved before he trudged into the damp morning on his way to the plant.

Today just minutes after closing the heavy door behind him, there was an insistent knock. She hurried to answer to avoid waking her little girl, finally back asleep after an especially early morning. She slumbered in a white metal crib in the corner, her lip puckering and quivering with a suckling motion after a fretful night, impatient with her teething.

Lovey swung the door wide to admit Alice Williams, who carried Rosie in her arms, the two boys trailing close on her heels. Rosie's face was flushed with pinkness just visible above the warm cocoon of blankets that held her. A chill wind raced in from the stairwell as another resident exited the building.

"Lovey, can you watch the boys while I take Rosie to the doctor? She spiked a fewer during the night." Alice looked flushed as well.

"You know I will." She ushered the group inside, hoping to keep the boys quiet, and reached out a cool hand to touch the baby. "She's burning up, isn't she?"

Alice nodded and pushed the boys forward. "I'll be back soon." She rushed away with the baby snuggled against her chest.

Lovey took a deep breath. She had heard yesterday that an epidemic of scarlet fever was running rampant through the neighborhood school and prayed little Rosie would be okay. She was just three months old.

"Alright, fellows, let's sit in the window seat and watch traffic until Melinda wakes up. Are you hungry?" She settled them in the large front room of the second-floor apartment that she and John had moved into just after the baby arrived. It cost a bit more and meant John taking on extra shifts when he could but it was an actual apartment instead of the large room they had shared their first year here. It included a tiny kitchen and a bedroom along with a bath. But best of all it faced the main street and the large window offered constant entertainment. Though small, the apartment was large enough for more children. They wanted more children.

Lovey walked into the small kitchen and uncovered a plate of cooling biscuits. She cut two open and placed them under the broiler in the tiny oven. Those boys never seemed to fill up and usually ate anything she gave them. She grabbed a jug of cold milk and poured a little into two small jelly jars and added water. She had to make the milk stretch until John received his pay on Friday.

"A truck," the smallest, Roland, yelled in the quiet room, and his older brother, Bobby, craned his neck to see better. Lovey came to stand over the shoulders of the little boys who now sat on the large window seat to allow themselves a better view of the black truck rumbling along Auburn Street, belching gray smoke from the exhaust. Although this city was filled with more automobiles than she had ever seen back home, watching activity out the front window was still enough of a novelty to interest her too. This was the children's favorite game whenever they visited.

Lovey busied herself with the biscuit toast, adding butter and jelly when she took it from the top rack of the oven. "Come and eat, boys," she called, and settled them at the small table.

She returned to the sink, rinsing a load of diapers in a galvanized tub. Wringing each one as tightly as possible in her red hands, she flapped it out and folded it to hang above the radiator that hissed steam most of the day. There was no way to dry the diapers outside in this weather. As the sun rose, she could see it would be a clear day but below freezing and anything would quickly freeze on the outside line.

Melinda awakened a bit later and had some lunch along with the boys and played for a while with her blocks, putting them one atop the other and watching with glee as the boys pushed them down. As the afternoon wore on, Lovey managed to get both boys to nap on a pallet by the couch. Melinda sat quietly at her mother's feet, not bothering the little boys who fidgeted on the floor, always in motion even in sleep.

Around 3:00 p.m. Alice returned, empty handed and confused. "What happened, Alice? Where's Rosie?" she asked, guiding her friend to the old brown sofa, which served to separate the living area from the kitchen table.

After eagerly reaching to touch each boy, Alice sat without speaking and Lovey brought reheated coffee from the stove. "You're frozen to pieces, Alice. Here, take a sip of this," she said as she pushed the cup into Alice's hand, closing her fingers around it when the other woman didn't respond.

Lovey fidgeted, wondering what to say to pull Alice back into this world she seemed to have left behind. More importantly, she worried about the tiny baby that had left with Alice but who had not returned. Perhaps she had been admitted to the hospital, causing Alice to worry. Lovey imagined her pain if Melinda became sick and had to be left alone in a big hospital.

Suddenly the door creaked open to admit John and his friend, Orville, quiet as two men could ever enter a room. Lovey rushed to her husband on the threshold, knowing instantly something troubling was wrong for both men to leave the plant in the middle of their shift. Orville walked heavily to his wife who sat as if frozen solid. He was on one knee with his head in her lap before she finally responded.

Her scream rang through the quiet room, sounding like a howl from a wild dog. Lovey looked to John and he shook his head with sorrow as he whispered, "The doctor called Orville to come home. The baby died as he examined her – probably scarlet fever. When he tried to talk to Alice, she ran out of his clinic."

The boys stirred and surrounded their parents in the dim light of the afternoon. Had the sun gone behind a cloud or had her vision dimmed. Lovey turned to go to Alice but John held her close. "Let them be for a minute," he urged.

Alice quieted. The comfort of her husband or letting loose with the scream had allowed her to awake but she was still stiff with grief. The children cried, not understanding but knowing instinctively the pain of their parents. Orville, his own eyes misted and dark, led his wife toward the door, which stood open to the hallway. Neighbors were gathering in response to the painful cry. The small boys followed their parents, the older with his arm curled around his little brother. Lovey reached to hug her friend - to offer comfort where none truly existed. Alice's eyes stared straight ahead, as if they were empty windows into an abandoned house. She held Alice tightly, knowing her silly soothing sounds made no impact to chip away at the boulder of pain that threatened to crush her friend. She released her, but continued to pat her strong back. "Go home, Alice, and rest a while but I'll be over soon to help you. Remember, you're not alone."

The Williams family walked through the small knot of people awaiting explanation without speaking - maybe not even noticing them. John followed to whisper the sad news while Lovey stepped back into their apartment to pull Melinda close, holding tightly to her own baby girl, as if that act alone could protect her from a similar fate.

Chapter 20

By the next summer Lovey again gave birth. She felt ignorant among these northern nurses and wished for granny. Evie Winstead delivered all the children on the ridge – if there was time to fetch her. Many women delivered their own young'uns, with the help of husbands or older children. These people at the hospital all treated her as if her southern accent indicated a lack of intelligence. She wanted to explain that the pitch of her voice didn't make her stupid but she couldn't find the right words. Maybe she was stupid.

She had been in hard labor when they arrived at the hospital around 2:00 a.m., and could barely speak between her pains, but she remembered the haughty voice of the admitting clerk.

"Who's your doctor, honey?" she had asked, after slowly filling in a lot of useless information, asking each question slowly and loudly, as if John couldn't hear or understand her.

"Don't have one," John mumbled for her. "Can't you have someone see about my wife while I stand here and answer your foolish questions?" John asked after a stronger pain ripped through her and she let out a small cry.

"This one's coming faster than the first."

"Oh," the clerk said, raising an arched brow. "Well then, let me just check and see who's on call."

Hours later Lovey clinched her teeth against more questions. What could she say when she didn't have the words? They spoke a common language but their thoughts and speech moved much too quickly here and she often couldn't think of a response till she was back at home. She was just a poor mountain girl but knew enough about manners to put others at ease.

The nurses finally left her alone after clucking over her like fat hens in a chicken house, telling her about spacing her babies and taking care of her own health. They had finally settled her into a clean bed and given her some food, and brought the baby. She enjoyed the quiet.

Her second child had come quickly into the world, impatient and scowling, another girl, much to John's disappointment. He had gone home now, to check on Melinda before going to work. They had finally talked of names during this last week and decided if this one wasn't their boy, they would name her Deloris, after John's sister who had died. The baby was olive skinned and had the startling blue eyes of her father in the tiny birdlike face. The deep blue of her bright intelligent eyes burned solemnly into Lovey's heart. She held the infant to her chest, thankful for her good health.

Spring of 1922 had again brought cases of scarlet fever to the building and around the city and reminded them all of Rosie's sudden death just over a year ago. Lovey feared for her own children's lives. Melinda was with Betty Templeton and her family upstairs and she was safe there. The Templetons had moved into the building in January and their daughter Kaye was great friends with Melinda. There was more danger here in the hospital, she suspected, with its wing of sick babies.

"How are you feeling, Mrs. Epperson?" a cheerful nurse in starched white uniform asked as she popped into the room, pushing a thermometer between Lovey's lips and picking up a chart to make notes. An answer wasn't expected.

The nurse, her tidy brown hair almost hidden under a stiff white hat pinned on her head, removed the thermometer and registered the number in her chart. "Your little girl checked out just fine in the nursery, though she's small. Did you get prenatal care?"

"We couldn't afford but a few visits," she explained, her face turning pink. The women from home birthed their babies just fine without seeing doctors, she wanted to add, but didn't.

"Well, you were lucky," the nurse replied. "She's a pretty little girl and should do fine. I'll take her now until she's ready for a feeding, and then we'll work on fattening her up." She pulled the baby off Lovey's chest and ignored the little whimper of protest. "You should try to get some rest while you can."

Lovey lay back and closed her eyes against the brightness of the room, oddly invigorated despite her lack of sleep. It was a warm June day and John had left after seeing the baby, his disappointment at another girl obvious.

John was accustomed to working on a few hours of sleep, she thought bitterly. He had been going out more often to drink with Orville.

Orville had been wild since he and Alice lost Rosie so she didn't complain despite her worry. Some men in the building seemed only to work and drink and didn't have much time for their families at all.

Her thoughts drifted back to her new baby girl. She was anxious to get her home and away from this hospital where they would force her to remain for at least a week. She worried about Melinda. She was bright for her age but wasn't quite two years old and wouldn't understand her mother's prolonged absence. The girl was sensitive and quiet. She had soaked in the sorrow from the building after Rosie's death and she might worry her mother was gone for good too, despite Lovey's efforts to explain before having the baby. "I'll be away for a while and then bring home a new baby," Lovey had explained.

They often talked about the mountains so she had drawn Melinda a picture of the family, including the new baby, sitting on a blanket having a picnic at the top of the ridge. The little girl carried the drawing around with her.

Light sleep came and went. Dreams offered the cool green of her Tennessee mountains rising over the ridge, as if sending good wishes from her family. The world outside Raven Ridge wasn't as friendly as she had hoped on that bright spring day she had left with John to start a new life. She craved a good life for her children but had learned those things didn't always come any easier away from the hills of home.

Chapter 21

The next year brought more of the same for Lovey and she almost welcomed the sameness of life in the cozy apartment. The drudgery of dirty diapers and dirty dishes filled her days. Caring for two small children zapped her energy and she found herself caring less where John was or if he were drinking again. The women in the tenement offered companionship and comfort and she had grown to love them like the sisters she had always wanted. She lay awake tonight, listening to Nervie and Ted fighting in the apartment below, causing her body to tense and her heart to skip for her friend.

Dislodging John's arm, she rose from her cozy bed and shuffled into the front room. Sleep wouldn't come over the harsh words she overheard. She couldn't ignore the cries as the other tenants seemed able to. Didn't anyone else care about the suffering of Nerva at the hands of her hateful husband? The bravado of Nerva's sharp tongue was understood after the first time she heard these frightening noises in the night, breaking open the darkness with misery. How did the children live with it and seem so happy?

With a cup of hot tea in her hand, Lovey sat in the big chair in front of the large window overlooking the empty street. She felt lonely and unsettled and wanted to do something but John had warned her to stay out of it. Talking to Nervie hadn't helped.

"And what would you have me do? Should I live on the street with my children?" Anger was evident in the set of the older woman's shoulders. Apparently, she had accepted her life for what it was so Lovey let it go. She would never tolerate a man raising his hand to her. Now she listened in the stillness of the night to the argument rage on and wished she could help her friend.

"You're a whore, Nerva, a useless whore who can't even please her own husband after he's worked hard all day to support you and a houseful of brats." The hateful words were followed by the murmur of soft pleading words that suddenly ended with the sharp crack of a slap. The sound of a swallowed sob followed a quick intake of breath. Lovey held her breath, feeling the slap herself. Children began to stir and whimper before Ned screamed loud enough to wake the entire house. "Get back to bed before I give you all something to cry about. Can't a man have any peace in his own home."

John mumbled a curse as he crawled from the bed. "He's bad again, huh?"

"He's worse when he's been drinking. It might help if you and Orville wouldn't take him to drink so often," she replied through pursed lips, running a hand through her uncombed hair. She shouldn't blame John, who was always even tempered and became more gentle with a drink or two. He came home after an evening with the men and only wanted to snuggle with her and sleep. She was sure Nervie wished her husband would do the same but instead the alcohol seemed to awaken some monster in him and he was ready to fight anyone in his path. Usually his poor wife suffered the brunt of his anger.

"There's no stopping him when he has some money in his pocket - all he wants to do is stop at the corner bar. The man has a devil in him and he would drink whether we went with him or not. He's never seriously hurt her."

"Not yet," Lovey said. "But who knows when he will go too far? We'll have to admit we did nothing to stop it." She jumped up to grab the long-handled broom she kept by the stove and rapped it against the floor. Sometimes the noise made him quiet and remorseful.

"Listen to the prissy neighbors, Nerva. I guess we woke them from their perfect little life of dreams"

"Please, Ned, let's just go to bed," they heard Nerva say before the sound of hard blows against soft skin reached them. Nerva's screams were muffled. Tears sprang to Lovey's eyes as if the torment Nervie suffered were her own.

She gritted her teeth and whispered in the quiet room. "The man who ever dares to put a hand to me won't live long enough to regret his actions."

John came to sit by her and took her gently into his strong arms. "He'll settle down in a bit, Lovey. It never lasts long."

"Why can't you do something to make it stop?" She burrowed her face into his shoulder and then pushed him away and stood.

Footsteps sounded in the downstairs hallway and out into the street. Lovey stepped to the front window to peer out into the darkness, and saw that Nerva was being pulled by the thick burnished curls on her head into the street. Ned glanced up. "I'm just taking out the trash," he sneered, shoving his wife away from him. She stumbled and fell on the sidewalk and lay there on her side with her arms coming up to cover her head. Lovey felt her anger bubble and boil over.

She walked back into the room, filled a bucket at the sink, hurried back to the window, and watched a minute more as Ned strutted and crowed like an old rooster under the window. She threw the cold water, bucket and all. The water hit him full in the face and made him take a step back in the street, almost falling to avoid the bucket.

"What'd you want to do that for?" he asked, beginning to whine like a spoiled little boy. He sat down hard on the curb and rubbed his face.

Despite her anger, Lovey giggled. Perhaps her stunt would make him quiet down for tonight at least. John leaned out the window to take his wife's place, pushing her back into the room. "Come on Ned. Let's get some sleep before work tomorrow."

Lovey strained around her husband's half nude body for a peek into the street to see what would happen next. Nervie rose and walked over to pull her husband to his shaky feet. He followed her lead like a docile child. She nodded up to her neighbors and called to them. "We'll be going in now. Good night."

Chapter 22

Morning came all too soon and Lovey was taking hot biscuits from the oven with sleepy eyes when John came into the kitchen dressed for work. She stood to face him and raised her chin as she said good morning to him and offered her cheek for his kiss. She refused to feel contrite over her splash of cold water on Ned last night. He deserved it.

Melinda, almost three, chattered to her daddy, and although he was confused he pretended to understand her as he looked to Lovey to interpret. She ignored him. Her stomach turned at the scent of the eggs as she scooped them onto a plate, quickly spooning a tiny bit onto two small plates for the girls before placing the larger plate in front of her husband.

"Thanks, Lovey." He took her hand to pull her close for a hug. "Did you finally sleep some last night?" He was trying to make up.

It had been difficult to sleep even after the neighbors settled down. She hadn't rested much but it wasn't only due to the disturbance downstairs and their disagreement about it. They were planning a trip home and she didn't want anything to cause a delay in their visit so she planned to wait until she was home again to announce this new pregnancy. It might cause a little strain on their finances and it would make her busier than ever but she was happy.

"I did despite the heat." She dropped into her chair at the old table and took a sip of coffee that had cooled in her mug, all the while reaching to spoon egg into Deloris's mouth. She pushed damp stringy hair from the nape of her neck and held it away from her as she smiled at John, ready to forgive and forget. She hoped her impulsive actions last night didn't cause him any problems with the neighbor.

"Maybe you can nap with the girls this afternoon. You do look a little peaked." Concern shadowed his freshly shaved face.

A breeze fluttered the curtain at the front window and Lovey took a deep breath of the fresh air. The baby gurgled and reached out a chubby hand for the spoon. Lovey handed her a piece of biscuit instead. This child was trying to feed herself at just over one year, and scooting around on her butt wherever she wanted to go.

John grinned at the baby. "She's a little pistol, ain't she?" He let her grab onto his finger and pull, dropping her bread on the floor.

"Is it today?" Melinda asked, big blue eyes looking like half-moons on a cold winter night.

"Not yet, sweetie, but soon."

"Morrow?" Melinda questioned.

"Three more days," Lovey explained, holding up three fingers. She grinned at John, their argument over the neighbors forgotten. She was happy with her family and as excited as Melinda about their trip home.

"Do you want to go for a long, long ride on the train, Mindy?" John patted the little girl on her head before he gulped the last of his food and stood. "Do you have my lunch packed, honey?"

Lovey stood, flustered. She had forgotten his lunch. "No, I'm sorry. But let me wrap you some of the fried chicken from last night. Will that be alright?" She asked, already wrapping the food from the ice box in some paper. He took it from her without comment and pecked her on the cheek again. He left without another word.

Returning to her seat, Lovey felt her stomach give another lurch and took a slow swallow of the cold coffee. She wondered if the nausea might be nerves from the horror of the night or the lack of sleep instead of pregnancy. Could it be? Anything was possible but she didn't think so. She recognized the signs now after having two babies in three years – another child was on the way.

She was no longer the naïve young girl who had first arrived in Michigan. Although John wasn't as attentive as he had once been, he still reached for her often enough to push out babies on a regular basis. But she was happy, if tired. Maybe this would be the boy he so wanted.

Chapter 23

Friday dawned bright and sunny. Lovey hurried around the apartment, packing up a special blanket for Melinda and a cloth doll Deloris slept with each night. They had scrimped and saved their money for the past three years in order to afford the train tickets for a visit home. The girls had never seen the thick forest and lush mountain valley of Tennessee and Lovey found she was beyond homesick.

John had a week off for the 4th of July and they would spend it at home. Lovey finally sat in the living room of the spotless home she shared with John and the girls and read again the short note from Granny.

"I can't believe I'll see you so soon. Mum and I are waiting to hug those little babes of yourn. I know my namesake, Melinda, has grown so since our visit and we can't wait to see baby DeeDee. Travel safely and we'll see you on Saturday.

Love, Granny

Lovey folded the letter and put it back in her black purse. "Girls, your dad will be home any minute. Melinda, go pee once more before we leave."

"I don't have to, mommy. I just went."

DeeDee mumbled something, copying her big sister in everything she did.

Lovey walked around the front room and checked the stacks of bags there. She had packed food to carry on the trip as well as water jugs. The matching dresses she had sewn for the girls were packed on the top of one bag. She wanted everything to be perfect for the trip home.

The door opened and John came rushing through, almost tripping over the folded quilt Lovey planned to make a snug bed for the girls to rest tonight. John halted. "You're ready? Me too," he agreed with a broad grin and pulled Lovey close to him as the girls ran to hug his long legs. "I just hope all this stuff fits in our compartment."

Lovey laughed. "Melinda, watch your sister while I help your dad load the car." Orville owned a car and had agreed to take them to the train station. She picked up pillows and followed John down the hallway to the steps. Lovey was winded on her return to the apartment but much too anxious not to help. They had everything in the car in short order and brought the girls down, John carrying the last bag of food as well as Deloris. They were on the way.

Orville backed out and pointed the small car toward Saginaw Street and downtown. John began singing to the girls, setting a happy tone for the long journey ahead. The train ride alone would take sixteen hours. He sang silly songs to make the girls giggle and mountain songs to bring the hills home to Lovey. He sang *Barbara Ellen* and *Wayfaring*

Stranger in a clear, strong voice that usually made her cry – but not today.

KATIE
November 1999

Chapter 24

Brown leaves crunched under Katie's short boots as she and Bobby hiked one of the more moderate paths on the Cumberland Gap trail. A gentle breeze dried the sweat collecting at the nape of her neck. She stopped, dropped her backpack at her feet, and removed her loose sweatshirt and tied it around her waist. Taking deep breaths, she watched two vultures take flight from the hillside ahead and fly west with the afternoon sun. Her breath was labored and rusty muscles stung. The brisk air invigorated her.

"Getting warm already? We aren't even climbing much yet." Bobby reached for Katie's pack, hooked it on his arm and stepped in front of her to take the lead.

"No, wait. I'll carry my own stuff." She hurried to catch up. A thick cluster of cedars shaded the path. Shadows danced through the almost bare limbs of the black walnut trees ahead. She heard the scurry of small animals in the underbrush.

Bobby stopped to wait for Katie and hand her the canvas bag, arching a brow at the independence on her face. He raised his hands in surrender. "Didn't mean to offend you. I know you can carry your own weight. I'm just delighted to get you out here with me before the colder weather cuts us off from these trails and the magnificent views they offer. That freak snowstorm so early in the season worried me but the return of sunny days have recharged me."

"It'd be sinful to waste this glorious day stuck inside." Katie gazed at the views around her as they walked. Deep blue sky, bright sun piercing in from above and cool breezes brought a thankful smile to her face. She was glad she had canceled her afternoon webinar when Bobby called with the invite.

"Sorry I'm a bit sensitive, Bobby, when it comes to hiking. Racing against my slightly older brother for everything created a competitive streak in me. We were always measured against one another and he usually won – at least until college when I started running cross country. After college, I embraced hiking but haven't been able to get out much."

She continued to walk the path behind him, gulping air deep into her lungs. She was so self-conscious around Bobby. She liked him but didn't know if he just wanted to be a friend or something more. Was this a date? She didn't know. The affair with Evan in medical school still haunted her and she berated herself over being so naïve.

Bobby slowed his long stride to match her pace. "Do you need a break?"

"Do you mind? Truthfully, I'm more winded than I should be. The clinic's been super busy since news of our special delivery the night of the storm spread through the community. There's been no hiking for me these past few weeks."

"That's a good thing though, right? I mean at the clinic."

"Oh, yes. I seem to be the doctor that everyone wants to see now. This is the first free afternoon I've taken for myself in a month at least."

Bobby stopped, threw down his pack and searched for a level piece of ground for them to sit on and drink some water. A meandering creek flowed alongside the dirt path they followed. He dropped onto the bank, crossing his long bare legs without effort. Katie followed his movements, folding and tucking her sweatshirt underneath her bottom. She retrieved a bottle of water and drank from it before rummaging in her pack for a bag of nuts. She poured a handful and offered the snack to him.

"So, have you considered my invitation to Thanksgiving dinner? Miss Epperson accepted so you'll be quite safe, doctor." He chewed and swallowed some of the nuts, poured a few more in his large hand and returned the bag. His hand brushed against hers, sending electric currents through her body. His brown eyes bored into her face as if he could read her thoughts and feelings there. Her face felt warm.

"My parents are traveling or they would join us but my son will be there. He'll charm you even if I don't." He grinned at her, his humor easing her doubts. He looked so harmless when speaking of his son she could almost forget his flirting.

"Sure, why not." She ducked her head but immediately raised it again, meeting his gaze. She refused to allow him to guess how he made her feel inside. She was a professional and a grown woman to boot – not some giggly freshman in high school wondering about the cute boy in algebra class.

"Should I bring something? I can pick up a pie at the diner." Katie had never learned to cook because her mother and father were both amazing in the kitchen. There had never been a need to learn, and besides, she had serious school-work to keep herself busy.

His perfect white teeth flashed a smile and she thought he might be mocking her. "No need to buy a dessert," he said. "Mathew wants to make an apple pie. Your praise at our culinary talents will be enough." He threw the last nut up in the air and caught it in an open mouth.

Katie stood, feeling dizzy at the quick movement of her head. "So, are you ready to move on? We're killing time here and I'd rather get to the top of the ridge and back before we lose the light."

He followed, close behind her. She felt the heat from his body as they climbed the steep path and she continued to move faster, feeling the chase closing in on her. Was she playing with fire here?

Chapter 25

K atie felt relaxed as she and Bobby trudged back down the ridge two hours later. The wooded trail was cool and dark in the late afternoon. Katie tried to orient herself in relationship to the small town and her clinic below from the top of Cumberland Gap. From the overlook at the pinnacle, she had seen Lincoln Memorial University and the mountain ranges surrounding it, one after the other. The red, orange, and gold of autumn still dominated the lower valleys, although the colors were fading and the barren spots where the trees had lost their leaves was beginning to show through.

A squirrel scampered just off the trail, digging for food before stuffing his cheeks full and climbing a towering hickory tree. Katie's legs burned. "It's all downhill from here," Bobby said, turning to smile at his silly joke. They both knew it could be as difficult to hike down as up and watched their steps. She appreciated his care to step in front of her and prepare the path ahead.

"Very funny. You're a regular clown when you're not on duty, aren't you?" She found herself liking him a lot when he relaxed his guard, or maybe it was her guard that had been relaxed. He was intimidating when he had on his sheriff's hat. When he reached back for her hand near the bottom of the path, she slapped down the little warning voice and allowed herself to take pleasure from the closeness.

At Bobby's truck parked in the tourist lot, he opened the passenger door. He stepped close for just a second, one hand resting on her left hip. "This was fun. Let's get some dinner with Mathew. He wants to meet you too."

"Oh, he does, huh. How does he even know I exist?"

"I may have mentioned you a time or two. We spend a lot of time together. He seems happier lately than he has been in a long time."

"I'm glad to hear that. Lovey told me all about him and I'd love to meet him but we shouldn't rush anything." Katie shuffled her feet but there was nowhere to go. His hand burned against her hip.

"No. It's good. It's time I brought someone else around." Bobby reached up to cup her face and leaned in for a quick kiss that promised more to come.

"Ok, let's go then." She was ready to do anything to avoid his closeness. He offered his hands to lift her as she climbed into the big vehicle. The truck was like many she had joked about as a young girl, calling them redneck rides. She had sworn she would never ride in one.

They were at Bobby's house in a short time. Katie looked forward to seeing his home and meeting his little boy. Bobby hopped out and came around to open her door and help her down, letting her body slide the length of him. She enjoyed the hardness of his arms around her. God, it had been a long time since she had allowed herself to feel an attraction for anyone. But they were moving much too fast. She didn't want to start something that might hurt her in the end.

"Hey, maybe I should go on home. I hold office hours on Saturday mornings until noon and should be fresh after playing hooky this afternoon."

"At least come in and meet my son, Mathew. Then you can leave if you want but I hope he'll convince you to stay. We can call for some pizza and I can drive you home after." He still held a loose arm around her waist and reached up to brush thick hair away from her face.

"I'll drive myself home. That's why I drove myself over here to meet you."

"Oh yeah. I forgot." He offered that big grin of his. His head dipped, and his lips brushed against her check before he whispered against her ear. "Please come in. I'm not ready for this nice day to end."

She tilted her head and smiled at him before answering. "I think you might have other things on your mind besides niceness." She blushed at his returning grin but agreed. "Ok, I'll come in for a few minutes."

Bobby kept a hand at the back of her waist as they walked up the brick sidewalk to his front door. The babysitter who had picked up Mathew after kindergarten and spent the afternoon with him, met them at the door, giving her daily report as she hurried out, explaining she had a church committee meeting.

Mathew sat on the sofa in the den, just off the entryway of the contemporary home with large windows along the back, overlooking a wooden deck. His feet were flat on the cushy sofa with bent knees providing a lap for the tablet he was playing with. Briefly, he looked up to welcome his dad. "Hey, I beat my highest score on Minecraft."

When he saw Katie, he became bashful. "Oh, hey" he said. "Are you Dr. Katie?" He put the tablet down on the coffee-table in front of him and turned to them.

"I am," Katie answered as Bobby motioned her toward the den. "I'm pretty good on that game but I can use some more tips. You'll have to show me some of your tricks."

Mathew stood and formally shook her hand as she stepped up to him, obviously well trained in his manners. "I'm Mathew," he said before he allowed his delight at her statement to burst forth. "You know how to play Minecraft?"

"I do. My best friend in medical school played it all the time between rotations so I had to learn too."

At Bobby's amused glance, she added, "It's a wonderful stress-reliever."

"Playing Minecraft is my all-time favorite thing to do. I can show you some things I do to beat my dad but you can't tell him. We play all the time but I always win." The boy with soft brown curls so much like his father's jumped up and ran to his dad. He leaned against the tall man. Bobby reached out to his tangled mop of hair, caressing his head.

"Ok, who's ready for some pizza? I can call for some or we can go out but it looks like a storm's brewing. The wind's kicking up."

Katie laughed. "I'm not sure that matters much after our hike. I feel grungy. Maybe I should go on home and let you guys settle in for the night."

"Don't go, Dr. Katie. Friday night is movie night and Dad got us the one with that funny dog. It's old but it's a good one."

"How can I refuse that?" She went and sat on the sofa as the doorbell rang. Bobby was on his way to the kitchen to phone in their order and stopped to answer the door.

"What...what're you doing here?" Katie heard him say. A tall willowy blond stepped in and the child jumped up and screamed with joy.

"Mom. You're here. I can't believe you're really here." He dove into her, almost knocking her over in his excitement.

Katie sat like a statue in the den, wondering how to get herself out the door. As the group moved into the house, the woman spotted her and walked on into the room, with her child clinging to one leg and Bobby trailing behind her.

The adults all stared for an awkwardly long moment. Finally Katie stood and stepped forward, her face a mask. "Hi, I'm Katie Cook."

"Yes, Regina. This is Katie, a friend of mine. We've been hiking today and just came in."

Katie reached out to shake the woman's hand. "Nice to meet you, Regina. I was just about to go home and get cleaned up. Excuse me." Katie walked quickly to the door, with Bobby following on her heels.

"You don't have to go, Katie. I don't know why she's here and I don't really care except for Mathew. He hasn't seen her since in over a year." He stroked his chin where a beard was appearing.

"Bobby, it's ok. You go on and handle this and we'll talk soon."

Katie hurried to her jeep, cranking it and speeding away as the first bolt of lightning struck. Yeah, fat chance they would talk anytime soon. She didn't need these complications and made a vow to devote herself to the clinic instead.

LOVEY
July 1923

Chapter 26

L ovey was droopy-eyed with exhaustion when they arrived at the
Epperson home early the next morning. The girls had slept through
the night and barely stirred while being moved from train to automobile.
In fact, they still lay curled together. Lovey had planned to go to her
family first but John's brother, Harrison, had picked them up and
insisted they stop by his mother's home first. She refused to argue.
Nerves prickled up and down her bare arms over the visit even though
they routinely mailed letters home and Mrs. Epperson wrote back often.
After four years, Lovey still felt like an outsider.

Mrs. Epperson sat on her porch in the early morning light, an old
swing creaking at the movement of one foot shod in high top black
shoes. The light was dim in the eastern sky but they could see her
waiting there, fresh in a crisp black dress. A cotton apron with tiny pink
flowers faded almost invisible covered her dress. Gray hair was pulled

into a severe bun on the back of her head. She was a slender woman and rose to her full height as they approached, a broad smile parting her face.

Lovey left the babies asleep in the car, hoping to move on as soon as possible. John sprang up the steep steps to greet his mother with Harrison close behind. He took his mother into his arms for a close hug. Turning to look for Lovey behind him, John felt his mother pull away and turn to the house, all but shunning his wife.

"I've got hot coffee on the stove," she called out as she crossed the threshold.

John followed her into the front room but Lovey lingered by the front door, watching the car where her children still slept. John and his brother followed their mother into the kitchen and it was only a moment before they returned with matching teacups and sat. John looked at Lovey raised brows. "Get some coffee, Lovey, and come sit."

"Will you have some breakfast?" Mrs. Epperson asked as she sat on an upholstered chair by the front window. Harrison sat on one end of the couch, quiet with his thoughts, but obviously happy to see his big brother.

"Don't bother, Mama. Lovey's granny is expecting us there and has breakfast planned for us." John sat on the edge of the couch facing his mother and waved to Lovey to join him. "The girls are still sleeping in the car but we wanted to stop in here first to see you and say hello."

"I had hoped to see the children too." Mrs. Epperson turned to Lovey and raised a haughty eyebrow. "I've never seen them at all," she said, and Lovey knew it was a reference to their life in Michigan, where she refused to travel.

"Oh, you'll have lots of chances – you'll be begging us to take them home, I 'spect." John laughed.

"They can be a handful," Lovey agreed. "I need them to sleep 'til we get home to the cabin." She crept closer and sat down between John and his brother on the couch.

"I see," Mrs. Epperson said. The old woman made it clear to Lovey that she was angry at her about this slight, as well as many others – real or perceived. Lovey wasn't sure she could ever make friends with John's mother but she would try.

John set down the tiny cup and saucer on the table and took his mother's small hand in his large one. "Where's Reuben living, still on the mountain?" he said in an attempt to distract her.

"They built a house back in Nat's Hollow, along the river, where Clyde Bunch lived. It's not a big place but enough for the two of them. There ain't no kids yet."

John dropped her hand, and finished his coffee in one gulp. "And what about Tom? What's he doing? Still cutting wood?"

Mrs. Epperson was smiling like a young girl at the attention John was giving her and Lovey relaxed a bit, settling back into the cushions on the couch, allowing her eyes to briefly close as she took in the cool morning air. Suddenly, she heard DeeDee cry out through the open car window, and her eyes flashed open. She rushed out the door.

Returning with both children, Lovey stopped just inside the door, where Melinda stood shyly in front of her grandmother. Pride brightened John's face as his mother surveyed the girls, both of them with coloring and mannerisms much like their father. Mrs. Epperson seemed pleased as John took Deloris from her mother and brought them both closer for a hug. Lovey sat but remained watchful.

The little girls hugged their grandmother, even though they had never seen her nor she them. They were at ease due to their father's easy manner. John continued to ask his mother questions about family and friends he hadn't seen in many years, and the girls grew restless, running from mother to father.

"Is it time to eat?" Melinda asked her mother in a clear, polite voice.

Mrs. Epperson moved quickly, coming out of the chair in a flash of energy. "I have biscuits fresh from the oven, and some cold milk from the spring house. Come on, child, and I'll see if I can fatten you up. You shore need it."

Before Lovey could intervene both girls followed Mrs. Epperson into the kitchen, where she sat them at the table and served them biscuits smeared with blackberry jam. Lovey looked at John but he avoided her glare which held a silent plea.

Chapter 27

O n Thursday Lovey sat on a blanket her mother had spread by the river for a picnic. Tall wisps of green grass shimmered around the women who sat basking in the warmth of the afternoon. All week she and John had visited family and friends around the mountain, driving Harrison's car over new dirt roads and walking or riding on horseback to more remote places. Today he had gone off with his brothers to their favorite fishing hole and she was free to do as she pleased with the women.

A natural pool of water in a rocky crevasse that fell into a stream trickling down the ridge provided a swimming hole near the top of Raven Ridge. Cold fresh water collected there and although it was low due to the lack of rain in recent weeks, it was just enough for the girls to splash in. Lovey stripped their clothes off and let them skinny dip in the deserted cove. Lovey's dress rose above her knees as she kicked off her shoes and stockings and dipped her feet in the icy cold water. The little girls splashed and squealed, racing back to their mother on occasion.

"Your life looks good, Lovey. I'm happy for you and John," Naomi said softly.

"I'm glad to see it too," Granny admitted. "I misjudged John and I'll be the first to tell it like it is."

Lovey blinked sleepy eyes and turned to the women beside her. Her mother and grandmother favored one another with squat bodies and had become quite round in their later years. Lovey shared the same coloring and facial features but was still slender and she had always towered over them in height. "Yes," she agreed. "John's a good man and mostly I'm happy but he drinks more than I would like. I worry."

Granny's eyes clouded. "It's the way of these mountain men to drink too much. I'm not sure why but the drink can be their devil if it gets a hold of 'em."

Lovey regretted speaking so freely. She had forgotten that her granny blamed drinking for the death of her Uncle Roscoe. And other hardships. Lovey didn't doubt that truth but she didn't think John had that kind of problem. She even drank a little on occasion with her neighbor women but she didn't admit that to her granny, knowing what her response would likely be.

"Oh, he goes out with the guys from work. It's not the drink as much as the time away from home that I resent. It's the way of married life, I suppose, and I have accepted it."

Naomi nodded her agreement, quiet as usual, but Granny spoke up again. "Yeah, they rule the roost, I suppose, and that's the way of it. God rest his soul, I loved your grandpa, but never wanted to marry again. Waiting on 'em hand and foot. And what do you get for your trouble? Hardship is all."

"You seem to like that Howard Davis well enough." Naomi said as she giggled and rolled over on the blanket, her elbows supporting her.

"What's this?" Lovey asked, following her mum's lead and rolling onto her stomach and bumping against her grandmother's shoulder. "Are you courting him finally? He's been after you for a decade at least."

Granny smiled but didn't confirm their theories. "Howard and I have been friends for many years – he cares for you too, Lovey."

"But mostly for you, Granny. He always has. He's always seemed kinda sad to me and his place over on Chucky River Road seems a lonely and deserted place. It's a shame there were no children before his wife died."

Lovey turned to check the girls and noted the sad look that creep into her granny's eyes as well. "We keep one another company sometimes. That's all it is," the old woman said. The lonesome words vibrated in the thin air.

Lovey jumped up and began unfastening her dress. "It's hot as heck. I thought it would be cooler up here."

Sweaty flesh stuck to the thin cotton as she gathered the material of her dress to push in down over her hips, wiggling a little. Squeals as loud as the children's escaped her throat as she dashed into the cold water in her slip. The chilly water splashed against her legs and hips before she ducked into the shallow water, coming up with liquid droplets dripping from her mass of dark black curls. Her laughter echoed out over the hills and the girls were delighted as they climbed on top of her, pulling her deeper into the stream. Lovey flicked water back at her granny and the women giggled in spite of their scandalized glances of reproach. It was good to be home where she felt so free.

Chapter 28

Sun blazed bright as the family gathered for the noon meal under the leafy maple trees sheltering the side yard at the Epperson home-place. Mrs. Epperson and her daughters-in-law had cooked all morning. Hams and fried chicken and biscuits and cornbread along with fresh sweet corn on the cob and several types of beans and sliced tomatoes, all fresh from the garden, covered the tables. Jars of pickles and relishes and jellies were gathered. Lovey tried to help but was rebuffed. The men had several brought tables into the yard and they were now covered with starched white cloths for the feast to come. It looked like the prodigal son had come home. It was Independence Day and everyone was happy. After losing her breakfast to morning sickness, Lovey was hungry and cranky, ready to eat and go back to her grandmother's for a late afternoon nap with the girls.

"Will you return thanks for us, Reuben?"

"Yes, ma."

After the blessing, fresh washed hands reached for the platters of food in front of them. The platters and bowls were passed from hand to hand in all directions and across the tables as well. Lovey counted 29 people at four tables. Two tables were fashioned of wide planks laid over saw horses. Newly discovered cousins, running barefoot in the rich dirt along with Melinda and Deloris all morning, had kept the girls entertained. Lovey passed half a biscuit filled with ham to each of her girls, who stood just behind her.

John sat by his mother at the head of the main table while Lovey was squeezed in by the other daughters-in-law on one corner. She reached for another biscuit and slathered it with butter and jelly. "When is this one due?" asked Ruby.

Laura, John's grown daughter looked across the table, eyes wide. "Are you expecting?" she asked, the desire for her own babe shining in her beautiful cobalt blue eyes. She was so like her father Lovey loved her already. The girl was married and lived in Middlesboro, Kentucky.

Lovey glanced down the length of the table before answering. John was caught up in conversation with his brothers and paying the women no mind. Lovey nodded. "I think so, the signs are there. John doesn't even know I suspect."

"Have you been sick?"

"You must feel awful, traveling and feeling sick, and in this heat?" said another sister-in-law.

"I'm so busy with my crew; I was six months gone with my last one before I even realized I was pregnant." Ruby took a long sip of cold water.

"I want to have a baby so bad I can taste it," Laura's truth was spoken in a soft breath of yearning. Mist collected in the corners of her eyes.

"You'll have several underfoot before you know it. Enjoy this time with the husband."

The women clucked around Lovey like hens on a nest of eggs, soon catching the attention of the rest of the table. Mrs. Epperson's attention turned toward Lovey with a sharp gaze. "What's going on down there, girls?"

Lovey got up and walked the length of the four tables to lean over John where he sat and whispered her suspicions in his ear. He grinned like a possum. "Sounds like we have another baby on the way, Mama. Could be that boy we've been waiting on."

The men sitting near John clapped him on the back as if he had done something grand but his mother soon interrupted. "Some women can't seem to produce a boychild. At least you have Thomas here if you ever come back to live in Tennessee. He wants to come to Michigan with you to find work but I forbid it. It's enough that you're gone but I refuse to lose another son to the north."

"Mama, the boy will do as he pleases and you can't hold him so tight. When will you learn that?"

Conversation stilled as everyone listened to the old argument between the two. "We'd be pleased to have him stay with us," Lovey added, happy to do whatever John wanted despite his mother's disapproval. She patted Thomas on the shoulder where he sat by his father and he turned to smile at her.

"Thanks," he said, ducking his head.

"That won't be necessary, Lovey. Please don't interfere with the family. Thomas will stay here where he's needed and continue to farm with his uncles and there will be no more talk of anyone else running off from home."

Lovey's face flushed at the withering look her mother-in-law offered with the harsh words. A full grown lioness would wilt under that gaze. The joy Lovey felt cracked and dried up as she walked slowly back to her seat. Why did the old biddy have to be so hateful? And why didn't John say something?

Laura smiled at her shyly from across the table, offering comfort. She was a kind girl who was already attached to Melinda and Deloris, loving them like the children she longed for instead of her much younger half-sisters.

Chapter 29

Saturday after supper, Lovey sat on a craggy rock on the hillside beside the cabin, gazing at the darkening sky over the ridgeline. On Monday she would be in Michigan, settling back in with John and the girls and all of her neighbors. A low rumble of thunder sounded in the distance and she hoped rain might blow away the humid air. Cool summer evenings in the north had become welcome as her tolerance for the heat of a southern summer disappeared. A light breeze touched the tops of apple trees bordering the back of the little farm. More lush green of large oak and chestnut extended down both sides of the rutted road that snaked down the mountain. They would follow that road off the ridge come morning. Her eyes misted.

When she blinked away the sudden tears and looked up again, Granny stood alone at the back of the house in the deepening dusk.

"Come sit by me," Lovey called. She moved her small frame aside to make room for Granny.

Granny fanned herself with the bottom of her flowered print apron as she walked slowly the yard. The apron with wide deep pockets was a staple she wore over the dark dresses she favored. The older woman reached for Lovey's hand as she climbed to reach the rock and squeezed in beside Lovey on the flat top.

"I think I will sit a spell, darling. I'm tuckered out tonight."

"It's been a long week for you. Having a family underfoot isn't something you're used to anymore. You'll say good riddance to us all."

Granny reached out an arm to circle Lovey's waist. "Lord, child. Forget such foolishness. I've ached to have you home again and those sweet little girls remind me how precious you were at that age. I hate to see you go."

Lovey leaned her head over Granny's where it had come to rest on her shoulder, taking in the fragrance of cinnamon and sugar from the fried apple pies the shorter woman had made earlier for them. "I hate to go but John has a good job. Our life is there for now but we've talked of coming home one day. We hope to."

A bolt of lightning lit the sky above them. The scent of cedar and pine from the evergreens competed with the clean smell of coming rain as the thunder crashed. She felt the waves of heat being chased away by a stronger breeze stirring the trees in the distance.

The women were still, enjoying the wind rustling their damp hair, cooling them after the long steaming day. It was time to go in, but Lovey lingered. Their bags were packed and John was settling the girls in bed for the night. His brother would come for them early because the train left at first light. She took Granny's hand, knowing the older woman was not well. It was possible they would not return to see her again in this life. No words came and Granny seemed to read her thoughts.

"Don't worry, Lovey. I'll be here, waiting, when you come home. Rolling hills of green velvet settle in a body's heart the longer they stay away. Leastways that's what my mama used to say – but she was talking about the old country then. Tears still come to my eyes and my heart hurts when I think of her never seeing the green hills of Ireland again after she came to America. These mountains were the closest she found."

Lovey felt tears prick her eyes too, imagining being so far from home. Michigan was far aplenty. Why she ever thought her place in life was somewhere besides here, she could no longer recall. Large drops of cool rain begin to fall and laughter rang out in the hollow as the two women dashed to the house.

Chapter 30

Just weeks after returning to Michigan, the weather was cool and rainy and the couple snuggled against one another in the warm cocoon of their bed. Lovey came awake in the night when she felt the first cramps niggle at her back. She reached for John's hand and placed it on the small swell of her belly before she fully understood what had awakened her. Another cramp rippled through her center and she brought her legs up, squeezing them tight as if she could hold the baby inside from sheer desire.

John pulled her to him and nuzzled the back of her neck, still mostly asleep but he awakened as Lovey pulled away and got up from the cozy bed. "It's the baby, John. I think I'm bleeding."

Lovey stumbled to the doorway, her bare arms prickling in the cool room, her hand sweeping along the wall for the light switch. The small bulb was dim in their room and she hurried on to the tiny bathroom. John got up as well and stood at the open door as she cleaned herself.

"I'm not bleeding much. Maybe it's nothing."

"What should we do - go to the hospital?"

Lovey's heart fluttered as she considered what she should do. John looked worried.

"You go back to bed. Early morning will be here soon and you need your sleep for work. I'll sit in the front room for a while and wait to see if I have more cramps."

Lovey had not seen a doctor to confirm her pregnancy but figured she was less than three months along. They couldn't afford to run to the doctor so often and with the girls she had simply gone to the hospital when she went into labor. She had not bled like this with the other babies though.

John took her hand and lead her back to the bed. He stood by her. "I'll wait with you, honey." He waited for her to sit on the side of their double bed. Encouraging her to relax back against the headboard, he added his pillow to hers and tucked her under the warm blankets topped by Granny's hand-pieced Dutch doll quilt from home. He came around to the other side and joined her under the bedcovers. With the dim light still shining, and one arm around her, they waited, neither speaking.

Lovey was afraid but tried to still her breath. She closed her eyes. John's large hand circled the inside of her upper arm, a rough thumb brushing against the bare flesh. It was soothing. She had seen him do the same to the girls when he snuggled with them before bed, telling them an old fairytale, and she felt protected in his ~~arMiss~~ Arms.

Watching the dial of the alarm clock as it ticked the minutes away, Lovey reminded herself to breathe with each movement forward of the long hand. She ignored the small cramps that continued through the next hour but as dawn arrived, her discomfort increased. When early morning light began to take away the shadows where their bulb didn't reach, Lovey stirred. "I think we better go, John."

They quickly dressed and after getting Nerva's oldest girl, now fourteen, to come sit with the two sleeping children, they hurried to Pontiac City Hospital, not far away.

LOVEY
July 1923

Chapter 31

Nurses took Lovey back immediately, fussing over her, while John was forced to wait alone in the cold empty waiting area. She lay on the narrow stretcher, tears flowing down her cheeks as the pains grew stronger and she felt the blood gush from her body. There was nothing to be done. Faintness threatened as the kindly white haired doctor leaned over her and spoke.

"We're going to take you into surgery now to see about stopping some of this blood loss." After that she could see his lips move but couldn't hear his words over the roar in her head.

When Lovey awoke, she was in a hospital bed with the sheets pulled tightly around her and John was sitting in a straight chair by her side, gently stroking her sun browned hand. The ache of her empty body hurt all the way to her center and she tried to speak but heard only a squeak.

John handed her a glass of water on the bedside table. "Here, drink something. They said your throat would feel scratchy."

She tried to raise herself in the bed but was too weak. John helped, placing an arm behind her as she sipped the water. Tears pooled in her eyes.

"It was our son," She set the glass on a table by her bed and covered her face. John pulled her hands away and helped her settle lower in the bed before he leaned his head closer, his forehead touching hers. They cried together. They stayed joined, head to head, until the nurse came and insisted he go home and let her rest.

***

It was August of the following year when Lovey lay in a hospital bed once again. She had birthed her third girl. John's pinched face betrayed his disappointment and she knew he had prayed for a son to replace the boy they had lost. His face also reflected the afterglow of too much liquor and she wished he had saved himself the trip if this was all he had to offer. Unhappiness shadowed their movements more each day.

"Have you seen her – is she alright?"

She had been in labor all day and half the night before she had allowed John to bring her to the hospital. He had left her at 6:00 a.m. to go to work, unable to miss his shift. Lovey pushed the pitiful little child from her wretched body around noon and they settled her in this room to rest while they cleaned up the baby. She must have slept. Now, the sun outside her window was lower in the sky.

John smiled, wiping the sorrow from his face as he leaned over and brushed back her still damp hair. She felt pleased that he touched her.

"She's tiny but strong, the doc said, not like…." His voice faltered as his face collapsed. He stopped the tears with a clinched jaw but the drinking was making him weak. Was his mother right that she couldn't give him a son?

Her tone was sharper than she meant. "It happens, John. Nobody knows why but it's usually because something isn't right, the midwife at home always said so." John couldn't forget his lost son. Grief had riddled her too but she had forced herself to look forward instead of behind them. They had three healthy girls. She turned to look out the window again and watched the white sheer curtain wave with the slight breeze. Slender, young trees reached for the sky across the street where new plantings lined a park. It would be winter again soon. She dreaded the coming cold.

Remembering this new baby had started with her loss of the previous one warmed her a bit and she raised her chin. There was still hope for a happy family. She and John had clung together after the loss of their baby and soon after the New Year she had been pregnant again. Dreaming of another boy to replace the lost child had given them hope. Now John was disappointed.

Tears were blinked aside as the nurse brought the baby, their tiniest yet at just under five pounds. Lovey propped against the soft pillows and pulled up her knees to rest her baby there on her lap, where she could count her fingers and toes and smell the lotion and powder on her delicate skin. Would this child's life be any easier than her own, she wondered? Life wasn't always fair to women.

Her lack of control over her life threatened to break Lovey some days. But not today. Moving to Michigan was supposed to bring a better life but the only difference was the scenery. The baby stared back at her with the blue/black eyes that would eventually lighten to an intense blue that sometimes matched the sky over the Smokey Mountains. The older girls bore the same deep blue color, just like their father.

John reached out a grease stained hand to brush against her tiny head covered with a coating of blond fuzz peeking from under a knit cap. He gazed down at this tiny creature that had been created from their sorrow. "She's a pretty little thing, ain't she?" he said, clicking his tongue as if calling a puppy.

Lovey looked at John and grinned, pleased he was coming around. "She is. And do you know what I want to name her, John?"

At the lift of his dark eyebrow, she blurted out her plan. "Jacqueline. That way we can have our little Jackie, boy or girl be dammed."

The silence grew for a full minute as he considered. He raised his head and stared into her face, his clouded eyes touching her tender heart. "I like it," he said, nodding.

He reached over to let the baby grasp his long forefinger. The baby's hold was strong. Lovey was glad. Only strong women survived in this world. She whispered a prayer of thanks just under her breath as John got up and left the room to go home to his two older girls.

Chapter 32

ovey told herself she was mostly happy. It had been almost four
years since the last birth and she couldn't seem to get pregnant
again. John still wanted his boy but the girls kept her busy and if John
was no longer as attentive as he once had been, the women in the
building were good friends.

John brought her his paycheck every Friday and treated her well
when compared to what some of the others got from their men.

The young man who suddenly appeared at her door this morning
spoke in hushed tones, asking about family members or neighbors he
might call for her. The words of this stranger ripped through her body
like bullets from a rapid-fire machine gun, one sinking deeply into the
softness of her heart, one nicking her lungs and stealing her breath, one
exploding through her torso, turning her into a puppet without support,
so that she sank to the hard kitchen floor. Her brain, the commander of
this disarray of body parts, ordered the limbs back to service as if they
had become disobedient soldiers who had broken ranks. The scent of
lemon came to her, as she sat crumbled there on the freshly washed
floor, refusing to hear the words that had been spoken.

Bright summer sun streamed through the large glass window
separating them from the street below and Lovey's eyes burned with the
heat as time slowed to a crawl. She noticed that the blue flowered house
dress she wore to clean her home had risen above her knees and she

tugged it down. She reached to touch the hair falling in strings around her face and her gaze settled on the chipped polish on one toe nail. Her bare feet looked cold there on the wooden floor, she thought irrationally. She recognized that her mind was in a stupor and tried to rein it in to take some much-needed action, although she had already forgotten what that should be. Something about John, was it?

Her friend, Alice, rushed through the open door, throwing herself down beside Lovey on the floor, despite her skirt and heels. Her neighbor tried to lift her, and even with the policeman's help, it was difficult. Lovey's body had no starch and she moved like one of the ragdolls the girls might play with. The two of them together managed to pull her up and into the living room.

"What happened?" Alice asked the officer, and Lovey thought the words sounded like marbles rolling around inside a metal dish pan. She understood the meaning but the sound was distorted in the large, open room.

She listened as the officer replied. "He stepped in front of a truck and there was no time for the driver to stop. They took him to St. Joseph's hospital but it was too late." Lovey noticed the young man in uniform looked uncomfortable and thought she should rise and put him at ease, but she could not move. This man didn't understand what he had done to her, bringing this dreadful news, his simple words making her a widow with three young children far from home.

The girls gathered around their mother, where she now slumped in the large brown armchair placed next to the front window, tears coming to her eyes. Her thoughts were jumbled. She closed her eyes, remembering the sweetness of her husband and allowed his love to wash over her. John had once loved her, as nobody ever had. *How would she feed her children? Who would help her raise these little ones? Should she go home – yes, John should be buried in the hills of home – not here in this cold city. But then what?*

She tried to stop thinking and pull herself together. Little Jackie, almost four, cried and reached for her mother and Deloris stood apart, her face panic stricken. Melinda spoke calmly but with fear straining the soft voice. "What's wrong, Mama?"

The officer spoke in undertones to Alice across the room before making an exit. Alice came to sit on the arm of the chair, leaned in close and spoke quietly, handing Lovey a hankie. "Breathe, Lovey, breathe. You will survive this because you must." Her friend continued to croon soft words of comfort as Lovey took a deep breath, coughed and tried again. She must bring her mind to the tasks at hand, she thought, blotting her face with the thin white handkerchief Melinda brought her.

She reached for Jackie, taking the tow-headed toddler onto her lap, hugging her gently to her chest, taking as well as giving comfort. She smiled sadly at the older girls. "Go play, babies. Mama's okay now." She touched Lovey's face and gently shooed them away to the other side of the room.

"What do I do now, Alice?" She held the other woman's hand in a grip that would bruise but she needed the lifeline to keep from floating away. "I'll do what you tell me because I don't know what to do. I just don't know what to do next."

Alice took charge as other neighbors began to fill the apartment, already responding with gifts of food and drink after the word of the unexpected death of John Epperson spread through the building. Lovey followed Alice like a well-disciplined child to the back room to change her house dress for something more appropriate. She returned to sit woodenly in the armchair that had always been her favorite here in the home she had created for her little family. Her thoughts continued to run wild and she felt the fear a small animal trapped in a room of rabid wolves might feel, her neighbors' teeth sharp and eyes watchful despite the words of tenderness they offered. Panic took her breath when she tried to speak. Alice brought her a cup of dark liquid that she drank without question, strangling on it as it went down, but the fear pushed back just to the edge of the room and she felt the blood return to her icy fingers.

The next day passed in a blur, tears of sorrow melting against the softness of her children's warm skin and they cried with her as she rocked them to sleep. They were too young to understand, except perhaps Melinda, who at eight watched Lovey with a shadow of fear in her young eyes that matched her mother's. Lovey knew the younger girls cried when she did so she tried to control her grief until the evening hours. Then she walked the floors alone, avoiding the creaks that were as familiar to her as her children's breath, begging John to give her some sign of what she should do next.

KATIE
November 1999

Chapter 33

Thanksgiving week arrived with a cool breeze and bright sunshine. Monday morning had dawned bright and clear with a sweeping cold front pushing into the Ohio valley, but the forecast had turned to heavy rain and fog for the holiday. Katie hurried through the crisp evening air on Tuesday night as she checked in on Lovey, who had developed a bad cold and possibly a mild case of pneumonia that might rescue them both from an awkward dinner at the Lanes on Thursday. She had decided to avoid the dinner but Lovey's illness would provide a legitimate excuse. Bobby had left several voice messages today. She planned to wait and call him with regrets tomorrow – when it was too late for him to argue.

"You can come and stay with me if you refuse to go in the hospital." Katie now demanded of her friend. "I'll pack you a bag. And I plan to put you a telephone in next week. You can't be stuck out here all on your own anymore."

She hurried into the cold back bedroom away from the fire and gathered two flannel gowns and a warm robe, along with underwear and socks. That should see the older woman through the weekend. Katie returned to the main room, and smiled as Lovey grumbled.

"This cough ain't no worse than croup I've had before. You petting me too much, Missy." Miss Lovey sat perched high in her rocker, ramrod straight, with a stubborn set to her chin.

"Maybe so but I want you in a warm house and not running outside bringing in wood and trying to keep a fire going. And didn't we have fun the last time you stayed with me?" Katie placed the small satchel on the floor beside the rocking chair and kneeled in front of her friend. She checked the woman's pulse. It was more rapid than usual as her body fought off the infection. "Besides, at my house, you'll be performing a public service, talking me through roasting my first turkey dinner. I bought one so we can have a small celebration at my house."

Chuckles filled the airy room. "Well, I always say, 'friends are God's way of taking care of us' so I guess I'll listen to the Doc this time. Bank the fire and set the screen. And grab those sweet potato pies I baked today. We'll take those along."

Katie did as she was told and after putting everything in the back of the jeep, came back and helped the grand old lady outside and then pushed her up into the front passenger seat. The second antibiotic Katie had filled would knock this out, she thought. She would watch Lovey closely tonight and if necessary she would order oxygen tomorrow.

Darkness had fallen early and clouds filled the night sky as Katie turned the jeep around to head back up the dirt road to her own house.

Just as she was about to take the curve up the hill, she thought she saw a light coming from across the river. She stopped and backed up. "Is that a light?"

Her passenger leaned forward to peer through the side window with rain streaming down it. "It sure is, honey. Flashlights. Somebody must be back over there tonight." Excitement cracked her voice and she began to cough.

Katie reached out a hand to pat Lovey's back as she struggled to catch her breath. "This is even more reason for you to come home with me. You'll be safer there." She offered a sip from the bottle of cough syrup in a drugstore bag on the console and waited till the woman was breathing evenly before she put the jeep back in drive and started to pull away.

"Shouldn't you call the sheriff?"

Katie caught a sparkle of mischief in Lovey's eyes as she stopped the jeep and picked up her cell phone. She held the tiny phone but hesitated. Calling him tonight would ruin her plan for canceling on him at the last possible moment.

"Should I get my shotgun?" Low laughter was smothered by more coughing from the sick woman.

"No. No..." Katie smiled in the dim interior of the jeep. "You're a troublemaker, aren't you, lady? I think you're enjoying this situation a little too much and that coughing serves you right. But keep it up and we'll have to do a breathing treatment when we get to the house."

Lying back against the headrest, the woman was silent as she took several shallow breaths. "Ok. I'll stop fun'in with you but I do think we should call. The sheriff and his deputies have combed that place looking for these young fools and it'd be a shame to let them slip away."

Katie reached across to loop the warm scarf around Lovey's neck and secure her seatbelt before she searched for the number. "All right, I'm calling. Just sit still while I do."

Chapter 34

Early the following morning, the two women sat together over a second cup of hot coffee, their bellies filled with a warm meal. Homemade biscuits and milk gravy along with hot red pepper ground sausage patties fried crisp by Lovey had been enjoyed by both of them. The food was ready to eat when she came from the shower at 7:00 a.m. and she relished it despite her sharp words to Lovey. "Aren't you supposed to be in bed resting?"

"I'm right as rain, girl. My fever broke during the night and I was raring to go but I didn't want to wake you before dawn." Lovey nodded her head as she reached for a cup of coffee.

Katie slathered another biscuit with blackberry jelly. She all but groaned as she took the first bite. "You're killing me with all this homecooked food."

Lovey took another biscuit as well and layered it with rich honey. She chewed slowly. After an appraising look at the slender body of Katie, she pronounced her verdict. "You can stand a little fattening up, child. Our mountain boys like their women with a little meat on 'em. Maybe you can run me on home as you drive out to work."

"No, please stay," Katie said, reaching across to take the older woman's hand. At least till we hear from Bobby, um, I mean Sheriff Lane." She withdrew her hand, leaned back and avoided the mischief in the eyes of her companion.

"Won't be long, now. He called while you were in the shower and he's on his way over to fill us in. He said they didn't arrest anyone but picked up some new clues."

Katie choked as she sat a little straighter. She took a sip of the cooling coffee and cleared her throat. As she continued to avoid the smug look on the mature face across from her, she heard the crunch of tires on gravel as the sheriff pulled his car close and stopped near the side door where they sat. She stood and met him there. The rain had stopped during the night, and a pale sun was rising, but he brought a damp chill into the house as she quickly pushed the sliding glass door closed behind him.

***

Katie brought another mug and poured it full as she invited him to sit. He greeted Miss Lovey as Katie pulled another chair over and settled beside him at the little round table just off the kitchen. "Have some breakfast," she offered.

"No thanks, but the coffee is great. I needed caffeine." He took a long gulp before continuing. "I've been up most all night chasing ghosts."

"Who'd you catch?" Lovey leaned forward - anxious to hear the details.

Bobby's eyes narrowed. "Do you have suspicions, Miss Lephew? Please tell me anything you think you know." He sipped more coffee as he waited for her reply, staring at her like a specimen under a microscope.

Laughter erupted in the quiet room as she broke from his gaze. "Oh, I don't know nothing much about it, Sheriff. I just know we got us a real bad drug problem in this county and I hate to see more young people lost to it. You'll catch 'em, though. Did you find some clues?"

"Not enough, although we have some fresh ideas about a connection with a gang out of Ohio. I want to set up an undercover operation in your cabin if you'll let me. If we're right, we can catch and stop this group for good. I've been in touch with some guys in Cincinnati and a drug task force there wants to come down and help."

"Wow, our little town's getting into the big time now. Sure. You can use my place. Whatever you need from me, I'm happy to help. This sweet doctor wants to coddle me anyway, so maybe I can stay here for a bit."

"Sure you can." Katie turned to Bobby to explain. "She has a bad cough and needs to finish her medicine while I keep an eye on her. She's incorrigible."

Bobby smiled at Katie and she blushed and dipped her head, remembering his kiss on Friday night in spite of herself. He looked as if he could read her thoughts and his smile widened, causing butterflies to take flight in her belly.

"Miss Lephew might not be the only one here with a stubborn mind of her own. What's with ignoring me all week, Katie? I've been calling about Thanksgiving."

Katie stood to collect the dishes and stack them. "I was planning to call you when I got a chance. We can't come for dinner tomorrow. Lovey's sick and you don't want to take a chance on Mathew catching this virus she has – and she needs to rest besides."

"Oh, pooh, I'm fit as a fiddle now, Katie girl. We can go."

With the dishes in the sink, Katie looked at her watch as she turned back to the table with a frown for Lovey. "You're going back to bed right now, woman. If I have to stand over you I will but I really need to get to the clinic to see a few patients before we close for the rest of the week. Will you be good?"

"Sure. The 'greatest wealth is health'."

Bobby stood as well. "I'll be going then. Hope you don't mind if I install a phone at your house, Miss Epperson. I've already called for it."

"Great idea, Bobby. I told her last night she has to get one."

"OK, then. It's settled. It's probably just as well that we cancel Thanksgiving dinner since I have this stake-out to run. But we'll talk real soon." Ignoring the older woman, his intense gaze raked up and down Katie's body as if he knew every inch of it intimately and she felt the heat rise in her cheeks.

LOVEY
Summer 1927

Chapter 35

John's son, Thomas, arrived in Michigan by train to help Lovey bring his father's body home for burial in the family plot on Raven Ridge. Mrs. Epperson had sent him and Lovey put aside her own pain to help the young man who was feeling his own grief. At twenty-one, Thomas was a handsome echo of his father, and the murmur of the mourners quieted as he entered the room. Father and son weren't close. He and his sister had tried to rebuild the relationship with John in recent years and although it was obvious they cared for one another, they hadn't stayed in close contact.

Thomas had lived with Lovey and John and the girls a few months the year before and tried working at the plant with his father. He quickly learned he hated the confinement of the job as well as the city. "I'm just not cut out for towns," he said after just a few months, packing his bag. "I guess Granny was right about me belonging on the farm."

Lovey remembered the day they put him on the train home. "Working inside isn't for everybody, son," John had said, reaching awkwardly to pat him on the back. "I miss the ridge sometimes too. Be good to your granny and tell her I hope to see her again soon."

Now, that would never happen.

She reminisced as she watched Thomas cross the living room filled with neighbors and friends. He stood over his father's body for a few minutes where it laid in the polished coffin. Lovey sat frozen despite the warm evening. She sat between Alice and Nerva near the coffin as she spoke to visitors and waited for Thomas to make his way to her. The boy's shoulders had grown broader and his hair was bleached light from days spent working on the farm without a hat. He stopped to speak to his three half-sisters who sat on the couch, turning the pages of a picture book.

Finally Thomas stood before her and she rose to welcome him. He enveloped her in a bear hug. "Granny Epperson bought tickets for tomorrow on the afternoon train and we're all to be on it," he announced. "I've already spoken to the undertaker and they'll prepare the body to be shipped home on the same train."

Lovey went limp with relief that he had taken charge and she squeezed his hand as he released her from the hug. She slid into the chair again. "Thank you for coming, Thomas." She had been so overwhelmed and indecisive, feeling like a washed-out shirt blowing in the wind, twisting away from any firm funeral plans. She welcomed someone else to tell her what to do. She had once been an independent, decisive woman. Had marriage and motherhood stolen that confidence from her or had it come from the devastating loss she felt without John by her side? Late that night she and Alice began packing her meager belongings in three large trunks.

Alice pulled out a stack of work pants from the bureau and laid them on the bed, already covered with clothing. "Do you want to take John's clothes, Lovey?"

She took a pair of the pants and held them to her face, inhaling. Although freshly laundered, John's scent came to her, woodsy and rain fresh along with a touch of automobile oil from the factory. Words choked in her throat and she felt faint.

Alice pushed her gently down to sit on the edge of the bed. "Take a break, honey, and I'll finish this. We'll pack everything and you can decide later."

Lovey watched her friend work, briskly rolling clothes and placing it into the trunk. She wondered if she would ever see Alice again after tomorrow. She knew she would miss her.

"Thanks, Alice. I don't know what I would do without you here. I feel as limp as a dishrag."

"I know. Just sit back and let us take care of you now. We love you and just hate so much what's happened to poor John. He was a good man, Lovey."

She lay back on the bed and turned on her side. She would do as Alice said. She would return home with her husband's body to see him properly buried and then she would see what life held for her and the children. She hoped after the funeral, this strange lethargy that had overtaken her would lift and she would be able to care for her children – somehow. A widow at twenty-eight, she wondered what the future offered.

Chapter 36

Lovey tidied her hair, pushing the unruly black curls behind her ears as the train slowed near the station in Tazewell. The trip had covered over 500 miles and stretched into long hours. After traveling with three small children she felt like a bag of worn-out rags. The younger two girls had taken turns and sometimes together had wallowed on her lap, seeking comfort. They had been fretful throughout the trip. Jackie had whimpered often for her daddy since his death and Lovey watched over her children through the long night of travel. She worried most about her oldest child. The girl wasn't eating and her face was as white and thin as a paper-doll.

The train came to a stop with a final squeak and a cloud of steam. Lovey stood and handed the smallest child to Thomas and took the older girls by the hand, one on either side of her. They moved forward to the doors to exit the train, and descended wooden steps that had been brought up and fitted tight against the train by the conductor.

The sun was high in the sky, blinding her, and the air was stifling. Her face brightened at the sight of Granny and Uncle Harold standing on the platform and she took the last two steps in a leap, dragging the girls along with her.

"Granny," she cried, running into the familiar arms. Allowing her tears to gush from red swollen eyes, she collapsed against the one woman she could count on to care for them all. She had swept the girls along with her, and they all shared in the warm embrace. The sweet floral scent of the 'Evening in Paris' perfume Granny dabbed on for special occasions filled Lovey's senses. She was home.

Uncle Harold moved closer to share in the hug. She grabbed him close, looping her arms around his waist and sucking back her tears. She managed a thin smile. He and Granny had married this past spring in a no fuss ceremony by the circuit preacher one Sunday afternoon, waiting till it was done to share the news. They belonged together.

"We got your wire, honey. I talked to Mrs. Epperson and we borrowed a car from Mr. Johnson to take you up the ridge to her house," Uncle Harold said.

Lovey stepped back to look at her family, took Jackie from Thomas and pulled a wrinkled handkerchief from her pocket to blot her eyes. "Thank you for being here for me. Both of you."

Granny hugged her again. "Where else would we be, girl? A body's family embraces you during hard times." She tickled Jackie under the chin, grinning at the four-year old.

Thomas went with Uncle Harold to get the large trunks from the baggage car and Granny herded the children away. The funeral home attendant arrived at the station to retrieve the body and assured Lovey they would get him ready and bring him to the house as soon as possible. She nodded. The laying out was to be at the Epperson homeplace. It was the only way, really, but she stiffened her spine, uneasy over Mrs. Epperson's genuine dislike for her.

Granny and the children had settled on a plain wooden bench outside the tiny station, and Lovey joined them, and watched as the men labored with the luggage. She felt numb. The musical lilt of Granny's hushed conversation with the girls buzzed around her like a honeybee. She slumped against the building.

Mr. Johnson owned the black Chrysler where Thomas had finally secured two of the trunks in the boot, hoisting the final one onto the top of the large car, and tied it with rope. Lovey watched without seeing, beyond caring if her belongings made it to Granny's in one piece.

Uncle Harold took the wheel, with Thomas in the front seat beside him. Granny and Lovey sat in the back with the three girls on their laps. Jackie clung to her mother, staring silently at these strangers. Lovey wasn't surprised that Mr. Johnson had loaned them the luxurious car. He and John had once been business partners and she had found the Johnsons to be generous people. They treated him much like a son and visited the small family often in the north, as Mrs. Johnson despised the heat. Lovey had come to care for them.

"I'm so glad you're finally here," Granny said, patting Melinda on the leg, but including them all in her words. "You need your family such a time as this." She nodded and glanced out the side window of the car.

"I thought we would ride that train for forever," Deloris said, looking at her older sister for agreement but Melinda was silent. "My daddy died, you know."

"Hush, child." Granny reached across to take her hand, and smiled at the youngster. "Do they still call you DeeDee?"

As the car turned off the black-topped highway, Uncle Harold drove slowly around the curves climbing Raven Ridge, and Lovey caught her breath at the sight of the rocky hills of home. Her chest was tight with tears. Her heart pounded and her hands clenched together, encircling the little one on her lap. The rich green of trees, scrubs and grasses tumbled over one another and covered boulders jutting though the uneven terrain by the side of the lane.

She watched the familiar ridge road rush by through the dusty glass window. She had never imagined this trip home alone. She straightened and brushed a hand across her face as if to capture any stray tears. She choked down her sorrow.

The car rose up the ridge, bouncing on the narrow dirt road, jarring her teeth. She clinched her mouth shut. Finally they reached the fork in the road across from the old white church where the funeral would be held and took the left turn that would carry them to the Epperson home. They arrived within an hour from leaving the station.

Lovey would remember the sight of Mrs. Epperson sitting by the front window for the rest of her life. The old woman's face was drawn with grief. Her eyes were dark, her faded hair pulled tightly away from her face and fastened in a bun on the back of her head, and her mouth was downturned. With anger or grief? She sat still as a raven staring onto the road - obviously waiting for them.

There were no words Lovey could offer to eliminate the hurt for either of them. She climbed out of the car and took the steps one at a time, one hand holding the railing, and finally stepped inside the house as Thomas took her arm to offer support. She made her way into the front room. "I'm so sorry, Mrs. Epperson," she said. "John was a good man and a loving father and his life has ended much too soon." She leaned forward to embrace her mother-in-law.

"Aye, that is the truth be told." The older woman stood and stared at her like a bug she would like to squash, and leaned close enough so only Lovey and Thomas heard her hateful words. "I hope you're happy now that you've pushed him into an early grave. Is that enough revenge for the Lephews?"

Lovey gasped. The impact of the words felt like a hard blow to the head and she stepped back. Mrs. Epperson reached up to pat the face of her tall grandson before she stepped around them both and walked away, her back held rigid and straight, long black skirts swaying with each proud step. Lovey stood speechless as Laura came forward and squeezed her hand before following on her grandmother's heels. Both disappeared into the back bedroom.

Others in the household hurried forward to pay their respects as if unaware the woman had shunned her. The coldness had been expected but it stung nonetheless. Granny and Uncle Harold walked behind her with the little ones in tow while Thomas settled her in a straight-back chair and sat down by her.

"Give her time, Lovey," he whispered. "It's been a shock for her."

She smiled at the young man as her heart squeezed. "I'm afraid all the time in the world won't change her feelings toward me, Thomas, but I'll give her my respect, as is only right for this time."

"We all know you aren't to blame for his death any more than you are for taking dad back to Michigan but I reckon Granny needs to blame somebody. And she's stubborn."

"I'm stubborn too, Thomas. But we'll get through the next days without doing battle. I promise." She patted his hand which was still looped through her arm.

Chapter 37

The funeral was held two days later at Raven Ridge Baptist Church
and was attended by most of the community. Many of the ridge
boys had followed John to Pontiac for work and he had helped them get
the jobs they sought. Some had even roomed with Lovey and John
temporarily. Their families offered sincere condolences.

John's large family were well known on the ridge, and Lovey
supposed everybody felt sorry for Mrs. Epperson over losing another
child. The older woman had buried her husband, one son and a daughter,
and now one more son, but she held her head high despite a stooped
posture. There was sympathy for Lovey as well but she refused to allow
herself consolation from the outpouring of love. She would fall apart and
be of no use to anybody, least of all her children.

She moved through the funeral as if in a fog, and stayed detached
from everyone. The heart-wrenching pain she had initially felt settled
into a dull ache that lodged deep inside her. She performed as necessary.
She walked in slow motion, a new black silk dress Granny had found for
her swishing against her legs, polished black shoes with chunky heels
echoing her heavy steps as she walked down the center aisle. The
original hand hewn heart pine flooring of the old church had seen a little
of everything. With her three children and John's older two seated with
her in the front pew, she felt empty and ghostlike, a hard outer shell of
the woman she had been just last week. Then, she had sat around the

kitchen table at her home in Michigan, gossiping with her friends, Alice and Nerva. She had complained about the man now lying in his coffin motionless as a buck blinded by the bright light of an careless hunter.

John's mother had taken the second row with her three remaining sons and their wives, and extended family took up five more rows. Friends soon filled it to overflowing, with a few men standing at the back of the church. She felt surrounded and judged.

Preacher Taylor led the sermon, not talking about John at all but repeatedly asking, "Are you right with God, today, brother and sister?" He raced from side to side across the small altar, searching each face assembled. John would have hated this spectacle. Lovey's family had fallen away from the church. She and John hadn't often attended either, preferring their own quiet soul searching instead of the organized religion of their childhoods. Sometimes she regretted not taking the children.

Pointing to the coffin, the preacher yelled, "This man didn't know his time was coming and you won't either. Today – this moment - is the time to accept our Lord as your Savior." He leaned into the aisle and said, "Yes, Lord, yes, sweet Jesus," as if he heard a silent command from above. "God demands obedience from his children. Come and repent your ways unto the Lord and receive salvation."

A long prayer followed and Lovey became lost in her own thoughts of the life she had shared with John. She thought of the day they had brought baby Melinda home from the hospital and she cried trying to get the baby's diaper fastened tight enough. He had laughed at her before he showing her how to do it. She remembered when Deloris had fallen on the furnace grate last year and burned her leg. John had been so calm and loving as he held her on his lap as they treated the burns for weeks. And when Alice's baby died, John had held her with arms of steel. How would she go on living without him?

The Younger sisters sang *Sweet Bye and Bye*. Their voices sounded so clear and pure in the old church with no music to accompany them. They ended it with a final verse of

In the sweet bye and bye,
We shall meet on that beautiful shore;
In the sweet bye and bye,
We shall sing on that beautiful shore

Another old favorite, *Swing Low, Sweet Chariot* came next. Both songs brought tears to almost all in attendance. Lovey felt her tears rise to the brink of her eyelids, where she held them through shear will. She refused to share with the family and friends here today but would save them for a private time between her and John tonight. Silly, she knew, but it was all she had left of him - their private time late at night when she allowed herself to think of him, talk to him and let tears run unchecked down her face.

John's older daughter, Laura, sat beside her, and also showed very little emotion. Lovey prayed the service would soon end. She felt sweat gather and trickle between her breasts and Laura dabbed at her face with a lace edged handkerchief. Laura, still without a child of her own, was devoted to the little girls of her father's second marriage and Deloris' head lay in her lap. The young woman used the back of her slender hand to brush lightly against the delicate skin of the little girl's pale face.

Melinda, soon to be 9 years old, sat ramrod straight beside her mother, her mouth tight and her thin hair combed into a straight bob, a blue ribbon pinned on one side.

Minutes later, the service ended with a rendition of *Amazing Grace* as the pallbearers came forward to carry the simple coffin out into the stifling heat of a late August morning. She gathered the hands of her older girls and stepped out behind the coffin as was expected of her. Thomas carried Jackie and Laura fell into step with her grandmother, taking her by the arm. John's remaining brothers and other extended family followed. Lovey's small group of family members followed quietly behind the others. Her father stepped forward to offer her support for the walk.

The wagon carrying the coffin creaked forward toward the wooded path. The cemetery was over a mile away, downhill into the lower valley, but would offer shade from the uncut forest. She would have chosen a more accessible resting place for John but the Epperson graveyard dated back to 1683 and it was expected. She refused to fight the family. Dried leaves and dead grasses scuffed her new shoes as they rubbed a blister on her heel. She prayed for strength in this miserable heat and wondered if perhaps the girls could ride on the wagon back to the church.

***

The graveside prayers were mercifully short. Although it was cooler here in the shade of large, leafy maple, sycamore and oak trees, she longed for the dreadful day to be done. Mourners stepped forward to offer words of comfort while she stood by the open grave.

"What will you do now, Lovey?" Houston Johnson asked, while his wife, Beulah, took her hand and hugged her, turning quickly to hide her own tears under a large black hat that covered half her face. They had lost a half-grown daughter the year before from a cancer that took her quickly. Lovey gave the woman's hand a tight squeeze before allowing her to move away.

"I really haven't decided, Houston," she answered, noticing that the group closest to them had fallen silent to listen, curious about the young widow's plans. She wondered too. She was sleeping in her old iron bed at Granny's house, with the girls on a pallet beside her on the floor. That couldn't last too long.

The kind older man patted her hand. "I loved John. You come and see me if you need help with anything. You hear, girl?"

"I will," she replied, accepting the warm hug he offered before he put an arm around his wife and stepped away. She turned with a sad smile to greet the next person, accepting sympathy. Men were mopping sweaty foreheads with large cotton handkerchiefs and using broad brim hats to fan themselves while their women were delicately patting their faces with lacy squares of silk.

The sun was high in the sky by the time the family drifted slowly away from the cemetery, most of them hiking the narrow dirt trail back to the church, but the wagon bed offering a ride for those who needed it. Her mother, Naomi, with a rare day off to attend the service, led her like a child back to the borrowed car for the ride down the ridge and home.

"I'm hungry," Jackie said as the car began to move.

"Me too," Deloris added. "I want a chicken leg."

"Shush, girls. There's plenty of food back at the house," Naomi assured the children, petting Deloris where she leaned against her. "We'll be home soon."

Lovey was glad the girls showed interest in eating. After these sad days she was relieved to hear their innocent chatter drift through her haze. Their laughter gave her hope she too would recover from this blow.

Chapter 38

As the unrelenting heat of late August swept down on the mountain valley, Lovey moped around the small cabin, finding it difficult to move. She watched quietly as Granny took care of her children for her. With Uncle Harold also living there, it was crowded in the little home, but he helped with the children. They quickly grew to be fond of him.

On Friday after the funeral she received a letter from the Hudson Motor Company, saying they would be sending a check in the amount of $4,000.00 from a life insurance policy the plant had provided its employees. She had thrown the letter in the floor and stomped on it before running from the house, blinded by grief. She couldn't find a way past her loss. Most days she stayed in bed, seeking the shade and stillness of the bedroom and the solace of sleep.

Finally Granny forced her awake. "Come on, Lovey. Hot biscuits are coming out of the oven right now," she announced one Sunday evening. "And Melinda's stirring up a pan of gravy. You know you hate cold gravy." Granny popped her head through the doorframe of the tiny bedroom, following the cheerful voice, urging her to come to the dinner table for her favorite meal, whether it was served morning, noon or night.

"Thanks, but I'm right swimmy headed. And I don't see how I can possibly hold down any food in this heat." Lovey turned to face her granny, her eyes half closed and lazy. Granny was the one constant in her life, the long gray braid wound around her head as always, the kind blue eyes in a plump face that spoke of a long life of her own heartache.

"Girl, you have wallowed in this bed way too long."

"I don't know what I would do without you and Uncle Harold to take care of the children." She blinked her swollen eyes against the late afternoon sun streaming through the open window. The white muslin curtains lay flat against the window seal, the air so still she could see dust modes floating through the room.

Granny came to sit beside her on the narrow bed and Lovey was annoyed at being forced to pay attention. She noticed the clothing and bed quilts still littered the floor that the older woman carefully stepped around.

"You have to try harder, Lovey. I know you're hur'in but your children need you." Granny picked up a little rag doll the girls had discarded and smoothed its yellow yarn hair back into place. She stood and handed the doll to Lovey. "Now come on and get up. I expect you at the dinner table in five minutes to eat with the family."

There was steel in her voice after the endless days of kindness and sympathy she had given and Lovey responded to her command. She felt like a child who knew when she had tried the patience of the adult in charge. She stood and smoothed down her wrinkled dress.

The small round wooden table, with four wooden chairs cushioned in yellow flowered fabric clustered tightly around, could barely hold the small family. Uncle Harold was holding Jackie and

Granny took her seat beside him. Lovey watched as her grandmother
nodded encouragement and slowly she put one foot in front of the other.
The older girls quickly moved to share a single seat, their small bottoms
fitting snugly side by side, smiling at their mother.

She sat in the vacated chair, anger choking her at the thought of
eating food. She tried to swallow the warm bread without losing her
stomach. She took very small bites. Her insides were hollow after the
past weeks lying in bed, eating only what Granny forced down her throat
late at night.

It was hotter here in the kitchen and the open window at her back
did nothing to ease the misery of the heat. She felt strangled. The food
stuck in her throat and her skin crawled with nerves. Each sound grated
against her head like a woodpecker hard at work on a post. She felt
light-headed and nauseous.

"I don't want to eat, Granny," Deloris said. "I only want cold
milk."

Lovey reached out and slapped her child across the face.
"You'll eat what's put in front of you and stop whining about it. You
hear me, child."

Deloris looked at her mother with large blue eyes, startled at the
unexpected slap. Tears pooled and stood in her eyes before sliding down
her cheeks. Lovey's anger melted and she stared at her hand as if it had
acted alone, without any input from her. She was shamed by the quick
look that passed between her grandmother and Uncle Harold and

reached across to pull her sweet little DeeDee into her lap. "I'm sorry, baby. I'm so very sorry."

Deloris began to sob, soft sounds escaping her open mouth. Lovey brought the child's head up to her shoulder to cradle her against her chest. "I'll never hit you again. I promise. You're mama's big girl and I love you to pieces." She brushed the damp hair back from her little girl's face and brushed away the tears with a thumb against her chubby check. She rocked the little body back and forth in her arms, bouncing a bit in the straight chair. "I took my anger out on you but I'll never do it again."

The others at the small table were silent while Lovey whispered and Deloris continued to whimper before finally popping her thumb in her mouth and growing quiet. Then the conversation resumed as if there had not been an interruption.

"The Almanac says we'll have a break in this heat by next week," Harold said. "It's about time."

"Not soon enough for me. It's hot enough to bake biscuits on the rooftop. And if we don't get some rain soon, what's left in the garden will be dried up to nothing." Granny waved the damp dish towel - trying to create a stir in the still air.

Melinda giggled at her grandmother. "I could put the biscuits up there for you, Granny, and sit in my special tree and watch them bake."

"Don't get any foolish ideas from your granny, Melinda. The roof is no place for biscuits or little girls." Uncle Harold pulled a silly face at Deloris where she sat still and quiet in her mother's lap, sucking her thumb, her mouth relaxing and curling upward over the playful talk.

"But I could climb over there from my tree," Melinda insisted.

"Lord no, child," Granny said. "The last thing we need is a broken bone to deal with if you fall out of that tree."

"School will start soon and that should keep her out of mischief," Harold said.

"You'll walk there with your cousins from around the ridge," he added to Melinda and Deloris. "It'll be fun."

Lovey didn't respond to any of them, still cooing over her troubled child, but she listened to the conversation floating around her. Granny was right. She had received all the time she would get for grieving. It was time to move on.

Chapter 39

By October life was returning to some semblance of order. Melinda and Deloris were enrolled in Baylor's Bridge School at the bottom of the ridge by Caney Creek. Lovey asked around about a small farm for sale. Willie Ray Singleton said he had ten acres with his old home place on it and she made arrangements to meet him at the small house. Uncle Harold and her father went along.

"It's small but it'd be a right good start for you, Lovey. It comes with a small tobacco allotment that would bring you a cash crop if you can find enough help to raise it." Her father had walked the acreage the day before. "It's got good rich earth and it hasn't been overworked."

Lovey peeked from lowered lids to gauge her father's words as they walked the overgrown path. He was a man of few words but added, "And I might be able to spare a couple of my hands to help you get the first 'baccer crop in."

"We can all pitch in," Uncle Harold offered. "Those girls will be a big help to you in a few years. And the place ain't too far from us."

The location and its closeness was part of the appeal for Lovey. She nodded at Uncle Harold. This farm was close enough to Granny to walk back up the ridge for help but it also offered Lovey and the girls a place of their own where they could settle in and become part of the community.

When Mr. Singleton showed Lovey the small house, she was pleased at the space, although it needed a lot of work, particularly cleaning. Old Mrs. Singleton had been dead for several years and it looked as if nothing had been done since well before that time.

"It needs a bit of work, I reckon," admitted Mr. Singleton. "I can help with some paint and varnish."

"That's kind of you." She stepped outside and still considered her options, her gaze sweeping the rolling valley below the small farm, trees in the distance still burning with the orange gold and red of another autumn. There was a small overgrown kitchen garden in the side yard just out the back door. The house had two small bedrooms for her and the girls, with a fireplace in each. The kitchen had a wood stove for cooking and the well was deep with good clear spring water feeding it.

The price was low enough for John's life insurance to cover with some left over to see them through until her farm prospered. "I'll take it, Mr. Singleton." Lovey reached out to shake his hand but he looked to the men for reassurance that the farm would be sold before returning her gesture.

"Alright then, we'll have the papers drawn up and sign them and it'll be yours," he replied, reaching to shake with the two men also.

The next morning she began cleaning the little house, cobwebs falling to tangle in her hair as she used her straw broom on the walls. Mr. Singleton provided paint, true to his word, and she coated everything that was nailed down with a new shine. Over the next week she moved some of their belongings there. She went into town to look for bed frames and a table for the kitchen. Granny sewed ruffled curtains from remnants she had on hand and by the time she and the girls moved in, it had become an attractive home.

The cool days of autumn found them settling in for the winter. She bought a milk cow and some chickens and Granny shared some canned goods she had put up along with a large ham from the smokehouse. She laid in stores of staples to see her through the winter ahead and began thinking of herself as a landowner despite being a young mother all alone, her heart often beating fiercely in her throat, strangling her with raw fear.

***

A few weeks into January, soup beans simmered on the cook stove as Lovey sat quietly near the fireplace, enjoying her solitude. She read her bible while the youngest child napped. Her eye-lids closed for just a moment.

The older girls came racing through the door, a cold rush of icy air following them. "Shut the door, quick, girls. Smells like snow out there today."

Lovey hurried to help them out of their coats and mittens, hanging them on a hook by the door, adding the matching pink knit hats and scarves she had made them for Christmas. The girls seemed content with their school work and the friends living nearby along the ridge.

"Do you really think it will snow, Mama?" Melinda asked, her face red from the bitter cold? "Should I get more wood in?"

"Not just yet, dear. Come by the fire and get warm first and then we'll do our chores. There's still daylight left." She brought both girls warm milk and a toasted biscuit left from the morning to the table and they joined her there, eager for their small meal after the climb up the ridge. She added a spoonful of Granny's blackberry jam to each girl's biscuit. Melinda reminded her of John, her brow thin and serious. She was a hard worker.

"It might snow, Deloris. Uncle Harold said it was predicted in his almanac." She took a sip of the warmed over coffee, listening for Jackie to awake from her nap.

"How can the book know?" Deloris, ever her doubter, asked, a drip of jam smearing her chin.

"Don't know, DeeDee. And it's not always right but is more often than not." Lovey reached across to wipe Deloris' mouth.

"Don't call me that, Mama. Jimmy Lee Mason made fun of me and called me a baby when Melinda used it at school.

"I've always called you that, haven't I mama?"

Lovey brushed a hand across her eldest daughter's worried brow. "We have, sweetheart, cause you couldn't say her name when you were so little but maybe she's all grown up now. We'll call her what she wishes. Does that suit you, Miss Deloris?"

"Yes ma'am. I'm much 'more growed' this year, since I go to school." She pursed her little lips in a pout that made Lovey laugh aloud, the sound tinkling in the quiet room.

Wind rattled the kitchen window near the table and Lovey shivered, remembering her winters up north. That first winter in Michigan, when the snow had lain on the ground for months, she had been beyond homesick. John had encouraged her to remember the spring times of her youth and look forward to the great times they would share ahead. But the good times had ended all too soon for him. Memories of her loss of John erased the laughter from her face.

Jackie cried out, awake from her nap, just as Lovey fell into bittersweet memories that often derailed her. Small flakes of snow began to pepper the glass window. "Coming, sweetheart," she called, getting to her feet. "Get ready for our chores, girls, while I get Jackie ready and we'll all go out together."

Both girls stuffed the remainder of their bread down and finished the warm milk as Jackie rushed out with a joyous giggle to hug her big sisters. She missed them so during the day. "There's snow," she announced. "It's on my window and woke me."

"Get your shoes on and we can go outside." Lovey added wood to the fire so the house would be warm upon their return and stirred the beans. She mixed a pan of cornbread and slid it in the oven. "When we finish outside, we'll have our supper and snuggle in for the night."

She helped all the children into coats and hats in preparation for their evening routine of milking the cow and getting in wood and fresh water before dark. The younger girls couldn't do much alone, but they were learning, and could each carry a little tin bucket of fresh water. She would milk the cow while Melinda collected kindling for the morning fire. Melinda did more than her share of the work.

The little family went out into the cold evening under a darkening sky of falling snow. Lovey guided her children through their outside chores while snow blanketed the hillside. The girls were delighted. Deloris and Jackie chased one another across the yard, scooping up little snowballs to throw. Although this life wasn't what she and John had imagined, she had managed to create some semblance of that dream and felt he would be proud of her.

The cold took her breath as she swung the milk jug over her arm. Melinda piled a stack of wood in her open ~~arMiss~~ *Arms*

As they trudged back to the house, Lovey planned for warmer weather, knowing the tobacco crop planted in the spring must succeed. She would do whatever became necessary, even doing the manual work alone if necessary.

KATIE
December 1999

Chapter 40

Katie removed her white coat late on Friday afternoon two weeks before Christmas and hung it over the hook on the back of her office door. The light was almost gone outside her window but she saw the misty outline of Clinch Mountain rising in the evening sky. Maybe tomorrow she would hike and be able to relish the cold fresh mountain air and clear the cobwebs from her brain – and her heart. The week had been busier than usual and her desk was piled high with loose paperwork that begged for filing but she planned to attend a rotary club meeting tonight and wanted to go home and change first. The bills were paid for December and the books completed so the filing could wait. A secretary would be nice.

A local lawyer, Brian Coffee, had asked her to dinner and to the Rotary meeting with him after. She suspected he might have more on his mind than helping her build her medical practice although Katie didn't feel any sparks between them. But he was attractive and smart and she needed the distraction.

She felt physically tired and after the evening ahead, she hoped the exhaustion would enable her to fall asleep tonight without thinking about Bobby Lane. Her dreams this week had been filled with him and his rugged good looks. Why did she find him so darn hard to resist? His kiss had burned all the way to her toes and she had been ready for more. She had really liked him and his son was adorable. Were all the good men taken?

Her practice should be all she was thinking about right now. Patient growth was up. Right now Misty was taking care of the scheduling, reception and nursing care but Katie hoped she could afford more help soon. Patients had started to come in after news had spread about the emergency delivery here at the clinic. The community was accepting her instead of driving to Morristown for medical care.

She swallowed the last bitter sip of cold coffee and set the cup down hard with a clank against the metal desk. She pulled her small purse from the bottom drawer of her desk and took a light step toward the door just as Misty came in. "Sorry, you have one more patient, Katie. Looks like a bad cold and sore throat with a high temperature."

"Okay, but then I have to go. Remember I have that Rotary club thing tonight."

Katie put her white coat back on as she stepped into the hallway. "Why don't you lock up and go on home. I can handle this one alone."

"I'll stay with you." They whispered in the hallway as they walked toward the exam room where the last minute patient waited.

"Are you sure? Don't you have to get supper for the family or something."

"It's ok." Misty cocked her eyebrow as if to say something more. "You might need me."

Katie stepped forward and entered the exam room without more comment. She didn't want the patient to hear them gossiping outside the room.

"Hello, I'm Doctor Ka…" she was saying as she opened the door and stopped just inside the room as she saw Bobby Lane and his son, Mathew. "Oh, it's you."

Chapter 41

Recovering, Katie stiffened her spine, put on her most professional smile and walked to the exam table where the young boy sat, wrapped in a soft blue blanket. She reached to touch his forehead, although she often scoffed at parents who thought they could determine a fever by touching the skin on their child's head. Her hand followed his pink cheek down to his delicate chin and cupped it tenderly for a moment. He looked so much like his father. "Hi, Mathew. Are you feeling poorly, little buddy?"

Bobby was jumpy and stood closer to them, placing a large hand on the boy's shoulder. He answered for his son.. "He's almost lost his voice. I've kept him home from school all week and thought he was getting better. His fever was under control until a couple of hours ago. When it shot up again I worried I should bring him in before the weekend."

The boy touched his father's hand, and looked at her with lackluster hazel eyes and a half-hearted smile as Katie listened to his lungs. She heard the rattle of congestion but his lungs were mostly clear. She would need a throat culture. She had seen several cases of strep this week. "Can I look at your throat, buddy? I can almost promise no shots."

He grinned at her, obviously relieved, and opened his mouth wide. Katie sat on her stool in front of the child. She grabbed a tongue depressor and a long swab and quickly took a sample. The child gagged a little as she finished and reassured him she was done. She patted his arm and handed the specimen to Misty, who had come to stand behind her. They would send it on to the lab but the weekend would delay any results. "It's all over for now. Lean back and relax against your dad."

Katie rolled back to the computer to fill in two prescriptions for him. "These will help while we wait for the culture to come back. I'm giving him something for his cough and an antibiotic because I'm pretty sure its strep and we don't want it to develop into anything more serious. Get these filled and call me if he isn't feeling much better in a day or two."

"I will. Thanks for seeing us so late, Katie." He smiled, his dimples flashing. " I tried to call you after Thanksgiving."

Bobby looked at her with those rich chocolate brown eyes, the lids partially closed in the sexy way that made her sweat. He looked hopeful and she avoided his direct gaze. Turning to Mathew, she asked, "Do you want Misty to take you to the treat box to pick out a toy? You've been very brave." She stood and lifted him off the table and sat him on his feet. Misty led him out to the prize box.

She turned to Bobby. "No problem, Sheriff. I hate to see little ones suffer so I'm happy you caught me before I left." She reached her hand forward as if to shake his.

He took her hand in his but held on. "Is this the way it is now, Katie? All professional? And we're back to you calling me Sheriff? I thought we were past that after our hike up the mountain." He took a step closer to her and she breathed in the scent of him. Maleness and fresh air.

She felt off balance and pulled her hand away. He released his hold on her and she turned to the printer to get the prescriptions she had entered. He took the papers she offered but didn't make a move to leave. He still stood a bit too close to her. His gaze held hers, overpowering. She paced backward in the small space of the exam room and changed the subject.

"I've been busy since the holidays. I haven't even seen Lovey or heard the details of the big drug bust. All I know is what Misty read in the paper. The article confirmed there was a Cincinnati connection and there had been some arrests."

"That's right. Mostly Ohio boys but I still think there's a local connection." He looked as if he wanted to add more but held his tongue. "Mathew and I hoped we could talk you into coming by for pizza and movie night again. When he's feeling better, of course."

"I don't date married men," she snapped. Hearing the harshness in her voice, she softened her tone. Bobby had no way of knowing about her past affair in medical school with what turned out to be a married resident. It had threatened her career and turned her away from any involvements. "Even if they're separated – I'm sorry. I can't afford that kind of reputation in a small town like this. It could ruin my practice."

Katie backed out the door and turned to lead the way back to the waiting area, where Misty and Mathew were examining the little junk toys she kept in a box for the children she saw.

"What'd she say, dad? Is she coming?" Mathew croaked the words out and tried to smile over the wince of pain in his throat.

Looking at the little boy, Katie couldn't help but smile back at him and wish things could be different. He was so sweet and a little needy and she enjoyed spending time with him. She wanted to let him down easy.

"I have plans. And besides, you need to go back to bed and rest. Doctor's orders." She tousled his hair. Misty moved to the front door to unlock it and Katie followed to see them out.

Bobby picked up his son and wrapped the soft blanket around him again. He held Mathew in his strong arms, and moved slowly toward her, his eyes holding hers. "We have our answer, son. But we'll work on her." Mathew peeked over the blanket and smiled at her again. He nodded his head as if to encourage her.

She watched the big man, moving so easily, his stride long and sure as he cradled his son. Katie didn't move as he came closer and then she quickly retreated, tripping a bit on her own feet. She could hear the voice of her brother as clear as if they were teenagers again. *What's wrong, Katie? That guy too much for you to even stay on your feet? You're a total klutz.*

LOVEY
Spring 1929

Chapter 42

The following spring, as her new farm hand, Clint, led the mare along a straight line, the plow made deep grooves in the rich black soil which was soft from spring rains and snow melt off the mountain. Lovey dropped each small plant in a hole and pushed the dirt back around the tender shoots of tobacco. She could have hired another hand to help Clint with the outside work but she had missed the activity of farm life while living in Pontiac. She wanted to work her own land and enjoyed the fresh air and the tightened muscles gained through hard labor. She was a strong girl and birthing three children hadn't changed that. She raised a newly bronzed bare arm to wipe away the sweat accumulating on her forehead. A sudden breeze felt like heaven.

Jackie played alongside the open field, drawing with a stick in the loose dirt as she sang.

> *London Bridge is falling down,*
> *Falling down, falling down.*
> *London Bridge is falling down,*

My fair lady.

The older girls had sung the little tune for her. She was a good little girl who played well alone and caused no trouble.

At the end of the last row, Lovey stopped to go inside and prepare a large noon meal. After trudging to the house she quickly washed up her smallest child, fed her and put her to bed for an afternoon nap. She felt breathless in the warm kitchen as she stood at an open window and watched Clint Collins clean up beside the barn. He removed his work shirt and stood in a sleeveless undershirt, splashing ice cold water from a bucket over his face and muscular arms His boots were caked with the soil of the field they plowed and he rubbed them in the wet grass.

He had walked behind Sassy, her lone horse, as the old mare pulled the plow with his guidance. Sassy, named by the girls, had been a work horse her entire life and didn't require a lot of instruction. Lovey bought her from the Tate family, who lived in Granger County on a hundred acres and raised horses. The old mare had been cheap and if she lived a few years, she fit into Lovey's plan for the little farm to grow.

Clint turned and noticed her staring. His sharp gaze snapped her attention back to the task at hand. "I'm whipping up some cornbread to go with the warmed over soup beans, Clint," she called through the open window. "It'll be ready soon."

He waved his agreement, showing white teeth in an easy grin, before stepping inside the barn to water the horse. Lovey moved away from the window, sliding the bread pan into the hot oven. Tearing her attention away from the vibrate man was difficult. He had worked for her only a few short weeks but was quickly becoming part of her daily landscape. He was slight, not much bigger than she, with light hair that curled on top and eyes so pale that in the glare of a strong sun they looked almost colorless. He was stout though, and thick through the arms and legs, with a cocky little stride that dared any man to mess with him. His temperament was quick, joy and anger interchangeable in a moment's span. Although she had mostly seen the lightness of his nature, he had one day become so angry at the old horse, she thought he might kill it with the whip before she intervened, demanding he stop.

Clint knocked on the screen door and stepped inside just as Lovey checked on the bread in the hot stove and decided it had a few more minutes to brown. She set two places at the table as she chattered. "Sit down, Clint. I know you must be done in after our work this morning. Jackie was plumb tuckered out and was asleep in minutes."

"She enjoyed playing outdoors, though. I 'spect she'll love farming like you. I've never met such a hard working woman." The legs of the chair scraped on the polished pine floor as he pulled it out and sat down at the table.

She blushed at his words and turned away to reach into the hutch for mismatched but clean beverage glasses. "What will you have to drink? Milk, coffee, water?" she asked over her shoulder, but pulled a large glass mug down before he answered, already having learned he enjoyed fresh, cold buttermilk with his dinner. This noon time meal was part of their financial arrangement; as partial payment she served him a hot dinner each day. He lived down in the valley at Mrs. Norton's boarding house, and she provided breakfast and supper. He had family over on Lone Mountain but there had been some falling out with them that he didn't like to talk about.

Lovey checked the bread. It had a nice brown crust on it so she pulled the hot pan from the oven with a dish towel. She inverted the iron skillet she used to bake her bread and popped the loaf onto a plate. She brought that to the table along with a bowl of canned peaches Granny had put up. Her homemade chow-chow was already on the table along with fresh churned butter. She was anxious for some of the early green onions and tomatoes she had been watching grow in her kitchen garden but it was still too early for them.

"You sure enough can cook, Miss Lovey," Clint said after swallowing a few spoons of the food he had put on his plate. "This chow-chow for the beans might be the best part of the job."

Lovey laughed, watching him shovel the food in his mouth. It was good to see someone eat after making food for them. She knew she wasn't a great cook but she had missed seeing a man enjoy her efforts. Another regret of widowhood. "It's my granny's recipe. It has a little kick to it, don't it?"

"Yeah, it does. I can't tell if it's the peppers or the vinegar that gives it that taste, but it doesn't really matter. It's just plain good." He scraped the last of his beans and chow-chow off the plate and followed it with the large hunk of buttered cornbread. He leaned back in the chair, wiping his mouth with one hand, before starting on his peaches like he was sucking out the last of the nectar from a stand of honeysuckle on a dry day.

Lovey concentrated on her plate as she felt his gaze fall across her face and the quiet space of the warm kitchen became thick with unsaid words. The mantle clock in the front room ticked away the minutes as time slowed like a dream. She knew he continued to watch her as she pushed the food around her plate.

Her stomach had growled as she trudged in from the field, but now she couldn't swallow at all. Cornbread stuck in her throat as she envisioned the man sitting across from her taking her into his muscular arms, pulling her close, and kissing her hard on the mouth. These physical longings had come over her unbidden in the past few days and she was ashamed. Her face flushed. She was still in mourning over the death of her husband, the father of her young children, and knew she shouldn't be thinking such wanton thoughts about another man.

"I've been thinking, Miss Lovey. Maybe I could come by here on Sunday morning and help you carry the young'uns to church up the way. It must be hard for you to tote that little one if she gets tired."

A stillness came into the room as Lovey held her breath. When she was able to breathe again, she inhaled and the soggy bread slid down her throat, freeing her voice but leaving her mouth dry. "I'd like that," she mumbled, despite herself. It was just church.

Clint continued to watch her with those pale colorless eyes. His eyelids narrowed, shifting over her sweat soaked body, and she smiled, acknowledging their relationship had shifted. She thought of the rat's nest of limp hair stuck to her head before allowing the newfound happiness this man had brought to her home to wash over her. She felt happy to be alive on this new spring day.

Chapter 43

L ovey slipped the cool satin dress with multiple petticoats over her head and felt it slide into place against her naked skin. It was pale pink with darker roses embroidered around the hips where the dress flared out to encircle her body and fall over her legs. The cash crop had been harvested, and she sent off to buy the first ready-made dress she had ever owned, from the Sears and Roebuck catalog. Black had been her only option this past year of mourning and she was desperate for color again.

The dress felt slick against her freshly washed skin. Her cheeks flamed from days in the sun despite her liberal use of face powder this evening. She tipped her chin higher in the empty room, as if daring anyone to deny her right to the new dress after the hours spent working in the 'baccer field all summer, right alongside the menfolk.

"You should buy yourself a pretty new dress, Shug," Clint had said when they had sold the tobacco. "Then maybe you'd let me take you dancing."

She smiled into her mirror at the memory. Brown chin length hair, lightened from days in the sun, had been pin-curled into waves and was now held behind her ears with tiny silver combs her mother had given her for her birthday. Tonight she and Clint were going to Red's, the local honky-tonk, while the girls stayed with Granny. Tongues had wagged about him coming to church with her but she had defended it, saying he was a hired hand who wanted to find the Lord. Although she wasn't sure she believed it any more than the church ladies and wondered now what the gossips would say upon hearing she had gone dancing.

She had never been dancing. Clint would teach her as he had taught her so many other things about farming. Their flirtation had grown through the heat of July and August as she found more work for him around the farm to keep him close. Now their bodies were at a fever pitch of passion and she knew he wanted and needed her as desperately as she did him. Hearing his quick step on the front porch, she rushed out to meet him.

"Evening, Clint," she greeted, stepping onto the wide front porch overlooking the green valley below. She pulled the door closed. This view of the valley spread out below her front porch took her breath in the early evening dusk and she paused to admire the thick growth surrounding her farm. Crepe myrtles and magnolia trees was in full bloom at the bottom of the hill, perfuming the still air.

"My, oh, my, Miss Lovey. You are a picture. You're just as I imagined you could be." He reached to take her hand and twirl her around on the wide porch, and she felt her full skirt lift and swirl around her knees, tickling the flesh through her new stockings.

"I dare say I'll have the prettiest woman in the county on my arm tonight," he said, pulling her arm through his and leading her down the steps.

Lovey felt content here on Clint's arm as if she just might be the prettiest woman in these parts after all. She had noticed how young girls looked at Clint when they attended church together. He had kept his word and gone to church with her and the girls most every Sunday through the summer. It was time for them to get married, which inspired her to plan for him to ask her before the night was done, and the way she felt right now gave her full confidence that would happen.

Chapter 44

CJ Cunningham brought Lovey a cup of punch from a table against the back wall. "Here you are, Lovey. I can't imagine why old Clint left such a sweet looking girl sitting all alone like this. Would you care to take a whirl with me?"

Lovey's face broke into a wide smile for this friend of Clint's she had just met. The handsome young man danced most of the evening, with first one girl and then another, most notable a woman named Mae, who seemed to dance every dance with someone. He was part of a group of three guys and one girl she and Clint had joined at the dance, sharing a large table with the foursome. "I think I better wait on Clint. He just went to the car for a minute with Burl Stadler." She turned to the door, hopeful Clint would soon appear. "He should be back any minute."

"He's doing a little business, I guess." CJ dropped into the empty chair beside her. "He's a fool, is all I can say, leaving you here alone. Run away with me instead and I'll give you anything your little heart desires." He put a long arm around the back of her chair, gently brushing her bare shoulder with light fingers.

So Clint was selling corn whiskey from the trunk of the car? She shouldn't be surprised. Many of the men nearby had a liquor still back up in the woods. Clint was friendly with the Wilder family and probably sold for them to earn extra cash and although she didn't like the thought of it, she supposed she couldn't blame him.

"So you go to school at Lincoln Memorial?" Lovey asked as she sat straighter in the chair, pulling away from his touch. He was a well-dressed dandy with a Yankee accent who couldn't be much more than twenty-one. "How did you meet Clint?"

CJ grinned at her, bright brown eyes flashing amusement in his sun kissed face as he settled into the straight backed chair. He was a handsome man although his face still held the smoothness of youth. Lovey was flattered by his attention.

"I'm studying engineering and working on the TVA project in Morristown as part of a project for class. I come here a few times a week with some friends from school and Clint gets us good moonshine when we need it."

Lovey took a sip of the fruit punch he had brought her and turned to watch the dancers. CJ's attention returned to the dance floor too and he whooped at his young friend, Stanley, who was slow dancing with the woman named Mae, who had seemed a bit too friendly with Clint when they first arrived. The pair was snuggled closely as they danced.

Joy filled Lovey in the darkened dance hall. She felt lighthearted again after such a long year of heartache and hard work. The rough wooden tables were on a floor covered with sawdust and each held a thick candle in a glass fruit jar, providing the only illumination. The dance floor was made of polished pine and covered the front half of the large room that might be dingy in the light of day but was romantic on this evening.

The song came to an end and the band took a break. Lovey and CJ were joined by another couple. CJ introduced the young people as Buck Ramsey and his wife, Julie, as they sat down and smiled at Lovey.

"You two are cutting it up tonight. Is that a new dance step?" CJ slid closer to Lovey to make room for Stanley and Mae as they also joined the table in the corner.

The Ramseys looked at one another and nodded before Buck turned back to CJ. "It's a variation on the Foxtrot we learned from a club in Morristown. We're going to try it out at the dance marathon over in Nashville next month."

Julie agreed. "We could win $100.00 if we can stay on our feet the longest. And the organizers offer all meals free while you're dancing. And cots to nap in. The rule is the couple must dance 45 minutes out of each hour."

"I think I heard someone at school mention that but I've never been to dance contest. Good luck, I guess. How long do they usually last?"

"Sometimes for weeks. But some we heard about only last for a few days. We haven't actually been in one before but it's worth a try. We can really use that money." Julie looked at her husband and took his hand.

Buck seemed to blush a little. "We lost our farm last month and need to raise some money before winter sets in. I haven't found any work much."

Lovey felt sorry for the kids but wished they could talk about something else. A lot of people were having hard times and she didn't want to think about it. Clint had shown her how to do a simple foxtrot. As the music started up again, she wished he would come back and dance with her.

Clint and Burl pushed through the swinging door of the building whose rafters vibrated with the lonesome sound of the mouth harp and banjo of the small group playing and singing of lost love and heartbreak. "Do you want a glass of fruit punch, Lovey?" Clint asked as he stepped up to the table. "CJ just brought me one," Lovey responded, noting the quick jealously that crossed Clint's flushed face before he laughed it off, slapping his friend on the back as he claimed the chair beside Lovey and pushed it closer.

"Not trying to move in on me, are you, little buddy?"

CJ held up his hands in mock surrender. "I confess. She's the prettiest girl you've ever brought around so I couldn't help myself. You know I have a weak spot for pretty women." CJ stood. "Speaking of which, are you ready for that dance you promised me, Julie?" He took the other girl's hand in his and led her back to the dance floor.

Buck stood too. "I'm going out for a minute," he said, winking at Clint. He walked none too steadily to the door and pushed through it.

"There seems to be lots happening in the parking lot. Maybe I should go out there to check on it," Lovey said, turning to Clint with a grin.

"No need. I brought it to you." Clint took a small bottle from his pocket and poured a stream of clear liquid that she recognized as moonshine into her cup of punch.

She took a sip and coughed. Recovering, she took another, finding it went down smoother the second time around. Her laughter was drowned by the twang of the banjo.

Chapter 45

L ovey dressed for church with a light step. She had officially dropped the mourning last night and she was overjoyed to wear colorful dresses again. She pushed aside the black dresses she had grown to hate. Two new dresses hung in the back, freshly sewed by her granny. Lovey pulled the light blue one from her closet. It was the color of the sky on a cloudless day. The other was a bright yellow dress with a crocheted border along the neck that brought a smile to her face. She loved color. She would save that one until the old biddies at church got used to her being out of mourning.

It was enough that she had gone to church with Clint the last few weeks, when she should still be alone. She had tried to follow conventions – especially for the Epperson family - but she couldn't deny she was in love with Clint Collins. She wore it on her face for the world to see.

Clint was exciting. He didn't play by the rules that others did and she found that intoxicating. Sadness had made her feel dead inside. But she had come alive dancing with him last night and knew she was ready to go again. Clint reminded her that life was made to be lived with a light heart instead of only duty and sadness. Primping for a man again brought joy. At the sound of a brisk banging on the screen door, she rushed to let him in.

"You're mighty pretty this morning, Miss Lovey," he said as she opened the door. "And after an evening of sin," he teased.

She no longer blushed at his compliments. His words were sweet. She boldly held his gaze and smiled, tempted to drag him back to her bed this morning instead of sitting in the small stuffy church and listening to the drone of the preacher.

She stepped outside to fall into step with him and they walked to his new car, one of the first on the ridge. The girls had stayed overnight with Granny and would be picked up on the way to church. "Dancing isn't a sin. God gave us the desire for movement."

"Well, I'm glad to hear it," he answered, catching her arm and swinging her around on the dirt lane before opening the car door for her. "I was afraid you wouldn't go again."

Her laugh bubbled up and echoed in the morning air. The heat would soon overtake the fresh morning breeze and disappear into a muggy August afternoon that forced them beneath shade trees or sitting on the front porch with neighbors, praying for a thunderstorm. "Why would you say such a thing, Clint? I had a good time dancing, and later was fun too. I'm not as backwards as you think I am."

"Oh, I know that now, honey. You showed me a thing or two, didn't you?" He closed the car door and leaned in the open window and kissed her full on the lips, his tongue pushing into her mouth.

Lovey had allowed him to take her to bed and considered herself engaged this morning. He hadn't actually asked her in so many words yet. But they would marry. She had forced him home last night to sleep and he would soon tire of leaving her warm bed.

With Clint at church with her and the children, she felt almost like a normal family again. Clint had to sit with the men but she caught his gaze on her often. What was so wrong about last night, she asked herself as Preacher Taylor started a sermon about sin and the corruption of strong drink. Lovey watched the children and tried to focus on the sermon.

If anything, Clint had brought stability to her family. He was particularly good with Deloris who needed a firm hand to keep her out of trouble. A stern look from Clint brought her facing front without a word. His help was welcome. Lovey only half listened to the words of praise and redemption as her body yearned toward the strong man across the aisle.

Chapter 46

J ust a week later, the engagement was announced and the couple was ready to set a date. Lovey invited Granny, Uncle Harold and her mum to Sunday dinner. She hurried the children from church to start her noon-time dinner. She killed two chickens, wringing their heads and hanging them from the clothesline to let the blood drain out. She quickly cut each still warm chicken into parts. She battered the chicken for frying, soaking each piece in an egg and milk mixture before dredging it in the flour and dropping it into the cast iron skillet of hot grease on the cook-stove. She mixed up a pan of biscuit dough and pitched them out between thumb and forefinger before dropping them into the pan and flattening each with the back of her fingers.

Granny had met Clint once before but Lovey wanted all of them to know him. He was fascinating. She had loved John with a youthful and innocent heart, and always would, but he had never offered her the kind of excitement Clint Collins did just by looking at her. When Clint brought his full attention to her, she felt weak in her limbs and was powerless to do anything but what he wished.

"Melinda, come get your sister out from underfoot," she yelled into the other room, high stepping over the smallest child playing with a new puppy on the floor, "and put this pup back in the box with his mum." She dusted her hands over the flour bowl and shooed all the girls into the front room. "You're all to be on your best behavior. You hear me?"

Not listening for an answer, her gaze moved from the sparkling windows, to the shine on her floor, and finally to the white crocheted tablecloth she had thrown over her small wood kitchen table. Yesterday she and the girls had picked wildflowers from the meadow below the house to fill an old canning jar with color. Now it set in the middle of the table. She smiled at the beauty of the mix of large sunflower, waxweed and delicate morning glories, their vibrant hue of yellow and purple adding an unusual beauty to the room. Her table was set with bronze glassware.

Stabbing a fork in each piece of chicken to quickly flip it to allow it to cook and brown on the opposite side, she next picked up a spoon to stir a pot of garden peas simmering on the back of the stove, and then hurried to her bedroom to take a final look at her reflection before her guests arrived. Her face had a glow that was more anticipation than heat from the kitchen and she pushed away a stray lock of hair and smiled. She would do, she supposed.

Hearing her family arrive at the back door, she rushed back to the kitchen. "Howdy, come on in the house, strangers," she called gaily, hugging each in turn.

Granny had brought a few late tomatoes and handed her the sack. "It's good to see you, child. You look none the worst for all your hard work on the farm this summer."

"It's been good. You know I love working outside." She would have said more but the girls rushed in then to hug their grandparents.

Uncle Harold handed out peppermints all around after making them promise to wait till after dinner to eat them. Deloris pouted but they all agreed and ran off, eager to return to the box of new puppies.

"Go ahead and have a seat at the table. Dinner's just about ready and Clint will be here any minute." Lovey called over her shoulder as she lowered the oven door and pulled out a browned pan of biscuits. She took the fried chicken from the pan and placed it on a platter as her mum came to stand by her side. Without speaking Naomi poured milk into a bowl for the gravy.

"We're anxious to know more about this fellow of yourn. He ain't known on this side of the ridge," Granny said from where she had settled at the table, crossing one swollen ankle over the other.

Lovey turned with a grin. "You've been checking up, have you?"

Granny nodded. "You could say that, I reckon. I asked around a bit."

Uncle Harold added from where he sat at the table, "Lovey, dear, you know we only want what's best for you. No harm intended."

Lovey nodded as a loud knock sounded on the screened door and she hurried to answer, leaving the gravy for her mother to finish. "Come in, Clint," she said, stepping back to allow him inside.

"Go take a seat at the table. You've met Granny and this is her husband, Harold Davis." Lovey's nervous laughter escaped her throat as the two men sized one another up. "And this is my mother, Naomi Lephew." Naomi, quiet as usual, nodded as she stirred the gravy.

"How you do," Granny responded quickly, taking the young man's hand in greeting, with Uncle Harold following her lead.

After a moment of awkwardness, Lovey called the girls, helped them get washed up, and they all settled at the table, the girls sharing the bench against the back wall. Conversation centered on the upcoming wedding.

"Have you set the date?" Naomi asked

"We've decided on November 1st. I've talked to Preacher Taylor and he's agreed to marry us after Clint joined the church." She turned to Clint who sat close beside her. "He asked after you this morning, Clint," she teased.

"Did you tell him I had a touch of the stomach ache?" Clint smiled at the group to assure them he was healthy despite his excuse to the preacher as he bit into a fat chicken thigh, grease running down his fingers.

"I told him you were probably at Red's too late last night," she teased back, passing a napkin to Deloris and nodding at her to wipe her mouth.

After a lull in the talk, Naomi asked about the wedding again. "What do you need mum and me to do for the wedding?"

Lovey smiled at her mother's offer. "Not much. It'll be very simple."

"We can take the girls for a few days at least," offered granny, nodding at the young couple. It was likely the closest they would get to a blessing.

"Time alone here to get settled in will be welcome, Mrs. Davis. Those little ones are sweet but can be a handful sometimes. "

"We can handle'em. What you say, girls?"

"Yea, no chores," Jackie said, making the grown-ups laugh.

Uncle Harold wiped his mouth and leaned back a bit. "So, Clint, what do you think you'll plant next year besides the 'baccer crop? Maybe some corn down that southern field?"

"I don't know yet. I have some other prospects to consider that might bring in more money without so much hard labor." He licked his lips and reached for his glass of cold water fresh from the spring. Although it was clear they all waited for more information he was silent.

"You ain't planning to work for any of them blame logging companies, I hope. I was against them from the get go," Granny said.

"Oh, no, I tried that work once but it's not for me."

"They're ripping up the mountains but you can't fight um, I guess." Granny allowed Uncle Harold to pat her hand.

"Yes, ma'am, you're right about that," agreed Clint. "But maybe it's not all bad."

"How do you figure that?"

"They've brought other work into the county. I work odd jobs and there's been more work to be had around these parts lately."

Granny nodded a bit but soon looked away. "Maybe so."

Lovey saw doubt cross the lines of the old face. Clint had some work ahead to charm the family as he had her. Granny didn't easily accept strangers.

"Who wants blackberry cobbler?" Lovey stood and began collecting dirty plates. "Come help me serve it, girls."

"Oh my, I do love me some blackberry cobbler. I'm afraid this woman'll make me fat and useless if I'm not careful."

Clint grabbed the desert plate from Deloris and dug in as the others were served.

Chapter 47

They were married at the little church on top of Raven Ridge, where she had sat still as a pond rock two years earlier as the preacher encouraged them to tell John goodbye. She thought she had died that day as well.

Clint had brought her back to life. Today was a joyous day instead of the misery she suffered then, although in contrast to the full church on that day, there were only a few witnesses today. She stood at the tiny altar covered with a few dried magnolia leaves and green ferns surrounded by candlelight that added warmth and beauty to the plainness of the church. She wore a silk and lace dress she had sewn with help from Granny and her mother. It was made of a soft lavender, the color making her eyes more purple than blue today. It had a wide circle at the bottom that flared around her calves. She felt beautiful. The fabric clung to her body, showing the curves of a woman instead of the girl she had been at her first marriage.

The last time she stood in front of a preacher, waiting to take her vows, she had known only blind love. This time was different. Most men, Clint included, seemed to have more flaws than not but life was easier with a man. That was a fact.

John had been quiet and spoke simple words of love. Clint, standing beside her, quite the dandy in a new black suit and white shirt with a red striped tie, sang a song of desire that turned her to him as if to the sun. He had but to whisper his honeyed lyrics to turn her hot with wanting. His burning kisses opened her fully as a mature woman.

Her daughters stood just in front of her, each with a small bouquet of purple cone flowers gathered from the hillside and tied into a bunch with lavender ribbon that matched the ribbon streaming from her dress. The church door stood open, allowing crisp breezes and warm sunshine to cheer the small altar.

Lovey's cheeks were flushed. Clint winked and squeezed her slender hand in his, claiming her as his. His gaze said she was his and she gave herself to him wholeheartedly.

"Do you take this man to love, honor and obey?" The cadence of the familiar words from Issac Taylor boomed in the quiet place.

"I do," Lovey answered with a clear voice. She smiled like a cat licking its whiskers and hoped her family didn't read the look for what it was. She was more than anxious to get this man back into her bed. After allowing him a sample of her sweetness, she had held him at arm's length until he offered a wedding ring. She had captured this handsome man to be a new daddy to her little girls and make them a family again.

Clint pulled her along in his wake as the couple hurried down the aisle after their kiss sealed the deal at the end of the ceremony. Guests threw rice as the newlyweds exited the church and walked out into the bright November afternoon. Lovey ducked her head as she ran to Clint's car, laughing as the hard rice pelted her body. She saw Granny herding the smiling girls along toward home as she and Clint drove away. Dust flew through the open windows of the car as they sped down the ridge. The newlyweds would have one night alone before settling into a new family routine.

Chapter 48

The first hard frost of the new decade found the newly married Collins couple cuddling in bed after all the girls had left for school. Lovey had arisen early, milked the three cows they now owned and fed the girls a hot breakfast of oatmeal dripping with butter, sugar and milk. She smiled at their giggles as she bundled them for their walk to school. Jackie was always in motion now and thrilled to join her older sisters this year at school.

Lovey stood at the window, watching the girls walk down the hill, Melinda holding Jackie's hand. She felt a wave of contentment with her family life. She collected a few sticks of wood from the kitchen hearth to bring back to the bedroom. She threw them on the fire.

As she leaned over to wake Clint, he pulled her into the small bed for some impromptu lovemaking. Now the thick featherbed enveloped the young lovers in comfort as a blazing fire burned in the corner fireplace. Lovey reached down with a slender hand to pull up the quilt to cover her nakedness. It was her Dutch Doll pattern quilt that had covered her bed for the past 15 years and witnessed much happiness as well as a few heartaches. That innocent girl who had traced the dolls onto her quilt-top was now gone. She had come into her womanhood. She stretched and yawned as she rolled to her side, grabbing the cover so it wouldn't slip off her, although she knew her nakedness would please him.

"I know we should get up but I feel so lazy I don't ever want to leave my bed again." Lovey backed into her lover and snuggled deeper into her pillow.

Clint spooned his body around her, covering her with his beefy arms "Stay. You deserve some extra rest." His hand caressed her arm where it was curved against her body and he nibbled her earlobe. She immediately responded to his touch but moved to deny herself the pleasure he offered by rolling out of his arms

She stood by the side of the bed, her naked body glowing in the firelight as she collected her clothes. She watched him in her dresser mirror as he watched her behind half-closed eyelids. She saw the blood of new passion come to his face and deliberately slowed her movements, confident in her newfound ability to please him.

She was brushing her hair into a neat bob when he came to stand behind her and began to unbutton her dress, letting it drop to the floor. She stood as if incapable of movement, allowing the hairbrush to clatter against the dresser-top as he slowly pulled her slip over her head, stopping to caress newly found sensitive spots. She moaned in response to his gentle touch and allowed herself to be pulled back into bed to delight in the tingle he produced in her, and enjoy the fresh explorations of their bodies.

Her hands roamed across his hairy chest and strong back. His body was tight and muscular and he was tireless in his desire for her and his attempt to impart pleasure in return. He now covered her neck with sweet kisses as he unhooked her brasserie and moved his callused hand across her breast, lightly tracing the curve.

"What about the chickens? I didn't feed them when I milked Jazzy and the new cows." Her voice was husky and her breath caught in her throat as his hands moved down her slender hips.

"The chickens can wait," he mumbled, gazing into her face with passion, already lost in his desire. Lovey allowed herself to follow him down into that sweet place he had taught her to find. Her face was flushed from the sudden heat in the room as she pushed back the quilt and allowed her bare skin to pucker in the cool air as he moved lower in the bed.

KATIE
December 1999

Chapter 49

The following Friday night Katie was dressed in black slacks and a new lacy red sweater as she walked into the Millhouse Inn with Brian for his small law firm's Christmas party. She was eager to meet his partners and their wives and girlfriends and make new friends in town. Next week she faced her first Christmas alone – without family. Her parents had booked a European river cruise to celebrate their 40th wedding anniversary on December 23rd and her dad's birthday. Loneliness washed over her at the idea of spending Christmas alone even though her brother had promised to come visit with his girlfriend after they spent the holiday with her family in Virginia. Fortunately, she had been invited to Lovey's for Christmas morning breakfast.

And maybe she would see Brian again. Who knew? He seemed interested although she held back a little from him, not sure about a real relationship. She liked him well enough but there was still no spark between them. She had allowed herself to like Bobby Lane and his small son too quickly and she reminded herself again that she had to forget about them. She refused to be a fool.

Brian and Katie joined the only other couple at the large round table with a white linen tablecloth and eight place settings. Introductions were made. The girlfriend of Brian's partner, Patrick, was a striking redhead with light green eyes and a determined chin. Her makeup was model perfect, which made Katie feel underdressed. The woman, named Brooke, touched Katie on her shoulder as a light fresh perfume floated in the air, and greeted her with a warm smile. "Patrick said you two met when Brian came in for a flu shot. Brian has some moves I didn't know about, I guess." She grinned at them both. "I should tell you he's my second cousin – at least once removed, I think, so I'm allowed to give him grief." They all laughed.

"And you went to the Rotary club for your first date?" The pretty girl crinkled her nose. "Really?"

"Yes, maybe I'm too easy but he seemed nice enough. And I'm trying to build my practice so I was planning to go to Rotary soon anyway."

"So you're the new doctor I've heard about. That work must be grueling." Brooke shrugged her shoulders.

"Sometimes, but mostly it's satisfying. I love medical mysteries and enjoy solving problems for people." Katie settled back into her chair, delighted with this happy couple, and accepted the drink the waiter brought.

"So, where are the others?" Brian looked around the room. The two senior partners and their wives were missing.

Patrick answered. "They're all coming together and got held up by a babysitter issue. But they're on the way." He looked at his watch and raised an eyebrow. "Shall we order an appetizer at least while we wait?"

"Yes, I'm starving. I hope they arrive soon." Brian signaled the waiter.

Brooke leaned back in her seat, long fingers wrapped around a martini glass. The foursome settled in to wait.

"Did you meet with the Campbells today, Brian?"

"No way, guys. It's time to drop the business talk." Brooke glanced at Katie and sighed. "Occupational hazard when you get these two together."

"What do you do, Brooke?"

"I'm a buyer for Margaret's Dress Shop in Knoxville. Do you know it?"

"Shopping isn't my thing so no. But if your dress is an indication of the inventory, perhaps I should bring my mother in when she visits. She loves to shop."

"Me too. So this is the perfect job for me. I get to go to New York City a few times a year and wear beautiful clothes and enjoy the glitz and glamour. Then I come home to this small town where I grew up. I'm close with my family and friends and can zip around town easily on my own, in my little car. I also help Margaret, the owner, with marketing and advertising."

Her smile was warm and Katie hoped they would become friends. She appreciated the other woman's passion for her work and the big city as well as for this small town where they both lived.

Brooke turned back to Patrick. "Hey, isn't that Regina Lane in the corner? I didn't wear my glasses but it looks like her – if a bit more worn around the edges."

Patrick looked to where she indicated and agreed. "I heard she was back in town but I haven't had a chance to mention it." He explained to the others. "She's my cousin and Brooke went to school with her. They were the cool kids."

"I was in the same class. At least in high school but Regina never liked me much." Brian glanced to the back of the room where they were concentrating their attention on a small table. "Thought I was a nerd. She always went for the big strong guys like Bobby Lane."

"We should go over and speak, I guess," Patrick said as he stood up. "Excuse us for a few minutes, guys. We'll be right back."

Katie finally turned also and watched as the couple she had just met walked to the dark corner where Regina Lane sat with a stocky blond man. Well, it was a small town and she supposed she shouldn't be surprised to run into Bobby's wife. Not really. But seeing her twisted the knife a bit more, reminding Katie why she couldn't continue the sweet relationship she had started to enjoy with the Lane men.

The woman stared at Katie, her gaze laser sharp. Katie felt her face grow warm and quickly turned back to her date. "So you know the sheriff too, Brian?"

"Of course. When you live in a small town like Tazewell, you grow up with the same friends all through school. I lost touch for a while during college and then law school at UVA but when I came back home, I found many of my former classmates still working and living in town. I thought at one time I would move to a larger city but I'm comfortable here and my family is here. It's home."

Katie nodded. "I miss my mom and dad and Chapel Hill – especially this time of the year. And even my brother sometimes. But I love the mountains so much and decided to keep the clinic open during the holiday. I'm still getting established."

Brian's attention wandered to where Patrick and Brooke were returning from Regina's table. "Bobby's a good guy and he didn't deserve what he got from Regina. She just walked away and never looked back."

The others returned to the table in time to hear Brian's statement. Patrick frowned. "Well, she's back now, buddy. And says she plans to file against Bobby for full custody of Mathew. She asked me to represent her but of course I explained that isn't our firm's type of case. Thank goodness."

Chapter 50

In the early morning hours Katie finally fell into a short and yet fitful sleep. She awoke to notice the night sky lighten from a weak morning sun coming over the ridge outside her bedroom window. She rolled from the warm cocoon of blankets and forced herself into a cool shower. The water stung. As she awakened more fully, she admitted her lack of sleep was due to her worry over Mathew and Bobby Lane. According to Bobby, the boy had hardly seen his mother for the last couple of years and now she wanted to tear him away from his father. That wasn't fair.

After rubbing herself dry with a large soft towel, she decided she needed a run this morning even if it made her late. She pulled her hair back, threw on sweats and laced up old running shoes. She gulped a glass of water, set the coffee pot to be ready in an hour, and left the house. She walked a few steps through the early morning mist before moving into a full jog along the deserted dirt road. Her mind cleared as she ran. As each foot struck black dirt, she felt more awake and her thoughts were less jumbled. This early morning run was five miles and she ran it whenever she had time.

Bare sugar maple and blackgum trees had dropped their branches along the ditch line near Lovey's and Katie stopped to stack them against a line of cedar trees along the back property line. If the ditch filled with too much brush, it would hold the run off from reaching the river and flood the old woman's yard.

Katie turned from the welcoming light shining from Lovey's kitchen window. The little cabin and the woman inside had offered Katie comfort and shelter along with understanding of her past choices by sharing some of her own youthful mistakes. Katie had opened up with Lovey about her past affair with the married man and Lovey's words had helped her heal and forgive herself.

Katie accepted that she had to decide on her own course of action this time. Should she contact Bobby and offer to testify on his behalf in the custody hearing? In her profession she had often offered proof of the rightness of one parent over another. She knew she should do it for the Lanes as their family doctor but was afraid to get more entangled.

What she felt for Bobby Lane was beyond anything she had felt before. Childish love affairs through school had not prepared her for the deep heartache she now experienced. Life was never easy but she couldn't mess this up. A child's heart was involved.

Breathing deeply, Katie retraced her steps along the empty road between her rental house and Lovey's home. The air was warming. She slowed, breathing in the fresh morning air filled with the scent of pine and cedar and wood smoke. Although she planned to spend the afternoon at the clinic, catching up on the endless paperwork, she was in no hurry this morning. She lingered by a turn in the path, taking in the magnificent mountain ranges across the ridge. She took her time and enjoyed the sparkling day as she stood still, mesmerized by the view.

An eager smile touched her face when she spotted Bobby running in her direction but it was quickly replaced with a look of bewilderment. She had never seen him run this road before. "Seems you're a hard man to avoid," she muttered under her breath. She might think she had conjured him if she believed in such things. Nervous laughter erupted despite herself.

His tall lean body was dressed in dark sweats and earbuds wrapped around his head. The eagerness that shadowed his handsome face upon seeing her warmed her heart and caused her pulse to quicken.

Coming to a stop, he pulled the plugs from his ears and slowly walked toward her. His deep brown eyes bore into hers, the color deepening with a flash of unmistakable joy. She watched him as he took in the look of her, a grin replacing his scowl. She raised a hand to smooth her hair, pulled up in a hasty bun that was coming undone. Her naked face held the flush of exercise and a welcome she didn't want to offer him. But he was a hard man to resist.

Reaching to touch his arm as they stopped by one another, she felt a jolt of fire race through her body. She yanked her hand away and took an unsteady step backward. He followed, smiling, the dimple in his chin winking at her in the rising sun now crossing the road. "I'm happy to see you, Katie. I was hoping to catch up with you sometime today."

He took her hand, brought it to his lips and just touched her fingers with the barest hint of a kiss. "Something brought me in your direction this morning and I didn't know what it was until this very moment. It was you, Katie."

Katie broke eye contact and stammered like a teenager. What could she say to that kind of declaration? " Act... Actually, I was going to call you later today, Bobby."

Raising his eyebrows, he reached for her again. This time he wrapped long arms around her slender body before nuzzling her neck with hot breath and sweet kisses. She responded to his touch and raised her mouth to his. When she finally broke away, she whirled away and started to walk toward home. He followed. Taking a deep breath, she cleared her throat and tried to think.

"I didn't mean it that way." She wiped her face and pulled off her sweatshirt and tied it around her waist. "I wanted to offer my professional help."

"I'll take whatever you can offer, Katie. But I need to come clean with you. We haven't known one another long but I've fallen pretty hard for you - maybe the hardest and deepest I've ever felt for anyone before. And Mathew feels the same way. We want you in our lives."

He was moving way too fast. She had finally decided to offer her help to him with the custody hearing but it was all coming too fast. She tried to lighten the mood. "Speaking of Mathew, where is he?"

"Spending the night at his grandmother's. The whole family is in an uproar over Regina. She's threatened to sue me for custody of my boy, Katie."

"I know. I heard." She stood as still as a doe upon hearing the snap of a twig in the forest, the soft hurt in his deep brown eyes causing her pain too. She admitted she might be in love with him too.

"I'll fight for Mathew but mothers are sacred around here. My dad swears he knows people who will speak on my behalf but I could lose him. That would kill me, Katie."

She shifted, leaning toward him. He pulled her against his hard body, wrapping an arm tightly, possessively, around her waist. His face lowered to hers and claimed a deep kiss that she couldn't have stopped herself from enjoying even if she had wanted to. Which she didn't.

As the kiss ended, he pleaded. "Won't you re-consider and take us on. I come with a lot of baggage but I promise it'll be interesting. Mathew and I are a package deal but I think you and I want the same things for our life." He choked on a laugh as he finished speaking, the emotion clear in his deep slow drawl.

"Well, Sheriff Lane, I think you've caught me whether you intended to or not." She dropped the Southern drawl she had tried for when it fell flat. "Seems I'm in this relationship up to my eyeballs. My heart's on the chopping block with yours, ready for whatever comes next. Let's go home." She took his hand and led him down the path and into her house.

LOVEY
February 1930

Chapter 51

Within months of their marriage, Clint's passion cooled, and it seemed the honeymoon was over. Clint went out more often, and alone, satisfied to leave her at home. She paced the kitchen floor on a cold Saturday night late in February, mad as a wet setting hen and feeling just as nervy. There was no one to let loose on. Clint was gone.

Lovey had put the girls to bed, muttering under her breath as they said their nightly prayers. She had a good mind to go to Red's and show him two could play this tune but she couldn't leave the girls alone – and she would freeze trying to walk to town anyway. If she were truthful, she was afraid of what she might find there. She knew Clint had an eye for the women and savored the attention he found in the tavern. He never took her anymore.

Many men left their women home alone and went out drinking but she had thought it would be different with Clint. She supposed he was bored with her. Men were like children, always wanting the next new toy to have and hold, and discarding them as soon as the challenge was over. Her disappointment was hard to swallow. Had she made a mistake?

Back and forth she walked across the floor as her mind worked this riddle of men and romance and love. Her anger simmered, although each step was measured and calm in the empty room, and she was lost in her dark thoughts.

"Mommy," Melinda whispered. "Is it time to get up?"

The soft voice in the poorly lit room startled Lovey. "What are you doing up?" she snapped.

Her daughter, eyes huge in a downcast face, stood peeking into the room from the open doorway from the front room. Lovey softened her voice and waved her into the kitchen. Settling on a hard chair, she asked more gently, "Why are you awake?" She pulled the gangly ten year old onto her lap.

Melinda snuggled against her, providing body warmth in the cold room. "I heard tapping. Where's Clint?"

"Oh, he's out with some friends tonight. I was just walking and thinking." Lovey brushed a hand across her daughter's forehead, threading her fingers through the thin brown hair. "We're snug as bugs here at home on this freezing night."

"Do you wish you were with him, Mommy?"

Lovey considered what to say to the girl, remembering her renewed happiness as she danced with him just months ago. Without waiting for a response, Melinda asked another question, her sleepy head rising from her mother's shoulder. "What's it like to dance, Mommy?"

Lovey gently pushed the child from her lap as she stood and reached to take Melinda's hand, pulling her closer. "Let me show you."

"There's no music, Mommy." Melinda giggled and ducked her head.

"That's okay. You can hear it in your head if you try hard enough."

Lovey began to hum as they stood close and swayed back and forth. She pulled Melinda along with her, their feet stumbling on the dance steps, their laughter subdued in the empty room.

"Mommy, you're silly."

"No, listen. Can't you hear the music?"

She twirled her daughter in the open room and smiled at the joy that lit Melinda's face, a face that was usually much too somber. Lovey regretted not giving her more time to play but she had always been so responsible and took on a lot of work for the younger girls. But now, she was ready to play along with the game.

"Yeah, I hear it." The little girl's long cotton nightgown flared around her ankles as they moved together and for a moment Lovey forgot where they were and that the gown was hand sewn from flowered feed sacks. Their life was simple but beautiful. The girls were precious and made the hard work of her daily life worthwhile.

As she tapped out the dance steps for her daughter to follow, her mood lightened. She and Clint could make a good life here for her children. Staying on the ridge was what she wanted for them and she needed a man to help her farm the land. Her life didn't have to be perfect. Security for the children was more important than anything else and she resolved to do whatever it took to keep this marriage together.

Chapter 52

Lovey stomped around the bedroom, gathering Clint's dirty socks and muddy bibbed overalls crumbled in one corner of the room. She fumed. Clint's lack of interest pushed her low in spirit. He was so loving in the beginning but had become a disappointment over the past year. She was doing all of the household chores - along with the farming – what little that was done. All Clint did was control the purse strings and she saw none of the money anymore. He visited the local joints more than ever, leaving her at home with the girls.

"Hell and damnation," she muttered, biting her lip around the curse that slipped from her mouth at the sight of lipstick on his shirt where he had dropped it beside the bed. It was bad enough that he didn't want more than a place to hang his hat and a little grub in his belly come supper. But she was damned if he would cheat on her and rub her face in it too.

"Lovey, quit your muttering. You're loud enough to wake the dead." Clint reached out for her in the dim morning light. "Come back to bed, woman. I have something to put you in a better mood."

"I'm mad enough to spit and there you lay up in the bed like you're the king of the manner, stinking from another woman's perfume and thinking to romance me. Why I ever thought you were the man of my dreams, I'll never know." She stood with a slender hand on her hip, his dirty clothes under one arm, her body held rigid to keep from shaking.

Clint's eyes opened wider in the morning light. "Now, Lovey. Don't be jealous. It's you I want but you're always busy with them young'uns or something else that you think can't wait a minute." He pulled the covers back, revealing his naked chest, inviting her into his bed with a sleepy smile.

She stood and gaped at him. His strength, youthful spirit and charisma had mesmerized her into believing in him but his lack of understanding now repulsed her. She suspected she was pregnant. Trapped in this hopeless marriage with a baby on the way, she didn't know what to do. Tears burst forward and began to run down her thin face. She brushed them away.

"What's the matter with you, Shug? You used to be a lot of fun but you've turned into a nag." He reached for her hand but she pulled away.

"I think you must be the laziest man in the holler, Clint Collins, and that's saying some. All you want to do is laze in the bed and have fun but it's time to work the fields for spring planting. Somebody has to bring in a crop of tobacco."

"Better watch that sharp mouth of yourn, girl." Clint pulled the covers over himself and burrowed deeper under the quilts. "It's still too early to plant yet. Anyway, I'm the head of this household and I'll decide my day."

"You do that," she yelled, and threw the dirty duds back in the corner. Let him worry about clean clothes.

"Watch out there, now," Clint hollered.

Lovey left the room, slamming the door behind her. He was all talk and bluster. She took a deep breath to calm herself before opening the door to the next room, where all three girls slept together in one big four-poster bed. She wasn't surprised to see them awake already, and regretted her loss of temper a moment earlier. The older girls were dressing in the cold room, but Jackie cowered under the soft quilt Lovey had pieced from old flannel when the girls had all been babies. It was Jackie's favorite.

On the corner of the bed, Lovey lifted the quilt and said, "Peek a Boo," her bad mood gone as quickly as it had arrived. She and Clint would work out their problems without involving the children.

The little girl looked at her mother with the turquoise blue eyes of all the girls, her mouth opened wide in her round little face. "Is Daddy mad?"

"Probably, but he'll get over it," Lovey reassured her baby, sorry Jackie had heard the angry words between them. Jackie considered Clint her father, having no real memory of John, and Lovey had encouraged the relationship between the two. The older girls still held him at a distance, preferring the memory of gentleness their own father gave them.

Fights were becoming frequent. What was it doing to the girls' acceptance of a new step-father? It didn't help. Clint often brought the older girls into their arguments, using some action by them to start a disagreement. Especially when he drank too much.

She pulled her youngest into her arms "Don't worry about Daddy, honey. Mama can take care of him." She watched as Melinda and Deloris pulled on their skirts and blouses, adding knee length socks and the little Mary Jane's she had bought for them when they sold the tobacco last year. Now she worried there would be no cash money this year. It was late and they still had no fields ready for planting.

As she cuddled with Jackie, she decided she would hire someone if necessary to get the tobacco planted. Clint showed no interest in working anymore but without the crop money there was only food, nothing for the extras she wanted her girls to have.

"Should we feed the animals before breakfast, Mommy?" Melinda asked as she combed her straight hair.

Lovey finished putting shoes on her smallest child and stood up, pulling Jackie along with her and stood her on the floor. "Let's do – we'll make it an adventure," she announced, crouching to lead the way as if on safari. The girls followed her lead, beginning to giggle in the quiet, cold house.

"Should we look for elephants and tigers this morning?" Lovey asked gaily as they exited the house. She gazed in one direction and then another, with a hand over her brow.

"I don't see anything but a muddy hillside," Deloris said. "We're not in the jungle."

The early spring had been a wet one and Lovey found herself secretly agreeing with the glum voice, but moving to her middle daughter's side, Lovey tried harder to bring her into the game, taking her by the arm. "Is that a rhinoceros ahead, Melinda?"

"Yes, mommy. I see it. There by the barn, right?"

Lovey smiled and looked back to Jackie, who joined in the game easily and said, "And monkeys. I see monkeys in the trees."

They all looked to Deloris, who giggled at their silliness and decided to play. "I don't see a rhinoceros and monkeys, but wait, there by the road is a kangaroo. We must be in Australia today! Right, mommy?"

Lovey nodded her approval, proud of her children, who were willing to see beyond the mountain ridges to other worlds she would teach them were out there to explore. They continued the game as they went back inside and Lovey made them a quick breakfast and packed their lunches before their walk to school.

Chapter 53

G ranny and Uncle Harold and Naomi came for dinner on Easter Sunday of 1930. Lovey and the girls arrived home from church to find Clint still in the bed, but he quickly got up and dressed to help entertain. While the women prepared the meal the men talked on the front porch and the girls ran in the side yard, playing a game of tag.

Lovey took a cup of coffee to the men. "There's time for a walk to the tobacco field before dinner if you want to walk down there, Clint. I know Uncle Harold can give good advice about how to get the best yield from this year's crop."

"Lovey," Clint said, his eyes darting quickly to her and staring hard. "That won't be needed. Thanks just the same, Harold," he added, not turning to the man sitting beside him.

Harold smiled agreeably. "Just let me know whatever you young folks need. I'm a man of leisure these days, although I've raised a lot of crops in my day."

Clint finally turned back to Harold. "I'm going to let the field rest this year after the lack of rain last year."

"That can be a good idea," Harold agreed. "A field has to regenerate."

"There are other fields to use," Lovey added. "Maybe the lower one down by the river."

Clint ignored Lovey. She stood just behind him, leaning against the screen door. "I have better plans but my wife wants her way with the running of this family."

She noted the look of concern in Harold's gaze before he narrowed his eyes and then turned away and looked off to the rolling valleys below the house, which were already turning green. "I'm sure it'll work out for the best. You might even rent out your allotment this year."

"Maybe so, that's what I told Lovey. I keep telling her I'm in charge here now."

Lovey felt her body slump a bit as she waited for Harold to speak up but he was silent. She had to let this recurring argument go. Maybe the man did have a better plan despite her doubts but she would have to let him do as he wished if she wanted to keep the peace. She retreated back into the kitchen, mumbling under her breath about stubborn men, but managed to smile for the women in the kitchen.

***

By late summer Lovey admitted to herself she had made a grave mistake when she married Clint. He was lazy. She stepped out into the dark cool night, allowing the screen door to close softly behind her to avoid the squeak she knew was there, and sucked the fresh air deeply into her lungs. She felt as if she had been holding her breath for the longest time and couldn't say what the need had been to do so. Everyone was asleep and the house was quiet.

Tonight had been the same as many in recent months. She was nauseous and found it hard to sleep. Despite the thin cotton gown worn soft by multiple washings, she was warm, her face flushed, but beginning to cool in the night air. An evening thunder storm had passed, leaving a mist drifting across the mountains surrounding her.

Dropping onto the top wooden step, she allowed her eyes to adjust to the faint light coming from a new moon barely visible in the sky. It was the darkest part of the night and the moon provided the only illumination. She remembered her mother often quoted that it was 'darkest before the dawn'. It had probably come from the bible. Her mother and grandmother couldn't read and only quoted others.

"What use is reading here in these hills – and for a girl at that," her father had said, but the women had insisted she attend the one room school located on the Ayers farm near the church. Lovey was proud she could read and knew that skill offered her a more promising future, even if it didn't look very hopeful right now. The original school had grown since Lovey attended and though it was still just one large room, it now offered more subjects for her children to learn.

As the night stillness washed over her, Lovey's breath came more evenly in her chest. She tried to avoid the thoughts of a coming baby but it was all she could think of. She had kept the news from Clint, although she was already feeling movement deep in her belly. What a fool she had been to marry again so quickly and now she was tied to a man who showed no ambition but had control over their lives.

226

The quietness yielded a rhythm of sounds not heard during the day, when wood was being cut nearby and trucks rumbled through the narrow dirt roads to move it to market, children laughed or cried, and the cycle of work was never ending. Only during the night did the valley sound as it had during her childhood. She heard hoot owls in the distance, calling out into the darkness; she heard cicadas busily singing in the trees; and if she squinted her eyes, there in the clearing she could almost see her ghostly young self, chasing lightening bugs with friends. She smiled as she leaned her heavy head on her knees, allowing her tangled hair to fall over bare legs, momentarily stretching her aching back.

The screen door squeaked, startling her and ending her solitude. Clint spoke. "What you doing out here in the dark alone?"

Just the squeak of the door irritated her, before he even spoke, and she jerked her head upright. She wanted to yell at him, to ask couldn't he fix the damn door at least. She wanted to scream out her pain and disappointment to him but knew the useless results of such an outburst. Instead, she spoke softly, denying her anger, and feeling the tightening of her shoulders. "I just wanted a breath of fresh air."

He stepped around her and stood facing her from the lowest step. She made out his shape from the white undershirt and boxers he wore. His jerky movements indicated his impatience with her and she prepared to give up this small escape she had attained for so short a time.

"What's wrong with the air in the house?" he asked, leaning forward to peer at her face but it was too dark here under the overhang of the roof. "It's freezing out here."

She had no privacy – not even for her worries. Clint was a bully and he was only pleased when she catered to his needs and desires – no matter how small and petty, and she often fought against that but she wasn't in the mood for a squabble tonight. There had been too many and she felt beaten down.

"I got warm inside. This cold feels good to me," she responded. Gazing at the new moon as it began its descent and a faint glow of light tempered the black sky at the horizon, she briefly dreamed of a new beginning for herself, against all odds to the contrary. She stood. "Let's go back to bed, Clint. Morning and another day's work will come soon enough."

Chapter 54

The next Sunday, Lovey sat on a ragged quilt under a large willow tree by Clinch River and watched as Clint chased the girls with a string of fish he had caught one after the other. The sun was low in the sky and the girls played near the murky water. Jackie ran to her mother and climbed into open arms as the older girls continued to race along the bank of the river. Clint slowed and dropped the fish into a pail of water before he sauntered to where she sat and flung himself onto the quilt.

"Are you hungry yet?" he asked, leaning close for a kiss, his pastel eyes open and staring into hers.

She read the hidden meaning in his gaze and felt a delicious tingle ignite in her body despite the child wiggling under her arm. Clint had a power over her that she no longer liked. Their marriage so far had been a year of fights and making up and heartache and a wild and carefree joy unlike any she had ever felt but she had grown weary of this kind of love. She was attracted to him still but she suspected he cheated when the opportunity arose and that knowledge broke her heart a wee bit each time she thought of it.

He pulled away and arched a brow before kissing her again, this time his tongue barely brushing across her bottom lip before he mashed his lips firmly against hers. He withdrew and leaned back on his muscular arms beside her.

" Just a bit," she answered, releasing Jackie and watching her as she scurried back to the riverside to join her sisters, her short legs pumping to catch the older girls.

Lovey watched Clint where he reclined beside her. His body was firm and taut despite his relaxation under the shade of the trees along the riverbank. She had kicked off her shoes and allowed her skirt to ride up her long slender legs. She had been reading a novel she had borrowed from her friend, Betty Jean, but threw it aside at his approach.

"Cat got your tongue?" Clint asked, poking her in the ribs. "What're you thinking about so hard?"

Lovey laughed and moved away from his probing fingers on her hip, tucking her thin cotton blouse back into the waistband of her skirt where it had escaped. "Nothing – I'm just feeling happy, watching the girls play and enjoy the day. I guess we've become a family of sorts after all, haven't we, Clint?"

"Yeah, I reckon so." She saw him glance at the children as they joined the Bundren girls, whose family had set up camp beside them along the river. Many families had come out to enjoy this unusually warm day.

"Those girls need more discipline though. It's time they worked harder around the house, especially now," he added, cupping his hand over the small swell in her abdomen. The unexpected change in Clint since learning of her pregnancy had been remarkable.

"Clint, they do plenty. Really they do." She placed a hand over his where it still rested on her stomach. "They do more than a lot of children their age. Anyway, I want them to concentrate on their studies so they'll have choices."

"High and mighty Miss Lovey," he mocked, "always thinking your kids are better than everybody else. Hell, you'll be lucky if Melinda can snag her an old farmer to marry. She's so skinny, I'm not sure even an old man would have her."

"Clint, don't be so mean. She's still a child but she'll fill out in a few years and make a handsome woman. And she's smart as a lick."

Clint's eyes narrowed as he took a swig from the fruit jar he had packed in the basket this morning and gazed at the girls. "Now, that Deloris, on the other hand, is becoming a little woman already. What is she now? Ten, eleven?"

Lovey watched as Clint gazed at the girls, his expression making her uncomfortable. "They're all still young and need us to care for them. They're good girls."

"You baby them too much," he said, settling the matter to his satisfaction and turning back to her. "Is there anything else here I can interest you in?" He pulled her down beside him on the quilt, trying to nuzzle her breast.

"Clint, someone will see." She giggled despite herself.

"So, we're legal, ain't we, Shug?" One hand brushed against her bottom, cupping it in his meaty hand. "I can't help it you drive me crazy just looking at you."

Lovey pressed her body full against him for a brief moment before pulling away and standing. "I better get those fish cleaned so we can have our picnic. Why don't you start the fire?"

Skipping away toward the riverbank, she gathered the fish and took them to the edge of the water to gut them and ready them for cooking. Other families lined the bank of the river, each fishing and enjoying a relaxing time away from working the farMiss Harvest was over for the year and it was a time to rest and get ready for a cold winter ahead. She had canned everything she could from the garden but still dreaded the cold winter ahead, wondering how they would afford the necessities with no crop money. She watched Clint from the corner of her eye as he rekindled the fire that had burned down.

Lovey felt more hopeful about her marriage since she had told Clint about the baby. He was tender with her since learning she was expecting his child. Maybe their life would get better. He needed to plant the damn tobacco next year, though, and quit relying on the dwindling supply of insurance money. She was still bitter that everything she had was now in his name at the bank. She could only obey as the little woman.

"Girls," she called. "Come and get ready to eat." As the fish browned in the iron skillet over the open fire, she pulled roasted potatoes and onions still in their skin from the ashes. Melinda unpacked the rest of the basket. There were pickled cucumbers and a melon for later.

The men grew louder and began to argue at the back of the wagon where she knew they sipped white lightening.

"What's that you say?" Clint demanded, bringing himself to his full height of 5'9", his face turning bright red. "I'll kill you for that."

Lovey rushed over in time to see Clint pull a switchblade from his pocket and swing it at Fred. "Weren't no call to say that. You'll watch your mouth."

Fred Bundren looked baffled at the sudden change of temper and stepped back to avoid a slash across his arm. "Now, Clint. I meant no harm. You're taking this all wrong." He continued to move away to avoid the knife, high stepping.

Lovey tried to intercede along with Iva Bundren, each stepping behind their man, who it appeared had become drunk on the white lightening and now wanted to fight. "Clint, what happened?" Lovey asked, trying to calm her quick tempered husband. "The food's ready and the girls are watching. Please come and eat."

"He said he reckoned I don't want to work or I could find a job in the lumber business. I won't have him tearing down my good name like that."

Fred continued to jump around, small and wiry and quick enough to avoid the sharp blade despite the spirits he had ingested. Lovey wondered if Clint really intended to hurt him. She had seen his anger flare before, usually over nothing and then quickly dissolve.

"I didn't mean no such thing," Fred protested, raising his hands in apology. "I just mentioned that Sawyer's was hiring, is all. I heard they was looking for cutters." The man still looked a bit dazed. "I'm sorry if I riled you, Clint."

Lovey touched Clint on the arm, trying to pull him away from the other man. He shook her hand away but stepped back and closed his knife. "Okay, then. Maybe we misunderstood one another. I don't want no trouble neither." Clint reached across to shake Fred's hand and the other man accepted but seemed eager to get away from Clint.

Clint put his arm around Lovey's neck, suddenly deflated, resting heavily on her as they stumbled back to their campsite. The girls stood nearby, trembling, watching in silence. Clint sat on the quilt and called them to join him there as Lovey checked the fish, which were burned to a crisp.

Chapter 55

Later that autumn, cold penetrated Lovey's cloth coat, and wind whipped around the mountain, whistling in the valley floor. She paced, stamping her feet on the frozen brush at the fence line she guarded. The shotgun felt heavy against her side where she let it hang, pointed harmlessly at the ground. Her teeth clicked against one another, and Lovey wondered if it was from the cold or her nerves. Her heart beat faster against her thin ribs.

A car motor ignited back in the woods, alerting Lovey to be on the lookout. She faced the dirt road leading down the mountain. She strained to see better in the early morning light, tears rising in her eyes at the effort. This was Clint's alternate plan to earn money -. moonshine running. The money was good but the threat was real too. It was her job to fire the weapon at the sight of any law. She unhooked and lowered the barbed wire fence at the approach of the black truck covered with a tarp hiding the load of clear glass canning jars filled with moonshine. As the truck drew near, it stopped and the driver handed her a folded bill before rolling quietly into the lane and on down the mountain.

Flushed, she hurried to replace the fence across the gap. Clint would work deep in the woods with Jim Wilder 'til sunrise, pouring moonshine for another load to run off the mountain tomorrow at dawn. She started off at a fast pace in the opposite direction, not walking more than a quarter mile before meeting a Ford truck with a star painted on the side, indicating the local lawman. She knew the sheriff well, but still felt a quick jolt of fear rise in her throat.

"Howdy there, Dan." She greeted as the truck pulled alongside her. She hoped her voice didn't waver as she met the questioning gaze of the sheriff.

"Hey, yourself, Lovey. What you doing out so early in this cold?"

Thinking fast and feeling reckless, Lovey met his gaze with her most innocent look, willing her face to relax, letting a playful light come to her blue eyes. She knew the man was suspicious.

"Looking for Clint and that no-good whore of his," she finally answered, the anger with Clint her only honest emotion.

The sheriff's head dropped as he considered her answer, his stare no longer as sharp. He believed her story, she thought, although he seemed to briefly consider her gun."

"You plan to shoot him?" he drawled.

Lovey laughed, the sound ringing bitter and true in the cold morning air. "I don't reckon I would although I thought the gun might be a good idea in case I ran into any trouble out here in the dark night."

Sheriff Dan Hurst finally smiled. "You're in Wilder territory, ripe with hidden stills and moonshine running but I expect you know that. It's not safe here but I don't think even the Wilder brothers would hurt a lone woman." He reached across and opened the passenger door for her. "Get in and I'll run you on up to your place."

She carefully put her shotgun in the back of the truck and slid in, feeling the cold. She shivered as she relaxed against the seat cushion. Dan asked after her grandmother and mother as he turned and started down the ridge toward home. A pale light flickered through the overhanging branches of bare tree limbs and announced the start of another hopeless day.

Lovey hugged her body with arms that shook, trying to warm herself against the iciness. The sheriff watched her, obviously concerned. A weak sun turned the sky pink as it peeped above the far ridge. They rolled to a stop on the rocky hilltop by her house and she exited the idling vehicle and retrieved her gun. "Thanks for the ride, Sheriff," she said, her bare hand resting on the cold metal of the car door.

"You're welcome, Lovey," he answered, ducking his head to look at her. "Will you send Clint around to see me? I was actually looking to catch up with him on the road this morning."

She froze, wondering if she had fooled him at all, but smiled. "What you want with Clint, Sheriff? I've never known the law to get involved with a woman's broken heart."

The sheriff watched her, his face serious, not speaking, letting his gaze rest on her before he leaned back in his seat. She saw the pity plain as day on his face and knew he knew everything. She supposed out of respect for her family he would only charge Clint for their involvement in the moonshine running, and leave her out of it. "Take care now, Miss Lovey. And be careful tramping around with that big old gun in your condition."

She raised her hand in a little wave as he turned and with a grinding of gears disappeared down the hill.

Chapter 56

Lovey mixed flour, milk and lard with her right hand and pinched out biscuits, filling the pan with them and popping them in the wood fired oven. The sausage sizzled in the iron skillet while all in the house still slept. The kitchen was cozy on this frosty morning. Lovey's back ached already and the day had hardly begun. She poured a second mug of hot coffee and sat, putting her feet up on another chair, waiting for the children to wake, enjoying the brief quietness in the toasty kitchen. They would soon wander in at the scent of the food. It was the Sunday before Halloween and the remnants of her sewing lay at the back of the table. She had fashioned angel costumes for the girls but lacked the final hemming. The girls were excited at the prospect of sweets, a treat they seldom saw. So, the little school they attended planned a party.

As the aroma of fresh baked bread filled the kitchen, she pulled the biscuits out of the oven and grabbed a platter to take up the sausage patties. She took her seat again. They slept a little later on the weekends, letting the chores wait until daylight. She wished for sleep herself but Clint had wandered in at dawn and woke her before he passed out across the double bed. Burning anger kept her awake after that. Before daylight she had climbed from the warm bed to build a fire and get the day started. Now she sat, almost dosing, the warmth from her oven thick in the air. The baby widening her waist was unusually quiet and still this morning and her eyes closed.

She jerked awake at the sharp knock on the back door. Hurrying to answer, she swung the door wide, and was surprised to see Sheriff Hurst there, along with two deputies. "What is it, Dan?" she asked, fear tightening her stomach into knots.

Dan Hurst removed his hat and shuffled his feet on the porch. "Is Clint home, Lovey? We need a word with him."

"He's here. Come on in the house," she offered, stepping back into the warm kitchen.

The sheriff wiped his feet and followed, nodding to his deputies to wait outside. Lovey took down another mug from the hook on the wall and poured him coffee without asking. "Set down, Dan. I'll have to wake him."

Lovey walked on tiptoes into the back of the little four room house, and called to Clint, who turned over and continued to snore. She reached over and pinched him hard on the loose skin just above his elbow, whispering. "Clint, the sheriff's here."

Clint blinked against the dim light coming through the window. "What?"

"I said get up. The sheriff's here with questions for you," she hissed, picking up a dirty shirt and pants from the bare floor and throwing them on the bed."

"What's he want now?" Clint crawled from the quilts and moaned, pausing on the side of the bed, his head in his hands. He slipped on his pants and tried to stand, wobbly. "I talked to him already. He ain't got nothing on me over the whiskey the Wilders are moving."

"I didn't ask but please take it outside. Do you think you can do that?" Lovey felt nothing for his trouble. She left the room without a backward look. Would Dan take her too? Damned Clint Collins for getting them involved with that moonshine operation. Although the work had given them easy money they hadn't earned with a crop of tobacco this year, it wasn't worth it if they both went to jail.

Deloris was sitting beside Sheriff Hurst when Lovey walked back into the kitchen, talking a blue streak to him. The girls knew Dan from church.

"Okay, who wants a sausage biscuit," she asked brightly, ignoring the sharp cramps across her stomach. "Is this about moonshine, Dan?" She wanted to slap her hand over her mouth to take back the blurted out question.

"No, Lovey. Don't worry, this is only about Clint."

She stared at her old classmate, feeling grateful. No telling what Clint had gotten into. She was sick of this life with him and if it weren't for this baby she was carrying she would leave him. Wouldn't she?

The other girls joined their mother in the kitchen just as Clint stumbled in, obviously still a little drunk from the previous night's activities. "Let's step outside," he offered, looking at Lovey and walking on through the door, leaving the sheriff to follow.

"What's happening?" Melinda asked and poured milk for her sisters as Lovey prepared a sausage biscuit for them.

"I don't know, darling, but I'm afraid we're about to find out."

Lovey and the girls sat quietly at the table, not eating. It wasn't long before the door opened and Dan asked Lovey to join them outside. When she did, she could see that Clint was about to be placed in the cab of the sheriff's truck. He didn't wear handcuffs but the deputies were on either side, leading him by the arm.

"Lovey, it's okay. It's just a misunderstanding. I want you to go to the bank first thing tomorrow and withdraw some money to bail me out. Okay?"

She stared at him, her eyes cold, not answering.

"You hear now, woman, I know you're mad as an old goat but I expect to be back here tomorrow night. I'll explain everything then."

As Dan got into the truck beside Clint and the younger lawmen climbed into the back, Lovey watched, silent. Her stomach cramped, and she felt blood run down the inside of her leg but she didn't care. Her love for Clint had died as surely as this baby had. So be it.

***

Lovey hurried to the bedroom to make a pad for herself to catch the flow of blood for the journey to Evie Winstead's. "Girls, hurry and eat your breakfast. I'm going to send you up to Granny's for a bit." Lovey spoke calmly as she entered the kitchen again. "I have some things to attend to." She pulled her warm jacket off the peg and ushered the girls to their coats, ignoring their last crumbs on the table and their questioning chatter.

"Why, mom? What's wrong?" Melinda asked, her face drawn and pale as she leaned over Jackie to help her button her coat. "Is it the baby?"

Lovey stopped for a minute and turned to Melinda, placed a rough hand on her face, cupping her chin. "Don't worry. Sorry you have to take on so much, girl, but you know how to get to Granny's place alright. We've walked it many a time."

"Sure, I can take us there."

"She should be home this morning but if she's out somewhere, just go on in and keep the little ones out of mischief until she returns." At the kitchen table, Lovey quickly tied the corners on a dishcloth she filled with the leftover bread and meat and handed it to her daughter. "Take this along with you."

Melinda watched her mother with troubled eyes but asked no further questions. Lovey considered before she added, "Tell Granny I've gone to the Winstead place for some help with a problem I have. She'll know what to do."

Melinda nodded quietly and reached for the hands of her sisters, but Jackie held back. "I want you to come too, mommy." Her little lips pursed out, and Lovey expected tears would soon follow.

"Come on now, Jackie. I need you to listen to me and be a big girl." Her voice was gruff as she herded the three children out the door and pushed them in the right direction. "Go on, now. Do as I say and mind Melinda."

Keeping the stern face in place until they were out of sight, her own face crumbled as she whirled and headed around the other side of the mountain at a trot. It might be too late but despite their troubles, this little fellow deserved a chance at life. If anyone could stop the early birth, Granny Winstead could.

The day was warming as Lovey jogged along the trail. It was at least two miles from her little home down the ridge to the fork where Raven Ridge Church nestled. Miss Evie lived more than a mile back up the other side and then a ways back in a secluded holler on the Upper Caney Valley side of the ridge. The ageless woman mostly kept to herself but was always there to doctor anybody who came for help with her medicinal herbs and roots collected around the valley. Some on the mountain called her an Indian medicine woman. Others thought she was a witch. But Lovey knew she was just a wise old woman who had learned the ways of medicine throughout her life.

A sharp cramp took her breath as it pulled at her stomach. She bent and panted. She figured she was at least five or six months gone by now and maybe even more. But it was much too early. She had first noticed the signs of a coming child in late June and had predicted a birth early in the year. Blood gushed from her and she began to walk again, but more slowly. She was at the fork in the road when the next pain came, almost doubling her over with its intensity. She wasn't sure she could go on.

Picking up a fat branch on the side of the road where a large limb had been ripped from an oak tree in the last storm, Lovey fashioned a cane. She leaned her weight on the stick as she climbed the rise in the road, praying for help. Blood had drenched through her protection and was running freely down her legs now. She kept moving, knowing this was more serious than she had first thought. The baby was surely gone and perhaps her own life was at stake. She begin to feel light-headed. She searched for the path to the Winstead place, assuring herself it was just around the next turn.

Feverish as she passed by the Epperson place, Lovey wondered what her former mother-in-law would do if she fell at her doorstep. She might allow her to bleed to death. Her mind began to play tricks on her as she saw one path and then another leading off the main trail. Her eyelids fluttered and she wiped sweat off her face. Her feet tangled over a loose vine and she stumbled and fell. Pushing herself upright, she continued to take one step after the other, hoping she was on the right path.

KATIE
December 1999

Chapter 57

Three days before Christmas, Katie and Bobby went out for what was technically their first real date together, despite their starts and stops after meeting one another the prior month. They drove almost an hour to Knoxville to have a nice dinner and do some last minute shopping. At the mall, Bobby picked up the latest popular toy. "Do you think Mathew would like this?"

Katie grinned at him. "Yes, probably, but doesn't he have enough junk already?"

He ducked his head. "He does, but the fear of possibly losing him has me wanting to give him everything within my power. Regina is buying him all kinds of stuff." He swore under his breath.

Katie took his large hand in hers. "You don't need to compete. He loves you." She pulled him out of the toy store and they strolled down the center of the mall with their arms linked and their bodies close. Stores were crowded with the bustle of people. Carols played, and giant trees were decorated with bright lights. Katie felt content. She juggled two wrapped gifts before buying a shopping bag for them.

Mathew had been at his mom's the past few days for a visit; Bobby planned to pick him up tomorrow. She looked forward to spending more time with both of the new men in her life. She definitely wanted to know the father better and the kid was pretty great too.

As Katie and Bobby walked out of the mall into the chilly evening, they met Regina and Mathew coming in from the parking lot. What were the chances of running into Regina in this crowded city of almost two hundred thousand. And yet their run-ins kept happening. It was almost unbelievable. Katie felt a cold chill run down her spine but then she saw the look of pure love on Bobby's face as he spotted his son. A warm glow filled her heart for them.

Mathew ran across the sidewalk toward them. He leaped into his father's arms and hugged him around the neck. "Hey, dad. What are y'all doing here?"

Katie held out the colorful shopping bag with a picture of a jolly fat Santa decorating the side. "I had some last minute gifts to buy," she teased. "One might have your name on it but I'm not telling."

Dimples spread across the boy's face. "It's almost Christmas, Katie. Santa's coming to see me. Mom said he'll come to dad's and to her house too. She said I'll get a huge haul."

Katie patted the child on his back. "I know, kiddo. Too much, huh?" She laughed aloud as he quickly shook his head, the sound echoing through the foggy parking lot. It had begun to rain. Street lamps cast dim shadows as a line of cars circled for open parking spots.

Regina stepped closer. "Mathew, you know better than to run away from me. This is the city and little boys can be snatched away from their parents by bad people."

She frowned at Bobby. "You of all people should have taught him that. It's basic." She pulled Mathew down to stand beside her on the sidewalk and gripped his little hand. He wiggled but didn't break the hold.

"He knows, Regina. He's just excited to see us. It's okay, buddy. Just be sure you stay close to one of us." He patted his son on the head, golden brown curls tangling in his fingers.

"Okay, dad. Sorry mom. Are we still shopping at the toy store?"

She considered for a minute, as if she might cancel the shopping, but then smiled brightly, her eyes glassy. "Yes. I need you to show me the largest, best, most expensive toy in the store so I can buy it for you."

"You mean Santa, right mom?" He pulled free and turned toward the glass doors ahead.

"Sure, son. Yes, the big guy in the red suit will take care of everything for us." She dug through a large leather bag and pulled out a matching wallet with wads of green bills hanging from it. "As long as mom has this, he will." She smirked at Bobby before she turned to follow Mathew.

"Be careful flashing your cash, Regina. We don't have much crime in Knoxville but there have been a few car-jackings recently. And this mall so near the interstate highway is the perfect place for it."

"Don't worry about me, Sheriff." Her words were sweet as sugar as she hurried to catch up with her son and looked back over her shoulder. Her high heels clicked against the brick pavement. "Remember, I don't leave home without protection. Mama's always packing heat." A brilliant, if somewhat artificial smile, flashed from her face as she slung the large bag over her shoulder and strutted into the mall.

Who was this woman? Katie stood and watched as the mother and son joined the mob inside, the automatic glass doors whooshing closed behind them. And where did she get so much sass? "She carries a gun?" Her words were barely audible as they turned toward the parking deck.

"Yeah. A lot of people around these parts think nothing of taking their guns wherever they go. I'm sure she has a permit. And if I remember correctly, she's a pretty good shot. Her father taught her how to shoot straight and bought her a little pink pistol when she turned eighteen."

Katie fell silent as she considered this. This was gun country but why did a young mother need to carry a gun around with her? And why was her speech a bit slurred and her reactions slow? Could she be involved in this drug gang? She fit the profile Bobby had mentioned except for her gender. But that was the perfect cover.

Chapter 58

Katie spent all day Christmas Eve with her guys - helping them decorate their home with a few final touches. Cold weather had arrived with a vengeance. Katie arrived in old jeans worn soft from many washings and a thick sweater but brought a pretty dress and heels to change into later for dinner. Bobby built a fire. After a hearty but leisurely breakfast, Katie entertained Mathew, playing video games with him while his dad wrapped gifts. Her eyes were crossed by the time they stopped.

After a light lunch Mathew agreed to a short rest while Katie and Bobby started preparations for the fancy dinner he had planned for them. He had a prime rib to bake and simple sides she might be able to help him with. Katie didn't cook.

His parents were coming, along with his older sister who lived outside of Washington D.C. She had arrived in town the day before and was staying with her parents across the mountain. Katie was jumpy as she watched Bobby roll out a pie crust, the flour smudged along his jaw somehow sexy. She couldn't sit still.

"Want something to drink? I'm going to make some iced tea."

"I have plenty made up in the fridge but its sweet." He stopped rolling the dough and watched her. "What's wrong, Katie? You're jumpier than a petty thief caught during his first big bank job."

She chuckled at his analogy as she shrugged. He made her smile through her nervousness. "Nothing, really. I guess I might be a little anxious about meeting your family. I'm nothing like Regina." Chapel Hill was a small town, but its rich culture made her a city girl through and through. She didn't shoot or ride horses or know anything about raising livestock or gardening. Heck – she didn't even clean house very well and she had noticed how neat his home was.

"At this point, that's a plus. Hand me that pie plate. Will you?" He waited as she placed the glass dish on the counter beside him. He held the crust above it and centered it before he lay it into the dish. He pressed the sides down and pinched the dough around the rim before using a butter knife to cut off the overhang around the edges. Using a fork, he made a fluted design around the rim.

"You're so domestic. How did you learn to make a pie?"

"My mama. She always said I should be able to cook and clean and wash my own clothes. So I did. And since I love pie, she taught me how to make those too." He poured the apple mixture from a bowl and popped the pie in the oven. He dusted his hands by clapping them together. Turning back to her, he captured her close to him and held her tight. "I know some things my mama didn't teach me too," he whispered in her ear. "Shall I show you?"

His mouth came down hard on hers and he pushed his hands through her loose hair, leaning closer still. He took a step, pushing her back against the large farm-sink and her arms came up around his neck. His hard body formed against her own.

Katie broke the kiss and pulled away, despite her immediate desire for him. She retreated back around the large kitchen island, breathing raggedly. She sat down and faced him. "I actually have something else I've wanted to talk to you about. I hate to bring it up, especially today, but I think it bears thinking about at least."

He came over and took a stool beside her, his deep eyes filled with lust. He touched her arm and pulled her hand closer to hold against his chest. "Sounds serious. You're not breaking up with me again, are you? Not on Christmas. Please." He cupped his hands around hers in a mocking plea before he reached over to brush a hand against her face. He was teasing but she didn't mind.

She couldn't think straight when he touched her like that. She looked toward the window over the sink, watching tree limbs sway with the wind outside and waited as a line of blackbirds on the power line took flight. When she looked back to Bobby, he had become serious too.

"What is it, honey?"

"I think Regina might be involved in the drug gang you're looking for," she blurted out before she could change her mind. "I'm sorry to say this but I've been thinking about it since we saw her the other night. It fits. She has loads of money and seems to be free as a bird as far as a work schedule. And she looks like she's on something." She was surprised to see Bobby throw his head back and roar with laughter.

"I wish she could hear you say that. I used to tell her she acted like an addict – but mainly over shoe shopping. Honey, that's just her personality. Always a little larger than life."

"Bobby, I'm serious. I see definite signs of addiction – and maybe even mental illness. You should consider this as a real possibility. Mathew could be in danger with her."

"No, I don't believe it. She fits my profile but she has too much respect for her body to get hooked on anything other than men and sex." He sounded bitter.

"Don't you think your past relationship could be clouding your judgement? Besides, I think I saw her yesterday over at the island when I walked up to Lovey's."

"Really? But she could be out walking too. A lot of people explore the island."

"Is she a hiker? She seems too prissy to want to get dirty to me." Katie heard the jealousy in her tone and evened her voice. "Sorry. That was mean."

"No, you're right. She likes to dress in fine clothes. And she likes money. But I can't conceive of her being involved. Not even to help her brother. They're close but she's always pulled him out of scraps instead of the other way around."

He reached forward and brought a hand back to her face. Moving closer, he claimed a kiss, ending the conversation. Allowing herself to be pulled into him, she enjoyed his clean masculine scent and the feel of his tongue on hers before he broke away. "Okay, you've got to stop tempting me if we're going to have dinner ready before the family comes. You better go get changed and maybe take a little rest too. You're too much of a distraction."

Katie decided to let it go. He couldn't conceive of Regina being a criminal and she would just have to wait it out and see what happened next.

LOVEY
October 1930

Chapter 59

When Lovey awoke, Granny sat by her side. She lay flat on her back in an old iron bedstead with unfamiliar quilts and was confused. There was a strong scent of lavender in the room. She noticed a small sachet lying on the dresser beside the bed, which surely was responsible for the sweet scent. Next she noticed the crocheted edging on the pillowcases where her head rested and then her voice came.

"Granny? How …? Where …?" Her voice was a croak and a wrinkled hand offered her a cup with cool fresh spring water. Probably from the stream she could see flowing outside the window. It looked cold outside and was growing dark. She heard a strong buzzing in her ears and took more water, swallowing deeply, trying to wake.

"I came as soon as the girls told me where you had gone. I knew you must be real sick."

Lovey's eyes blinked in the dim light of the room as she turned back to Granny and saw Evie Winstead hovering over her as well.

"Of course you've lost the baby. I 'spect you know that." Granny's hand brushed her cheek.

Miss Evie Winstead patted her hand where it rested on the outside of the soft quilt. "No time for worry about that now, girl. What's done is done. Concentrate on recovering yourself because you've lost a lot of blood."

Lovey couldn't speak. Maybe it was for the best that this baby was gone but she felt sad nonetheless. She closed her eyes as the women continued to talk above her.

"If I hadn't been out tramping the woods, she surely would have died out there in my lane all alone," Miss Evie marveled. "In all my years, I've never seen such a sight of blood."

"I'm beholden to you, Evie. I don't know what those children would do without their mother. Should I bring a wagon to get her back home?"

"I'll nurse her here for a bit, Melindy. She's young and strong and will be back on her feet in no time." Lovey felt the soft covers pushed up higher on her shoulders and tucked under her chin against the evening chill. Someone patted her face and leaned in to kiss her cheek. She felt warm and lazy, and she couldn't respond as she should. Her eyes fluttered open briefly and she watched her Granny step away from the bed, turning her back and hugging the other woman in the room.

"I'll bring a pot of soup over. You let me know of anything else she needs."

"She'll be all right. It's all natural, and things happen as they should."

Lovey felt the damp tears on her face and let the wave of dizziness take her under but continued to feel the presence of someone watching over her and heard the creak of a rocker leg on occasion. She was safe. She allowed her body to rest despite thinking there was something Clint needed from her.

Chapter 60

Clint's trial was about to start by the time Lovey was back on her feet. He was facing six months in jail for the beating and cutting he had inflicted on Jim Wilder. She wanted to let him rot in jail, but couldn't do it. Instead, she visited him. They sat on a hard wooden bench at the back of the office where the sheriff allowed Clint to join her, although he cuffed him.

Clint tried to hug her but she shrugged him away. "I've arranged for a lawyer from Knoxville to represent you but Dan says it won't much matter."

"It's too late now. Buying myself out of this was a pipedream anyway." Clint hung his head and looked at the floor. "I heard about the baby, Lovey. I'm sorry." She thought she heard grief in his voice but wasn't sure. She was learning she didn't really know him at all. Why had she fallen so fast? Anger and grief fueled her sharp tongue.

"The lawyer's fee took the last of the money, Clint. Is what they told me at the bank true? How did we go through my money so fast?" She whispered in the large open room, watching as the sheriff filled out a form and the deputy hung photos of what looked to be gangsters.

"Don't worry about it now, Shug. I'll be out in time to plant a great big field of tobacco in the early spring. We'll get back on our feet quick as a pig can eat his slop." Despite the cuffed hands in front of him, he again tried to reach out to her, allowing the back of one finger to rub against hers where it rested in her lap. She jerked away as if his touch burned her.

"Now don't be that way, honey. I don't even remember the fight at Red's." Clint rubbed his face and shook his head as if to clear it. He was clean shaven and his hair was slicked down, scraggly curls visible against his neck.

"They say you busted things up something awful. Jim almost died." She turned to face him. "How could you do that?"

"It was the liquor. I swear."

"Sure it was but you'll be lucky to get out of this alive, Clint. The Wilder gang takes care of their own and you'll suffer more for this when you get out of jail. You know that."

"Don't worry none. I can take care of myself. The Wilder boys cheated me and they won't get away with it."

Lovey slid farther away from him. "What happened to the man I married, Clint? You don't seem to care about being a husband and father anymore."

"I'm still right here." His grin was wide as he winked at her. "And I promise I'll be back in your bed soon enough."

His words confused her. Did she still love him? Clint stared into her eyes and grabbed at her hand again. She allowed his hand to circle one wrist. He caressed her hand with a stubby thumb, and then held tight, trapping her in his grasp. He leaned close. "Listen, girl. I know you're angry but pay attention to me. C.J. owes me $200.00 for the car I sold him and he's good for it. Go collect from him."

"All right. I will." The money might be enough to feed them through the winter, she thought. She pulled her hand away and stood, swayed slightly at the quick movement but then took a step back, out of his range. Weakness still hovered but she was determined to follow through on her plan. She pulled a lacy handkerchief from her pocket and twisted it in her hands.

"Let's wind it up, folks," the sheriff called to them.

"This is it, Clint. I've done all I can for you and I want free of this disaster of a marriage." She took another step back. "Don't come back to the house when you're released. I'll not have you there after this."

"Now don't fret, honey." Clint smiled, shaking his head at her, as he called out loud enough for the others to hear him. "I won't be gone long."

The man was infuriating. She stomped her foot on the creaky floor as the sheriff moved forward to take Clint back to the cell. "You listen to me, Clint Collins. I mean what I say." Her voice had risen too. "Don't come home."

She turned and walked out of the room with her head held high, and felt the men staring at her back. She closed the door hard behind her. Clint didn't believe her but she would show him if he dared come looking for her after this jail sentence. The children had suffered enough, losing their dad so young, and it was up to her to protect them from more hurt and distress. She would do that if it was the last thing she did in this world.

LOVEY
March 1931

Chapter 61

Cold rain dotted the glass windows and dusk came early on this wet March evening at the top of Raven Ridge six months after Clint went to jail. It was Good Friday but without yet much promise of warm weather. Lovey let the heavy logs she carried drop into the firebox, adding dry brush and twigs from her kindling box over the top and lighting the whole. She stepped back, waiting for the fire to blaze and provide more heat in the little house – and in her heart that grew colder with each passing winter day. She had waited till now to restart the fire from this morning, trying to make her wood last. The money from C.J. was almost gone. He was a good man and did not quibble over the amount.

She turned at the sound of the girls rushing in the door from school. "It's freezing out there," Melinda squealed. "It's beginning to ice over, Mama. We better hurry and feed the chickens."

The young voice filled with such hope and happiness despite their dire circumstances brought Lovey out of her reverie. "I've already done it, Melinda. Come by the fire and thaw out. Both of you." She didn't tell them she had sold most of the chickens today in order to buy needed supplies for them as well as to feed the few cattle they had. At least they still had milk and she hoped to sell some calves soon in order to try to get a crop in the ground. She planned to turn her life around. With Clint gone, it might work.

Pinto beans simmered on the stove and the girls read their lessons as Lovey hummed a favorite song called *Barbara Allen*. Betty Jean had encouraged her to take comfort in her religion but Lovey wasn't able to find it there. She was lonely and scared on this cold night.

By early evening it was pitch black outside and Lovey lighted the oil lamp on the table. She called the girls to come eat as she pulled fresh cornbread from the oven, hot and crusty and ready for fresh churned butter. As they finished their blessing, there was banging on the door. Lovey scurried to see who was out in this poor weather.

Clint stood on the threshold, hat in hand and looking bemused at her shock. The girls sat still, watching their mother for a cue. She was no longer angry at Clint, but she didn't want him back in the house either. Her options were limited because she couldn't leave anyone standing out in the pelting ice to freeze to death. She stepped back and let him enter.

"Thank you, Lovey, for letting me in. I know I don't deserve it."

She closed the door and walked back to the table. "Will you have some soup beans with us?" she offered, wondering if she had lost her mind.

"I would love that," he said, his most charming manner surfacing.

Jackie offered her chair and stood by him as he ate. "I missed you, Daddy," she said, hugging his arm.

Chapter 62

Winter had brought ice and snow to soak into the earth with the nutrients needed for a rebirth. It was a natural preparation for new life to burst forth in the springtime. Hope and joy had briefly returned for Lovey as she allowed Clint to come home for Easter despite her misgivings and brave promises to the contrary. After weeks of romancing, she held firm in her decision to keep him from her bed. It wasn't much but it saved her pride.

He was mostly useless but had brought much needed cash into the household when they needed it most. He might be running moonshine again but Lovey didn't want to know and didn't ask. Now, as he reverted to his sorry, old ways after just weeks at home, she was ready to kick herself. The days had become long and dreary again.

The morning sun came over the top of the ridge to warm her with hardly a breeze stirring the air and Lovey's hope was renewed as she watched her father walk up the hill. "Thanks for coming," she said, as they moved across the dry field, lighting stalks here and there with a torch, setting them ablaze. The fire spread quickly across the open land, bordered by a creek bed on one side and the slope of a rocky hilltop on the other.

There was only a hum of response as he walked to the edge of the field. He was a tall man, with no extra fat on him, but muscular through his shoulders and arms from hard physical labor of his life on the farm. His long arms waved the blaze of fire he had set on the outer limits of the field, and it began to spread back to the center, taking the brown weeds in its wake of destruction.

She would get her tobacco in the ground, even if she did it without Clint. He was useless, laying up in bed all day and going out at night. She refused to fight. She decided she would go about her business and ignore him. Any love or respect she had once felt for Clint was gone.

Lovey's skirt rustled with the energy of the blaze and she stood back, watching the weeds go up in smoke. Later they would rake the ashes into the dirt to add richness for the coming crop of tender young shoots of tobacco. The ash would nourish the young plants to produce a healthy crop.

Her father came to stand by her. They stood watching the fire, mesmerized by the flames, and the roar brought peace to Lovey as they watched.

"I'll bring some seedlings next week to get you a start. Can I do something about Clint?"

She looked at the man who had once loved her mother, watching as his eyes followed the snap and crackle of the fire and she wondered if he had spoken or if she had imagined the words. He wasted few words. But he was known in the valley for feeling the pain of others and was generous in spirit. She loved him in spite of his absence from her childhood.

"No, I'm taking care of it." Lovey replied. She stood solid and silent, not facing her father in the air filled with the sharp scent of smoke. She knew her face flamed pink, and not from the fire.

Chapter 63

Lovey ran through the squishy ground to avoid the huge drops of rain that had begun to fall in the dusty evening. Her blouse stuck to her skin, and mud climbed her bare legs. She ducked into the small barn and paused to take a deep breath, the scent of damp earth and hay strong as her eyes slowly adjusted to the gloom. Raindrops sounded like a cascade of pebbles as they hit the tin roof. Bessie, the last cow after selling Jazzy and the new calves, bawled to be milked and Lovey saw that Melinda was struggling to get the stubborn animal to stand still while she straddled the three legged stool to the left side of the ornery old cow.

"Here, let me help you," she said, stepping closer and putting a hand on the cow's head to steady her. She reached for a handful of hay to feed her, shaking her skirt free of rain.

Melinda pulled on the swollen teats and warm milk splattered into the metal bucket. Without looking up she said, "Thanks, mommy. Is it raining hard out?"

"Just a quick downpour, I think. Big drops, so it shouldn't last long. I got most of the biggest weeds pulled out but can do the rest in the morning. I want to get some more manure spread too while we're still getting plenty of rain."

"I can stay home tomorrow and help."

"No, darling, you help plenty, but I want you to study and learn so you'll be able to do other things with your life." She nudged Melinda off the stool and took over from her, knowing her fingers were larger and stronger and could complete the job faster.

"Miss Bunch said we must study hard if we want to make a teacher, but I think I'd just as soon get married and have some babies." Lovey watched her daughter pick up a pile of straw and play with it, slowly straightening it into an even bunch, like a broom head, without being aware of what she did.

"Well, that's alright too, but it's good to know a trade in case your family needs your support. I've always farmed, at least some, I guess, and that's come in handy."

"But you don't like it, do you?"

"I do but mostly I haven't had a choice. At least it allows us to feed ourselves if not much else sometimes."

Melinda took the little broom she had crafted and used it to sweep aside the dust on a wooden board that ran along the length of the single room barn as if she were cleaning the floor. "What would you do if you could do anything in the world, Mama?" The girl's dreamy blue eyes came to rest on her mother.

Lovey set the full bucket of milk to one side and took the empty one that Melinda offered in its place. "I used to want to be a nurse. Evie Winstead and her skill with a handful of herbs picked up in the woods has always fascinated me."

"Why can't you do it?"

Lovey smiled at her girl. "Maybe I will one day. But for now I think we need to get this milking finished and get in the house before the little ones tear everything apart. Did you put our cobbler in the oven before you came out?"

"Yes, and I told Deloris to take it out if it was ready before I came back." Melinda persisted with her questioning as they performed their evening ritual. "But you could study with Mrs. Winstead, couldn't you? I mean unless you're scared of her."

Lovey laughed. Many of the children and even some grownups were afraid of Evie Winstead, whose reputation in the county was one of witchcraft and trickery. "I'm not afraid. Miss Evie and Granny are friends and I've learned about plants from her but I don't know enough yet. Besides, I'd need some book learning too."

"I guess people might trust you more with book learning," Melinda said.

Lovey finished milking and set aside the second bucket. She stood and led Bessie into her stall and gave her fresh hay. "I think they would. Mrs. Winstead knows a lot but sometimes people shy away from her advice. With education to go along with her knowledge of medicinal plants, a body could do a lot of good in these hills."

"Couldn't you still do it, Mommy?"

"No, it's too late. Schooling's for young people."

Melinda took the second bucket, which wasn't as full, and Lovey picked up the first one. The two left the almost dark barn and trudged up the final hill toward the house, a light steady rain falling on their bare heads. Lovey hoped the change in the rain meant a nice long drink for her newly planted tobacco. Tired from her full day of work around the house and the late evening hoeing she had managed to get in after supper was done, she was ready for bed. A berry cobbler would provide a sweet treat, made with berries the girls picked yesterday. Lovey's mouth watered.

Coming into the house, she noticed Clint was dressed to go out. He swept past her, his glance daring her to object, but she had no fight left for him. She went to the oven to remove her cobbler, deciding she would have it with a glass of milk and go to bed early. She was spending back-breaking days in the field, determined to make a cash crop this year and show her no good husband what a good woman could accomplish on her own. Let him do as he pleased. She didn't care.

Chapter 64

It was still raining two nights later when Clint came home drunk and badly beaten. It was the dead of night when Lovey came awake at the sound of a slamming door outside and hurried from her bed. Clint stumbled through the front door and fell into her as a rusted old truck rattled down the drive under a new moon. She half carried him as he shuffled to the bed that was still warm from her body.

"Who did this, Clint? Why?"

"They can't tell me not to sell whiskey. It's a free world," he proclaimed before falling across the bed, crying out and clutching at his ribs.

"Somebody's message looks pretty strong," Lovey mumbled as she pulled off his boots. She managed to get his dirty pants off before he rolled over into the bed, unmindful of the blood smearing the clean bedding. "Are you selling moonshine again?"

"I've got me a little still up near Slim's place. Me and him are partners."

"Clint, must you always take the easy way? I have a large healthy field of tobacco started and this rain is just what we need to nurture it. We'll have ready cash in the fall." She yanked an old quilt from the bottom of the bed and pulled it over him and went to warm a pan of water. She searched out some lavender oil for his scrapes and bruises.

At the sting of the disinfectant on his face, he roused and cursed at her, wincing at the movement against his ribs, which she suspected were cracked. "They won't get away with this. I'll not take it lying down, I'll tell you that." One eye was swollen almost shut and she wrapped it with a poultice of scrapped out potato as he mumbled a drunken plan for vengeance.

After tightly wrapping his ribs with a strip of old bedding, Lovey moved her hands over Clint's battered body and checked for broken bones. He drifted off, as she finished her nursing, and she hoped he would sleep off his anger as well as the drink.

Lovey sat awake the rest of the night. Apparently Clint and the Wilder brothers had fought. She knew the Wilders didn't take kindly to anyone encroaching on their whiskey selling territory but was shocked at what they'd done. There might be more to the story than she was hearing. Clint should have learned his lesson after his last run in with the Wilders.

Clint was up at first light, mostly sober and raring for revenge. He dressed slowly. "Where are you going, Clint. Please don't mess with that Wilder bunch."

"Don't you worry your pretty little head none about this, woman. This is a man's battle and I'll handle it." For the first time in forever Clint reached to embrace her. He kissed the top of her head, gently brushing the tousled hair to one side before grabbing his shotgun and running out on an empty stomach. Lovey watched him walk slowly up the hill, her hands clenched in tight fists. Whatever he did wouldn't bring them any good.

***

Lovey didn't have to wait long. The girls were reading in the front room when Sheriff Hurst dashed through the rain to her back door late that afternoon. She quickly opened the door and let him inside. "What is it, Dan? Clint?"

He removed his hat and took the warm mug of coffee she poured for him. The steady rain made the day chilly as they stood and faced one another in the dim kitchen. "I have Clint locked up in the Tazewell jail, Lovey. He's fighting with the Wilders again."

"Did you see the ugly bruises and broken ribs they gave him, Dan? It might not be all one sided this time." Lovey's mouth tightened. Clint was a sorry excuse for a husband.

"I suspect you're right, Lovey. I'd bet my last dollar the bad blood is over some moonshine business gone wrong but neither will say." Lovey felt her fair skin turn warm under the sheriff's close scrutiny. She considered telling him about Clint's still but held her tongue. No need to add a moonshining charge.

"Sit down, Dan, and let me get you some food to go with that coffee. I don't know where my manners are today." She pointed to the small table, and warmed his coffee before she uncovered a small stack cake and placed it on the table. Then she joined him there.

"Nothing to eat, Lovey, but thanks for the offer. It's miserable out there today. This rain isn't likely to let up anytime soon and the bridge is almost out now." He took a sip of the coffee.

She covered the cake and glanced at the cross decorating the wall above her table. "I prayed for rain but maybe not this much." Lovey listened for a minute to the heavy downpour as it hit the tin roof and rolled off. Dan waited, silent as he took a gulp of the fresh coffee.

"What exactly did Clint do?" Did she want to know? She didn't want to hear but felt she should ask.

"Clint shot into a herd of cattle that belonged to the Wilders, taking down two jerseys. They came in and swore out a warrant for him and he isn't denying it so unless he wants to fess up about what the Wilder clan did to him, my hands are tied."

Chapter 65

The rain poured for ten days straight, ruining the maturing tobacco crop. Creeks overflowed, ravines filled with runoff and the roads washed out along with the river bridge. All of that could be rebuilt. But the bushy green tobacco plants she had put so much work into lay scattered across the field, wilted in muggy heat that returned after the wind and heavy rain had done their damage. The unusual weather this time of year came from a tropical storm off the coast of Carolina. The Collins weren't the only family on the ridge to lose their crop. A complete failure of most crops in eastern Tennessee would cause many to go hungry.

Dan released Clint from jail after the flood and he hired a boat to bring him across the swollen Clinch river. They had been stuck in the house together for days, arguing, while the sun cooked the uprooted tobacco plants.

This morning after making the bed, Lovey felt sick to her stomach and lay back across it. She pulled her old Dutch Doll quilt to her and rubbed the worn fabric against her face. She was cold despite the sun streaming through the open window. She suddenly dropped to her knees on the bare wood floor at the side of her bed, clasped her hands together and prayed, for what, she no longer knew. She and the children had not attended church the past two Sundays and their school had been canceled until the roads were repaired.

Clint strolled into the bedroom and chuckled. A cold weariness washed over her as she anticipated more fighting. She thought he had gone already. It was a hard pill to swallow but maybe Clint was right. Prayer didn't seem to help.

"You find some humor here, do you?" The words were mumbled through her crossed arMiss "It wouldn't hurt you to do some praying too," she said as she pulled herself up and slid from the room like a ghost. "But that might keep you out of the liquor joints," she mumbled under her breath, not caring anymore if she made him angry. He should share in the misery.

Lovey drank a cool dipper of water and sat in a hard chair at the round oak table in her sunny kitchen. Bowing her head into her hands, she felt numb. The house was damp although the sun had already raised the temperature to boiling outside. It seemed Clint took joy in her failure with the tobacco. But how could he want her to fail?

Clint followed her into the kitchen and she raised her head to watch him without a word. He checked his wallet for bills and counted out three dollars before replacing the money in his wallet and then his pocket. She thought of reminding him they needed coffee if he was going to town but decided against asking him for anything. She was exhausted from hearing him talk on and on about selling her little home. She knew they needed money but how could he even think that selling the house was the right thing to do?

She stood and took a step toward the door, deciding to check on the children in the barn where they had gone to play. Maybe their innocent chatter would cheer her spirits.

"Wait, Lovey. We've got to settle this – once and for all." He sat and pulled on the freshly polished boots laying by the door before coming close to her where she still stood near the door. "I've found a buyer for the house and I'm going to town to sign the papers whether you agree or not."

Lovey raised her arms as if warding off physical blows. "Please, Clint. We can't do this. Not over this silly feud with the Wilders." She stood near him, her blue eyes pleading.

"It's not a feud. I got angry."

"I told you to stay away from them."

"They beat me up. I couldn't let that go."

"Why not? See where it got you."

"When I found my still busted up like it was - I couldn't see straight. They deserved worse than they got."

"But you knew you'd have to pay for it?"

"I've heard enough nagging from you. Lovey. I didn't plan to get caught. But I did. Now I have to pay for the livestock to avoid jail."

"Clint, there must be some other way."

"It's the only choice, Lovey. The money will clear this up and will give us a fresh start too." He tucked his shirt into the dress pants he wore before yanking the belt higher on his waist and pushing out his chest. Sometimes he reminded her of a fussy little peacock.

Lovey looked at him with a long face. Her voice was weary. "This home is all I have for my children, Clint. Their father's death bought it for them."

"Woman, there's other, better places to live than this. And I have to have the money to pay my court fines or serve time. I won't do that again." He took her arms in his hands and squeezed, his fingers digging into her soft skin.

"How will we live without a place to grow tobacco?"

"I can work. I already have a job lined up over in Middlesboro if you would just listen to reason. You're the most stubborn woman I've ever known. You refuse to consider a good plan iffin it ain't yourn." He stomped his foot on the worn wooden floor, settling the heel of one foot into a boot before pulling on the other.

She felt contrary and wanted to object but wondered if his words were true.

"Lovey, you've never believed in me. How do you think that makes a man feel?"

She broke eye contact and sat down hard in a nearby chair. Ducking her head, she peered at the scratches on her once beautiful old oak table and felt the tears gather in her eyes and begin to fall. She wanted to trust Clint. She wanted to love him as she once had. She wanted to let him take charge of their fate and take care of her.

He sat too, moving his chair closer. He lifted her hand from the table and held it tight in his, bringing it up to his rough lips. He cradled her chin with his other hand, making her feel safe and protected for just a moment.

Against her better judgment, she nodded. "Do whatever we need to do, Clint. I don't know any more so I'll leave it to you."

Tears of defeat rolled down her cheeks as he strutted out the door.

Chapter 66

"Let me take that," Clint said. It was moving day, and he reached for the box Lovey carried, charm dripping with each word. Lovey let him have the box, turned without a word, and relished the bang of the screen door behind her as she walked back inside. She had packed their belongings yesterday, surprised at all they had accumulated in the past three years since John had died and she and the girls had settled here on the ridge.

There had been some happy times here. Sad times now outnumbered those early days and she was ready to leave this home behind, despite the tears that clogged her throat. Her high-topped shoes whispered against the shine of the freshly waxed floor as she walked to the bedroom she had shared with Clint. It was empty, much like her frozen heart.

She bent to retrieve a small yellow ribbon from the floor. It was once attached to a silk slip she often slept in when she and Clint had been newly married. She longed for the strong arms of a man around her – while at the same time she rebuffed his attempts. Clint had ruined everything for them.

"I'm sorry, Lovey," he said, promising to make better decisions, and she wanted to believe him.

"What about the job in Middlesboro?" she asked, still hopeful. But he had lost that too, after more trouble at Red's that put him back in jail for a couple of days. The job went on without him. They had been forced to rent an old house in Poor Valley instead, and Clint assured her he would make this work. He got a job with Sawyer's Lumber Company.

Poor Valley was on the opposite side of the mountain and the land was dry and rocky up there due to the over cutting of trees. Dust flew in Lovey's face as they made their way higher up the ridge. Could she even grow a vegetable garden here, she wondered? Maybe - with any luck. What choice did she have left? She couldn't and wouldn't try to grow tobacco anymore. She didn't have the heart for it.

With a shake of her head that almost rattled her teeth, Lovey allowed her gaze to return to the empty room and sweep the space that had once been hers and Clint's. The room was bare. The window glass was clean and ready for new curtains. She planned to cut her old blue drapes for the new house, which had fewer and smaller windows. She might use the leftover for some throw pillows.

"Mommy, tell Deloris she has to bring her sewing box. She wants to leave it behind." Melinda yelled as she ran into the room, her footsteps tapping on the bare floor, with Deloris close on her heels, pulling at her.

"I won't need it, Mommy. I don't even like to sew anyway," Deloris said, trying to pry the small box from her sister's grip. The top came off, spilling the contents, the ping of buttons dancing on the floor of the empty room.

Heat rose in Lovey's face and she bit hard against her bottom lip to keep from yelling. The girls were unsettled about the change to their routine but they had worked hard alongside her yesterday, preparing for the move without complaint. Deloris and Melinda bent to recover the contents of the sewing box without being told to do so and briefly it was so quiet Lovey could hear her own breath, fast and uneven in her throat. "Take those last boxes from your bedroom to the truck," she said. "As soon as Clint takes this load, we'll get the last things ready."

"Okay, Mommy," Melinda answered, taking her sister by the hand.

Lovey was afraid they wouldn't like their new home but at least she had kept them out of the lumber camp, where Clint had wanted to live. He would have a longer hike to work from the rented house but the walk to school for the girls, although long, was manageable. The new place was more secluded. It was so far off the main road back in one of the hollers, most folks didn't know it was even there. Their church and friends would be far away.

Following the girls from her bedroom, Lovey peeked into the children's shared room next door. "Have you taken everything out already?"

"Just about," Melinda said. She handed Deloris her sewing box and reached for her own where it sat on the floor. She hurried outside to add the small box to the truck.

"Scoot. Go help her, Deloris. Maybe I should have sent you to Granny's too."

Deloris raised herself to her full height. "I'm helping. I'm old enough to help and I'm helping more than Jackie could."

Lovey's heart lightened at this response from her independent middle daughter. The girls had been a big help getting all their things packed and ready for Clint and Bill Singleton to move in the truck Bill had provided. Her father had also brought a wagon and loaded the bed frames and feather mattresses in that. He and Uncle Harold were at the new place now, putting the beds together and getting the large items in place for them. After this load, Clint and Bill would return for the last few items along with Lovey and the girls. By dinner they would be at the new house. Granny was bringing food and staying to help Lovey get the family settled in. Lovey didn't hold out much hope for their efforts but she resolved to make the best of her new life. She was out of choices for now.

KATIE
December 1999

Chapter 67

Christmas day dawned bright with a brilliant sun that belied the bitter cold outside. Wind whistled through the cracks and crevices of the mountain range and whipped around Katie's little house like a dragon blowing ice instead of fire. The weather reporter called for freezing rain and possibly a light accumulation of snow before the end of the day. Katie dressed warmly and drove to Lovey's to have breakfast before going to Bobby's. She had promised to come see what Santa brought for Mathew. Bobby had happily agreed. Now she yearned for the quiet day ahead, inside by the fire, with Bobby and his little boy. And no talk about Regina.

Turning off the ignition after the short drive, Katie stepped outside and hurried to Lovey's back door, her hands filled with several small gifts. Lovey waited by the open door, the scent of pine smoke strong from the burning fire inside. She ushered the young woman inside before pushing the heavy door closed against the cold wind. "Come in girl, near the fire. It's so cold out, I expect the milk cows can only spit out icicles this morning."

Katie laughed. "It is at that. And I guess you've milked your share of cows in this kind of cold weather high on this mountain."

"That's true enough. Thank the good Lord I don't have any to milk this morning. Or babies to deliver. Seems those who came in the cold always had more trouble than the spring babies."

Lovey's eyes were shadowed with secrets from long ago as she took the young girl's coat and hung it on a peg. "The fire will warm you. And some coffee." She scurried for a mug of the rich brew and the sugar bowl and they sat together at the old table pulled close to the kitchen fireplace in the rustic cabin.

Katie crossed one leg over the other and settled in with her friend, in no particular hurry. A generation gap didn't exist between the two women, their lives so different and yet their interests so similar. Lovey knew a lot about illness and healing despite her lack of formal education. She still helped people with her dried herbs and medicinal plants from deep in the forest but she encouraged Katie to build her medical practice, as the old mountain ways were dying.

"I have something to tell you, Katie. I might should of told it long ago but I thought not at the time. Now might be the right time. But then I decided it should wait till today, on Christmas Day. Your daddy's birthday, right, honey."

"How do you know that? You remember the day he was born, Miss Lovey? I guess you were there."

"I was. And so was your granny, my very best friend in this life I've lived, Betty Jean. But there was somebody else there too that freezing cold day. I told you about my oldest daughter, Melinda. I told you she died young. It was on Christmas day, in 1938, in childbirth - although I did everything I could to stop her bleeding. The child she delivered was tiny, he came early and he was all shriveled up and sickly."

Katie waited, holding her breath.

"After Melinda was gone, her husband almost went insane with grief. I was still trying to work at the hospital in Knoxville, take care of Deloris and Jackie while they finished school, and my own mother and granny needed me more than ever. I couldn't take the tiny baby. Betty Jean still yearned for a child and it seemed the best solution to let her adopt him."

"My father? We always knew he was adopted but he was never told who his birth parents were. Grandma always told him that she and Grandpa were the only parents he needed to know about." Katie stood and leaned over this old woman she had come to love so much. Her own great-grandmother. What a trip? She dropped to her knees and hugged Lovey's legs, putting her head in the woman's lap. She sat that way for a long time, letting Lovey stroke her head, pushing the curls that were so like the pictures she had seen of Melinda, away from her forehead.

"Miss Lovey, dad will be so proud to learn about you and his mother. He's been lost a bit since his folks died. Family is all important to him and always has been. He and mother are planning a visit after they return from their cruise."

"All right then, girl. Let's get on about our celebration – and we'll do it all over again when he comes to visit. It's been many years since I've seen him but he's a fine looking man. The only one in our family since I only have daughters and granddaughters and we couldn't even claim him for our own."

The women exchanged their simple gifts. Katie unwrapped a colorful hand-pieced quilt and a jar of red striped peppermints. She had brought Lovey bath salts with scented powder and perfume, along with a grocery store gift card and a huge box of store-bought chocolates. They had finished eating breakfast and Katie was stacking dishes in the old sink, preparing to wash them before leaving. The sun had dimmed and rain was starting to fall outside. The rain hitting the window sounded icy.

Chapter 68

"So you're going to spent the rest of the day with the Lanes. Bobby's a good man. You can have your doctoring and a family too, Katie. Not like in my day." The woman seemed to know everything Katie worried about. It was as if she knew things before Katie told her.

"Are you sure you don't want to come along with me to Bobby's?" Katie looked over her shoulder at Lovey, who had moved to her rocker by the fire after adding another log. "You know you're welcome."

"No. Deloris is coming from Nashville this afternoon and I 'spect I might see some of the closer grandchildren before the day's done. Usually, some of the family come visit sometime during Christmas Day, although with my big birthday coming so soon, they may wait. Jackie will surely call from Memphis." The fire popped as Lovey replaced the screen in front of it. "Don't worry none over them dishes. I can clean them up later."

"It's no trouble. It's the least I can do after that breakfast of country ham and biscuits, along with the milk gravy you made for us. And that honey you had for the warm bread was too much but I loved it. I've enjoyed my morning here with you so much. It feels like home." She turned on the faucet and let the water run warm.

There was a knock at the door and then it flew open and banged against the back counter before either of them moved. Regina entered along with the blond man Katie had seen her with at Old Mill Restaurant. A taller, younger man came in behind them. He pushed the door closed as Regina stepped forward.

"Sorry to break in on you like this, Miss Lovey. But we need a word with the doc." The hard stare she turned on Katie was as cold as the ice outside. The two men, bulging muscles apparent even with the heavy coats they wore, stood as silent as sentries on each side of her.

"What is it, Regina? We don't have anything to talk about." She looked at the older woman, raising her brows. What did Regina want with her? Lovey's expression was as blank as her own.

"Is something wrong with Bobby or Mathew?" Katie's heart skipped at the thought.

A snicker came from Regina. "Let's step into the other room." She nodded toward the wide parlor at the front of the house and took a step toward it.

"Don't you worry about my boy," she hissed, close behind Katie as she passed. "He's just fine and doesn't need the likes of you to take care of him."

When Katie paused, Regina took her arm and the two sauntered into the front room as if they were the best of old friends, arm in arm.

As soon as they cleared the doorway, Regina produced a small handgun from somewhere, confirming Katie's worse fears about her. She waved the gun in Katie's face before putting it back in her pocket, raising her raincoat to show it still pointed toward the doctor. "We can do this the easy way or the hard way, Dr. Cook. Someone's been hurt and I want you to come along and take a look at him. Leave Lovey out of it or we'll have to take her along too. And this weather isn't exactly friendly right now, especially the way we'll travel."

Katie's words stuck in her throat and intelligent words refused to form. "What? Why...?" She stuttered before she finally nodded silent agreement. What was this all about? Obviously, she had been right about Regina? Too bad Bobby hadn't listened to her last night.

Katie had to protect Lovey. As they walked back into the kitchen, she avoided Lovey's gaze, sure her fear would give her away. She had to get these thugs out of the house. "Okay, Miss Lovey. Looks like Christmas is over for me. I've been summoned to the clinic for an emergency but thanks again for the delicious breakfast. Your friendship is cherished."

She leaned forward for a hug as Lovey stood. The older woman's eyes flashed with a quick wit. Nobody was fooling her but Katie prayed she wouldn't say or do anything stupid. She risked slightly shaking her head.

"Ok, dear, I'll call Bobby and let him know you've been delayed. You hear me?"

Katie knew what she was trying to say and winked before she turned away.

The two men were already at the door and had it open in a flash. They stepped through and walked ahead. The rain had let up but it still misted. Katie grabbed her coat, pulling it on as she stepped outside, with Regina bringing up the rear, closing the door with a bang.

"What's wrong? Regina? I don't like this?"

Katie hoped Bobby came quickly. But as they walked around the side of the cabin, she noticed the cut phone line dangling from the pole. Her hopes were dashed. Katie would have to figure a way out of this mess herself.

LOVEY
August 1931
Chapter 69

The family settled in the big old two story house set back under the overhanging rock of the ridge over Poor Valley. On clear mornings they could see all the way to the bottom of the mountain where Clinch River curled like a silver ribbon through the dark green of thick forest land. Lovey and the girls cleaned and waxed every wood surface in the house during the long hot summer, and it began to feel like home to them. There was a rotten board on the roof that still leaked in the back bedroom but it was in a corner and Clint promised to fix it before winter.

The house had once been a grand old lady but had fallen into disrepair through years of neglect and emptiness. Faded paint and curling paper that covered the walls showed her age. Clint had repaired several leaks in the roof. He had taken charge of what purse strings there were and Lovey left him to it, trying hard to avoid fighting with him.

The weather would soon change and the children would return to school. Lovey and Granny worked in the kitchen side by side on the last

Elizabeth Wilmoth Solazzo

Saturday in August. Granny handed her another jar of preserves and she lined it up on the open shelves at the back of the kitchen. "This will sure taste good with some hot biscuits, Granny. I thank you for it."

"You worked so hard in that ruined tobacco crop, I suspected you could use some canned goods. Do you have enough of everything?"

"I'm sure I do," Lovey lied. "Anyway, Clint's bragging on the canned food he can buy over in Knoxville. He's making another trip next week with the cook for his work crew and planning to bring in some beans and tomatoes in those tin cans for the crew and he said he would bring some home too."

"They may not be fitting to eat at all. You reckon?"

Lovey laughed at the look of horror on the older woman's face. "He likes them. The girls aren't too hard to please either and I remember eating those wax beans from the store when we lived in Michigan. They didn't have a lot of flavor but they were filling."

"Not in my lifetime am I planning on eating those when I can grow juicy tomatoes and fresh beans on my own land." Granny sniffed as she placed a half gallon jar of peaches on the bottom shelf alongside others. She had brought a dozen and Lovey knew they would make delicious cobblers in the dead of winter. There was nothing better on a freezing winter day than the scent of peaches filling her kitchen as they were baking in the oven, making her dream of the warm days ahead and the fresh peaches on the tree.

"Home-grown always taste better. Maybe next year I'll get a chance to put up more than I did this year. I noticed there are blackberry vines down the hill. And the water is fresh and cold as ice here."

Clint was working but not bringing in much cash. The family still had Bessie for milk and some chickens so hopefully that would see them through. Clint told her not to worry about it.

Granny leaned back on her heels and pulled herself upright by holding onto the old oak table. She slid into a chair and crossed her arms over her amble bosoms and rested one ankle over the other. "You're a good girl, child, and I'm proud of you for making the best of a bad situation. Your mother is too. She wanted to come up to see you today but had to work."

Lovey leaned down and hugged her granny before sitting herself. "Oh, well, what else can I do? I'm tied to him now and hopefully he'll provide for us."

"I'm sure he will. A man wants to be in charge of his home and you having a home already might have caused some problems for y'all. Maybe this will be a new start for you."

"The house isn't too bad and the girls are settling in. Melinda likes having a room of her own although I sometimes find them all in bed together come morning. They're growing up fast and ready to go back to school."

"Good. School will keep'em busy. It's a long walk to get over to me but I hope to see you some this winter if the weather doesn't get too bad. I have several quilts to piece and could use your help to finish them in the spring."

Lovey saw the girls hurry across the yard as Uncle Harold pulled his wagon to a stop at the top of the hill. His old mule yawned and nickered as he released the reins and leaned back against the wagon board. He had dropped Granny and the jars of fruit off a while ago and drove on to take some hay to the Wilmoth farm.

Granny reached for her large black pocketbook on the kitchen table and slipped it over her arm. "He'll be ready to go quick before it gets dark. I love you, child. Get word to me if you need help with anything." She scurried out the door, grabbing for each girl and offering quick kisses before she climbed into the wagon with a spry step.

Lovey waved from the doorway. "Thanks for everything. We'll see you soon."

The girls and their mother stood and watched the wagon disappear down the hill as the sun sank lower in the sky. The woods nearby were already filled with darkness and she wondered briefly, although she no longer cared, where her husband was tonight.

Chapter 70

L ovey punched up the fire as the evening grew cooler and returned to her rocker in the front room. The girls were in bed after a warm bath, with strips of brown paper wrapped around damp hair to create curls. She flipped open her old childhood bible and restlessly riffled the pages, reading short passages here and there, looking for answers. She planned to walk with the girls to Raven Ridge Church in the morning, the first time she would attend since moving to Poor Valley. The walk would take a good hour but she missed the companionship of her church family. Maybe they would go on to Granny's after church and visit for a spell. It would make for a long walk home but it would be worth it and they could rest at Granny's before they started back.

Hearing the whine of a truck motor as it climbed the steep drive, Lovey closed the crumbling pages of her old Bible and walked to the door to see who had arrived at this late hour. It had to be Clint. The lights of a vehicle blinded her and she paced in the open doorway as Clint, and then a woman, stepped out. The truck backed around beside the house and rolled back down the hilly road. Clint and the woman walked toward the house. Lovey brushed back her unruly hair and stepped aside for the pair, seeing the glint of alcohol in Clint's bloodshot eyes.

"This here's Birdie. She wants to rent a room from us." The couple shared a glance and giggled as if they told a very funny story. They were very drunk.

Lovey was speechless as the tall, handsome woman stepped forward and held out an unsteady hand. "I know it's late but I'm looking for a place to settle near the lumber camp. Clint here offered your spare room." The woman's hair was as red as her wide lips and the heavy powder that covered her face almost hid the smell of white lighting. Clint didn't have the benefit of anything to mask his stench. What kind of woman would come home with a man she didn't know? Or maybe they knew one another better than Lovey knew.

"We don't have an extra room, Clint." Lovey smiled and tried to motion Clint into the kitchen but he wouldn't move away from the woman.

"Well, the girls can bunk in together and we can give her the big room Melinda's using. Or even this large front room could be turned into a room to rent." He waved his hands around the room expansively, as if showing a fancy hotel room. "She's a paying customer, Lovey. That should make you happy."

Lovey stood, staring, shaken at this strange turn of events and considering her options. Was he serious? The driver of the truck had gone so the woman had no way off the mountain. She supposed they would have to put her up for the night. They could sort it all out when everybody sobered up.

"Git, now, woman. Move the girls into one room and get her a cozy place ready." He pushed Lovey's shoulder before putting an arm around the strange woman. "Unless you'd rather give her a spot in our bed." Clint laughed at his little joke. "She might add some warmth."

Lovey heard the laughter from both of them as she hurried up the stairs to do her husband's bidding, her mouth clamped tight. Shaking Melinda awake, she walked her over to the other room to the big bed where her sisters still slept soundly. "We have a guest, Melinda. Move in with your sisters for tonight."

Melinda complied without complaint or question as Lovey tucked her in beside her sisters and spread out the old patchwork quilt that was her own favorite. The pattern was of cut out dolls in different colored outfits, with matching shoes and hats. Lovey pulled the quilt over her children and looked at the silent dolls decorating the quilt as tears came to her eyes and ran down her face. She brushed them aside and pulled the door closed as she heard the shuffling of feet on the steep staircase.

The woman called Birdie climbed to where Lovey stood. They moved together into the darkened and cold bedroom, lit only by a kerosene lamp, Birdie stumbling and giggling. "It'll be okay in the morning," she whispered, her head resting briefly on Lovey's shoulder as she patted her unwilling hostess on the back. The strange woman immediately fell into the newly emptied bed and passed out cold, leaving Lovey to stare blankly at her.

Chapter 71

As *The Old Rugged Cross* was sung in the high sweet tenor of the Wilmoth Sisters quartet, Lovey's body itched to move. The hard wooden bench cut into her backside and she resisted the urge to twist from side to side. She and the girls had been attending church regularly the last few weeks and Lovey awaited an answer to her prayers. 'Please God,' she prayed, 'What am I to do about my sorry sad life?' But there was no answer coming and she wondered if she was wasting her time. Her faith had grown weak.

The alter call seemed to last forever and she was restless with pent up energy. When Pastor Buddy Wolfe finally ended the service, the worshipers exited the old church with rough pine beams and stepped out into the freshness of a cool sunny day. Lovey nodded to neighbors and friends, but her thoughts were already home, with Clint. She wanted to talk with him, try to make him understand what she needed from him. Melinda took Jackie's hand and led her down the lane with other children running ahead of them, obviously feeling the same impatience for freedom as Lovey.

Betty Jean joined her at the open church door and Lovey felt her friend's smooth hand take her by the arm, stilling her with a gentle touch. "Are you alright?" she asked, gazing into Lovey's eyes.

"I'm well," Lovey answered and looked away, pulling free from her touch, avoiding the kindness in her friend's hazel eyes and the softness of her hands. This gentle friend could bring tears to her quicker than any small harshness from another.

"You look skittish. I watched you during the service and you didn't make a move but I could see the energy jumping around you like summer lightening."

Betty Jean always knew her best but Lovey wasn't sure she was ready to share her troubles with the preacher's wife just yet. "I need to hurry home. Deloris is down with the measles and I left her home with Clint. You know she can be a handful."

Betty Jean stepped away. "I won't hold you up but come visit me this week, will you? I'd love to have one of our long talks and spend some real time with you."

Lovey smiled and waved as she walked away. "Maybe I will. I'd like that too."

Catching up with the children who had waited by the dirt road where a few cars were slowly moving away and more families were walking toward homes sprinkled around the church, she relaxed a bit. Her friend's loving touch had added a livelier step to her gait. Surely things would improve at home soon.

"Are you hungry, girls?" she asked, as they begin their climb, leaving others behind. "I have some chicken cut up and ready to hit the frying pan when we get home." Lovey took Jackie's small hand and helped her jump a puddle left over from last night's rain shower.

"And some hoecakes with butter and jam?" Jackie asked, as she looked up at her mother with wide open eyes of happiness and a gap toothed smile.

"Yes, my little sugar cake. You'd be happy if we only had sweets, wouldn't you?"

The group trudged slowly up the winding hill as Lovey puzzled over the future. At least Birdie, the term they were now calling their guest, was paying for her keep and that allowed them to buy supplies like flour and salt and sugar. She was trying to ignore what might be going on between Clint and Birdie, almost not caring anymore, although she knew she should. She could barely remember the Clint from their courtship and wondered where it had all gone wrong. Was he right that their troubles were all her fault for not letting him be a man?

How did she make him less a man just because she wanted him home at night? She didn't care if he drank a bit as long as he came home and tried to help make a family with her. The girls needed a father but he seemed indifferent to all but Jackie. Dare she hope for a change, she wondered as she and the girls finally made the turn to their lane and began to climb the steep hill? Melinda and Jackie skipped ahead of her, happy and full of energy, and Lovey began to feel more hopeful as well. She was surprised to see Deloris sitting on the front porch swing, wrapped in a quilt.

"What're you doing out here in the cold?" she asked, hurrying forward.

"It's not cold, Mommy. The sun's shining."

"But you're sick, child. Where's Clint?" She took Deloris by the arm and pushed her ahead into the house as she moved through the front door. "Back in bed with you, sweetheart. I can't believe you're outside in the cool air. Clint should know better."

"Be quiet, mom," Deloris whispered, turning to hunker against her mother, burying her face in Lovey's waist. "Clint and Birdie are taking a nap together and they said I should stay outside and be quiet."

"What did you say?" The strangled voice trailed off as she marched her middle daughter back to her bed and tucked the covers over her. She leaned to kiss her cheek automatically. "Stay in bed!" she demanded.

Lovey's body was cold and stiff as she took measured steps back downstairs and stood in front of her bedroom door, her breath held tight in her chest. The sound of the tiny squeak the knob made as she touched it prompted her to fling it open even as her imagination raced ahead at what she might find. Her suspicions were confirmed. The couple separated and reached for clothing to cover their naked bodies as Lovey stepped into the room.

"Out," Lovey screamed. "Get out of my house right now. How dare you do this right under my nose, in my own bed." She pulled at the other woman, throwing dress and slip and stockings, along with blankets and pillows; anything she could get in her hands. She was beside herself with rage, pushing at Birdie, still partially undressed, to leave.

"And you," she said as she rounded on her husband. "You can leave too. I don't need this in my life or the lives of my children. I'll not tolerate it. Do you hear me?" She took a breath, her vision momentarily blurred as she felt the slap of Clint's open hand across her face. The cold crack of his hand awakened her to the reality she faced here, and she backed away. Her hand rose to caress her cheek where it stung with the slap and she continued to back out of the room. She had never been hit by anyone.

"Be gone when I come back," she said to Birdie, her stare pinched and hard against the obvious pity in the other woman's gaze.

Chapter 72

Lovey felt possessed by demons as she whirled and ran out of the house and back down the path, ignoring Melinda's beckoning call. She dropped her shawl and her full skirt flew out behind her. She was ashamed. Clint had left her no room for saving face. He had taken the last of her self-respect and she could no longer lie to herself.

Screaming wild words of hurt as she ran helped stem some of the disappointment and discouragement she felt. Her body was on fire with hatred for the very man who had once so charmed her and she was warm despite the coolness from the overhanging limbs along the path. He was the same man, cocky and sure of himself. His self-assurance had attracted her in the beginning when she once watched him strut around the yard, kicking at the hens if they didn't move out of his way quickly enough. The fact that it was she who had changed instead of him angered her most. How could she have been so blind with love? She slowed her steps and took several deep breaths as she approached the fast moving stream tumbling over rocks into the river below.

She stood a short distance away from the water, bent at the waist as she recovered her breath and the roar in her head subsided to a softer whisper of water racing over rocks. The scent of damp earth and dying vegetation awakened her to her surroundings and she spied Evie Winstead bending over the opposite bank to fill a small bucket and swing it to the long grass beside her boot shod foot. Renewed breath allowed her to smile and murmur hello to the elderly woman. She hoped she looked presentable.

Lovey moved closer. The two women had developed a friendship of sorts after her miscarriage. It was said Widow Winstead knew everyone in the valley and all their business just by looking at them but Lovey didn't mind. She respected the woman's knowledge of medicine and tried to learn from her at every opportunity.

A cloud came up dark and gray as the old woman stepped closer, only the thin thread of a the stream separating them. A cool breeze tickled the bare skin on Lovey's arms and the scent of mud and crushed grass rose in the air. A mist enveloped both women as the older one stepped closer, her feet almost in the water where she stood on the opposite shore. Lovey shivered.

"Tis good to see you, girl." Mrs. Winstead dipped her head in a little bow that reminded Lovey of a country gentlewoman some said the old woman had been when her father first came to preach at the Raven Ridge Baptist church in 1895. Questions filled the sharp eyes of Widow Winstead as she turned to the young woman but. Her face lit with a kind smile.

"How are those sweet little girls of yourn?"

"Fine," Lovey answered, pinned by the dark penetrating gaze.

"And that young buck you took up with? He treating you right, I hope." Lovey started at the words, thinking the old witch really could see right into her hurt heart and know everything she was thinking. How was that possible? There were lots of things in this world that were hard to explain but that notion didn't make them unreal.

The two women stood still, and stared at one another for a spell, a young woman with her heart breaking and an old woman who had lived so long there wasn't anything she hadn't seen or heard of, even in these backwoods. They didn't speak until Evie Winstead nodded as if the girl was spilling up all her secrets.

"Huh," she murmured, "some men don't know what's good for um, I always say." She used her cane to beat back some brush by the side of the path. "I used that little precious right there on one or two men in my day." The cane brushed against a small bush with yellowish green leaves that sprouted white flowers in the spring. Lovey had seen the plant and was taught never to touch it by hand. It was poisonous.

The old woman's dark brown eyes were lit and alive as a bitter smile curved her mouth. "It's called doll's eye." The tip of her cane dug underneath the leaves and pulled forth a ball of berries with a large black dot on each. They looked strangely like eyeballs. "It'll simmer a grown man down all right. The leaves can cause a horrible rash but the fruit that comes in spring are quite deadly if boiled up with some food. A little or a lot – depending on your trouble."

Lovey didn't speak as the woman pointed with her gnarled cane, indicating the wild plant that grew here under the overhanging willows dipping into the water. She gave Lovey a hard look. "A woman has to do what a woman has to do. Remember that, girl. It don't make it all-together wrong."

The old woman stepped back from the water, picked up her pails of water, and climbed up over the rise on sure feet before she disappeared into the thick brush that grew on her side of the stream. She hadn't uttered another word. Lovey stared at the almost hidden little plant a long time before she began the climb home, deep in thought, her breath coming strong and even. She didn't know exactly what she would do yet but it was time to take action - that much was finally clear to her.

Chapter 73

Lovey's breath came easier despite the steep climb as she retraced her steps back up the ridge. Evie Winstead had reminded Lovey there were options where she thought there had been none. Using poison was silly. Wasn't it? Not something she could do, but this pitiful inaction wasn't like her either. It was time she did something. Her children were the most important element in this puzzle of a life she had created. She must protect them. They deserved more than she had given them to this point and her mind worked to factor a solution.

The wind blew colder and she shivered as she trudged home on the rutted dirt road that led back to her place. She jumped to the far right of the road as an old gray truck came into view, bouncing down the trail. She saw it was Birdie, along with her brother, Slim, with all her belongings piled in the back of the truck.

Lovey was glad to be rid of the woman although they had relied on her small room and board fee to see them by and by these last desperate months. She was pleased Clint had listened to her. As the truck slowed on the bumpy road, the two women stared at one another, their narrowed gazes speaking volumes.

Lovey had grown to like Birdie after getting used to the idea of another woman in her home and was disappointed in her now. Hadn't they become friends in recent weeks? Bird Baylord was a beautiful widow woman with no children, who lost her husband in a burning car crash near the top of Clinch Mountain. After Clint and Slim had started up a new ~~steal~~ STILL in Poor Valley last year, Bird's man, Johnny, had been their runner. He loved racing. He lived for speed and outrunning the law even when it wasn't necessary. He relished a story for himself among the local population, dreaming of one day being written about, somewhat like the story of the Bunch gang of Claiborne County. Johnny's luck ended when he tried to outrun the revenuers for his last time in January of last year and rolled his car into Dead Man's Curve.

Melinda and Jackie were waiting on the porch swing, huddled together; looking almost as forlorn as the day their daddy had died. They ran out to meet her as she walked back into the scrawny patch of yard surrounding their home. Melinda had retrieved her mother's knitted shawl and brought it along to wrap around her. Lovey clutched it to her breast as the children circled her and each placed a hand on their mother, their sticky but warm fingers welcome on her arms, leading her inside. She was chilled.

Lovey's sturdy body moved forward step by step, into a sudden cold gust of wind kicking up around the corner of the house. She pushed herself home although her legs were leaden. Home was where a mother belonged, a father be damned.

Chapter 74

Pushing the girls ahead of her into the house, Lovey shushed their questions about Clint and the strange direction the afternoon had taken. "Melinda, check on Deloris – make sure she's in bed and covered up and then come right back to help me in the kitchen. It's late but that chicken still needs frying."

Lovey stepped into the kitchen as Melinda went upstairs to do her bidding. Clint sat in a kitchen chair in his sleeveless undershirt, head hanging low and damp hair fashioned into a curl atop his head, drinking reheated coffee. He was almost sober.

"She's gone, Lovey. Bird walked down to Maw Riley's and made a call for Slim to come pick her up. I hope you're satisfied. We'll need her rent money before the end of the month."

Lovey slammed the iron skillet on the stove for an answer. She saw no need for words as she put in a generous portion of shortening and placed the pan over the burner. She quickly readied the chicken with an egg and milk mixture and then coated it in flour and dropped it into the hot skillet, trying to ignore her husband's presence behind her at the table.

"Now, Shug, don't be mad. You know I can't be accountable for what I do when I've been drinking. I didn't mean no harm."

Moving briskly around the small kitchen, Lovey added canned corn and a jar of chopped collards to the stove, along with boiled potatoes and hoecakes. Each familiar step provided a balm to Lovey's anxious nerves and she was soon humming under her breath.

Melinda set the table when she came back down, also ignoring Clint where he sat, but Jackie climbed into his lap and began to chatter. Clint cradled the small child in his muscular arms, leaning close, his hooded eyes on the child, but he occasionally glanced up at his wife, awaiting a word that was not forthcoming.

After putting the food on the table, Lovey left the room without a word.

Her steps calm and measured on the bare wood floor, Lovey began stripping the sheets from her bed, ignoring the perfumed scent of Bird and remaking it with fresh linen. Her breath came even in her chest and she refused to think beyond the next moment in front of her. She didn't know what would come next but decided she could only trust in herself to get out of this mess she found herself in. Somehow.

Something would surely come to her soon.

Chapter 75

Frozen brush crackled with each step Lovey made along the trail. It wasn't especially cold but the sky was gray and cloudy with the promise of rain. Bare tree limbs announced that the long Indian summer they had enjoyed was over. Lovey felt trapped in an endless parade of poor choices and was just as glad her husband had not come home last night. She trotted along the lower valley road to her friend, Betty Jean's house, the movement helping her stay warm against the early winter chill. Being outside lifted her spirits.

Rounding a curve, she stopped and stared at the high porch of the Wolfe's home tucked into the little cove. "Howdy, anybody home," she hollered.

Betty Jean opened the door immediately as if she were expecting her friend. It was only then that Lovey remembered Wednesday afternoon had once been their visiting day. She hadn't consciously planned the long awaited visit for a Wednesday, but perhaps that's what had drawn her here today. That and her despair over the miserable life she had made for herself.

"I'm so glad you've come, Lovey." Betty Jean took her by the arm as she climbed the steps and pulled her inside the house, allowing the screen door to slam on the outside world. She pulled Lovey into the front room where a large winter cactus filled with buds rested on a long table against the window behind her couch. Betty Jean's smile split her face, and Lovey found herself returning the gesture although the movement felt strange on her face, which had not known much laughter or joy in recent years.

Betty Jean bustled about the room, pulling a whistling kettle from the wood-fed stove that sat out in middle of the floor in the front room, offering coffee and a little snack cake she rushed to the kitchen for and brought back on a delicate glass plate. The green glass dishes were offered in each box of their favorite old fashioned oatmeal.

Lovey gazed around the homey front room as she waited for Betty Jean to settle. The curtains were lace trimmed and stiff with starch. There were doilies on all the side tables, hand crocheted and also starched. The wood floor had a gloss on it set off by the rag rugs scattered around the room. Lovey's home had once held this kind of shine and the faint scent of lemon to it but no more. Now she was ashamed for anyone to visit, what with her lack of housekeeping and the stink of Clint's cigarettes.

Betty Jean fluttered to a stop and took a seat next to Lovey in front of the warm stove. There had been no fire for the girls this morning beyond the kitchen stove they used for the breakfast cooking. Lovey had a moment of unease as she saw Betty Jean fluff out her dress and felt tears dampen her lids as she imagined how she must look in her old work clothes.

"Lovey, are you alright? I've been worried about you this whole past year." Betty Jean reached over to put an arm around her shoulders.

Blinking back the quick tears, she nodded. "It's not easy but I guess this is what I deserve for jumping blindly into a second marriage. What's that saying? 'Marry in haste, repent in leisure'. I was just so lonely without John."

"You've done nothing wrong, Lovey. You wanted to love and be loved. It's not your fault Clint has let you down. You deserve so much more."

"Maybe so but I don't guess that matters now, does it?" Lovey looked at her rough hands, darkened from hauling wood. There was a fresh splinter that spoke of her manual labor. She wanted to curl her hands away but felt her friend stretch them out and reach for a needle in a pin cushion on the side table. She begin to work gently at the splinter, pulling it free from the puckered skin.

Betty Jean clucked like a mother hen and Lovey knew she didn't say what she really thought of Clint. She was too much of a lady. But her eyes flashed fire. "There's divorce," Betty Jean whispered. "You've tried so hard. You can't go on like this."

"It may come to that but I would hate to lose my church family. You know I'd be shunned." Lovey wondered what Betty Jean would say if she knew about Birdie and the worst of it but she didn't want to say more. "I'll work it out somehow, Betty Jean. Don't worry so about me but just let me rest here a minute." She leaned her head against the back of Betty Jean's sofa and sighed. She closed her eyes and saw the happy life she had once planned alongside her childhood friend. The image was a welcome relief from feeling like a dumb animal caught in a cage.

Chapter 76

A few weeks later, Lovey gathered eggs in the bottom of her apron. She wore an old wool coat against the cold morning but her hands were bare and her legs uncovered from the bottom of her dress to the high galoshes she wore. She backed out of the chicken coop and turned toward the house only to stop in her tracks, her back pressed hard against the rough wooden door of the old structure. A red fox paced in front of the building, wary and watchful, his golden eyes drooping with hunger. The winter had been hard for animals as well as humans and she felt a moment of pity for the wild animal.

Quickly coming to her senses, she raised a hand to shoo him away, imagining what one of the girls would do in her place. Melinda usually gathered the eggs each morning but she had come instead because of the hard frost last night. There was a layer of thick ice on the ground and she planned to keep the girls home from school as it would be too treacherous out.

The fox held his ground, not responding to her waving, and then even moved a little closer, growling low in his throat. She reached behind her with the hand not holding the apron full of eggs, searching for something to throw at him. Clint kept a shotgun in the house but it wouldn't do her much good there. Her body shivered.

Melinda jumped off the back steps with a clatter of noise, wearing old boots that had belonged to her father. "What's taking so long, mama?" she yelled as she slid along the path in the oversized boots.

"Stop, Melinda. Don't come any closer," Lovey said, watching the fox turn to her daughter.

Melinda spotted the fox and turned back to the house. She lost her footing in the ice and came sliding down the path on her bottom. Lovey moved to place herself between the wild animal and her child, throwing an egg at the fox.

The fox stopped to lick up the remains of the cracked egg as Lovey positioned herself in front of Melinda. They huddled together on the cold ground before the fox again advanced on them. Lovey threw another egg, this time just past the animal. As the skinny creature turned in his tracks to lap up the splattered egg, Lovey pulled Melinda to her feet and they took a step backward to the old house. Foxes didn't usually attack people but her heart thundered in her chest. She felt a cold sweat on her body despite the freezing temperature. The wind howled around the side of the house, blowing stringy unwashed hair around her face. The light was still dim in the valley but her eyes focused on the wild animal as mother and daughter inched backward, ready to toss eggs as needed.

Each time the fox turned his attention to them, Lovey lobbed an egg, each one giving them another step to retreat. She only had a few eggs left as they reached the bottom of the steps. She let loose with one more, tossing it as far as possible, grabbing Melinda with her free hand as they stumbled up the steps into the house. Allowing what remained in her apron to fall free on the floor, crunching eggshells beneath her feet, she raced for the gun in her bedroom.

"Stay in the house, girls," she yelled as she stepped outside with the weapon, preparing to protect her children and her small flock of chickens.

The fox was back at the chicken coop already, on his hind legs and searching for a way inside. Although she didn't think he could get in, foxes were notorious for their ability to wiggle into tight spaces to capture a prey. She moved forward on the ice, taking each step carefully, the fox so desperate for food he didn't respond to the sound of ice cracking under her boot. She would have to shoot him, if not today, next time. She raised the gun to her shoulder and sited before she squeezed the trigger.

She felt as desperate as the fox, the two of them fighting for survival. The shot sounded loud in the stillness of the cold morning and the animal dropped on the ice outside the chicken house, unmoving, his blood quickly freezing on the hard ground.

Before retreating to the house, Lovey leaned her shotgun against the shed and grabbed the cooling paws of the dead fox to drag him into the edge of the woods, knowing other scavengers would soon feast on his remains. She lost the contents of her stomach on the ground beside him. Although she had often shot guns with her father, she had never killed another living thing.

Turning from the dead animal and her own vomit, she saw a glimmer of sun crest the hill. She used the back of her coat sleeve to wipe the bile from her lips and ignored the sour taste in her mouth. Holding her body tall as she walked to the small house she called home, she wondered what she would feed her children this morning.

Chapter 77

The last Saturday night in February of 1932, Clint came rolling in during the middle of the night with Bird and her brother, Slim. He had been gone since the New Year, and Lovey had hoped his departure was permanent, although she was becoming increasingly desperate for food. She had sold her milk cow the last of January and the chickens had gone to market just yesterday, traded for canned milk, flour and lamp oil. The whine of the truck motor climbing the hill and drunken laughter woke the children and Lovey from a deep sleep. She sprung out of bed and ran to the front room, her children close on her heels. Anger burned hot as fire by the time she got there. Clint had a jar of moonshine and the three passed it around to one another.

"What're you doing here, Clint? And what about her?" She poked her finger out at Birdie. "I won't have this again. I tell you, I'll not stand for it." She motioned for the children to return to their beds. Melinda and Deloris hesitated. Her sharp glare convinced them to take their smaller sister and retreat to the upstairs bedroom, where they all slept together now.

"I thought you had left home for good."

"What kind of man would I be if I did that, woman. I've been working with Slim and the boys over on Lone Mountain and have some money for you." He pulled a small wad of bills from his pocket and held it out. She took it, knowing the money would feed her children next week, but hating herself for having to. She stuffed the bills in her night clothes, noting the satisfaction in Clint's smug smile.

"How about a little kiss now?" Clint moved closer and tried to hug her, but he was sloppy drunk, falling into her and almost bringing them both down.

"Forget it. You smell like a still." She pushed him aside. "All of you need to go on back to where you come from. There's nothing for you here."

She walked to the bedroom and Clint followed her inside and closed the door behind them. "You should be a little more friendly, Lovey. What's the matter with you?" He drank from the open jar again and carefully set it on the dresser.

"Clint, I'm tired of this. Get your whore out of here and you can go with her for all I care."

"You don't need to act like that, woman. Birdie and I ain't nothing to one another. Just old drinking buddies."

Lovey heard the sound of the front door opening and closing in the other room and assumed Birdie and her brother had gone. She was relieved but wished they had taken Clint with them.

"Now see what your bad manners has done. My friends have left."

Lovey watched as Clint took a pre-rolled cigarette from the back of his ear. He lit it with a stick match and blew smoke in her face as he replaced the box of matches in his pocket. She waved it away. "What happened to the man I married?" she asked, true puzzlement in her voice as she crossed her arms in front of her body. "You're a lazy, good for nothing bum who only cares about drinking and carousing with these trashy folks?"

"Lovey, I'm warning you – you're going too far." He took an unsteady step closer to her, his face turning red and his fist balling by his side.

She stood her ground. "As a matter of fact, I want a divorce. I won't have my girls living like this no more. Never knowing when some drunk will come in and wake them in the middle of the night."

"Miss 'high and mighty' Lovey! Always thinking you're too good for common folks. Maybe I'm tired of you too. Did you ever think of that?" Clint dropped the burning cigarette on the floor and stomped on it as he reached out his hand and slapped her hard across the face, as if he were swatting a fly. She didn't flinch and her stare dared him to do it again. Her eyelids didn't flicker and her face was stone.

After his hand came up again to backhand her, this time harder, she felt his fists pound into her chest, taking her breath. "Stop it, Clint," she yelled, as she tried to move away from him in the small room, but only fell backward on the bed instead. Clint tumbled over with her, repeatedly slapping at her and using his fists, straddling her on the bed. Lovey managed a few swings but mostly missed.

"Clint, stop it." Lovey thought the plea came from her own lips until she saw Melinda standing behind Clint, pulling on his stout arm.

"Stop. You're hurting her," the little voice begged, the sound soft. From blinking eyes Lovey saw the younger girls in a corner of the room, crying and pleading for the violence to stop.

Clint flung Melinda from his back and roared at all the children. "Get out of here and back to your bed." The voice sounded horse and strained and his breathing was heavy. Lovey rolled to her side, floating somewhere above herself. She coughed and saw bright blood on her Wedding Ring quilt Granny had made as Clint stood and chased the girls out of the room.

Clint was eerily calm when he returned and she prayed he had not hit the girls. "See what you made me do, Lovey. This is how much I love you. I'm crazy at the thought of losing you and I won't ever let you go." Clint cooed soft words of love as he pulled away her bloody nightdress and wrapped her in clean blankets, putting her to bed like a small child.

Lovey didn't speak but lay quietly, her mind looping in and out of consciousness. When she was lucid, she was busy making her plans to end this misery once and for all. She was done and would accept no more punishment from this man. It stopped right here.

Chapter 78

L ate the next week a strong wind blew for two days. The storm knocked down trees that blocked the rural road three miles down the mountain. Lovey lay in bed, her body healing from the beating. She remained quiet, letting broken ribs heal and dark bruises fade but her mind was a busy place as she planned.

The storm brought damage but also brought fresh spring air that was heady. Clint joined neighbors to help clear the road and restore power to lower Caney Valley. There had never been electrical power this far up the mountain so life changed little for the Collins's. School was closed so the children helped her with farm chores.

She joined them as they gathered eggs this morning in the bright sunlight of a fresh day. What she suspected were the Lane's chickens had drifted north with the storm and had been roosting in her empty chicken house, providing more eggs. Lovey decided she would bake a cake for dessert after the evening meal – something she rarely did anymore.

Jackie squealed as the chickens flew blindly into the sun streaked air of the dank building as they were disturbed. The older girls laughed at their baby sister and Lovey chided them. "It's okay to be startled, girls. Life can take us by surprise."

Deloris ran around in circles, trying to scare her sister again. Melinda joined in the game and Jackie soon chortled with the fun the older sisters provided. It was a relief to see them so carefree. They had not spoken of the night of the beating but each watched their mother more closely than ever. Lovey smiled at her growing girls as she placed three large eggs in her apron to carry back to the house. She only had canned milk but it would do.

Later that day the scene was set for a lovely family dinner. Lovey and the girls had cleaned the little house until the threadbare and shabby furniture and fixtures literally shone in the late afternoon sun. Clint arrived home to a happy family scene and seemed in a good mood despite the hard work of hauling limbs out of the road and sawing up wood. "Come and sit down, Clint, and rest a spell before dinner."

The little man glanced at his wife with narrowed eyes as he sauntered into the front room. He had been especially attentive and caring all week, but that no longer mattered to Lovey. He sat down and began to take off his work boots. Lovey made no mention of the mud he tracked over the hard wood floors shining from a fresh coat of wax although she saw Melinda frown and run to get the cleaning rag. "Where'd the chicken come from?" he asked.

"The Lord provides," Preacher Wolfe says. "Seems he's right this time. Chickens from next door have taken up residence in our barn." Lovey rushed back to the kitchen to see about the old hen she had killed for supper, fearing it might be a bit tough. "I decided if the Lord brought them here, he wouldn't mind if I accepted the gift. The larder's almost bare."

"Get washed up and come on to the table." She took up the few side dishes she had prepared and placed them on the table, adding water to five mis-matched drinking glasses. She finally brought the chicken to the table. She had used an old recipe, adding bare roots and herbs with the last of the potatoes and carrots to bake around the bird.

"Who wants a leg?" she asked, knowing she would have to use part of the wing for Jackie in order to satisfy her three children's desire for a leg. Too bad a chicken only had two, she had often pondered, but almost giggled at the silly notion today. A chicken can't have three legs and a tiger can't change his stripes and a bum will always be a bum. She carved Clint a large part of the breast and transferred it to his dinner plate, ladling on the rich gravy she had made just for him after a quick walk down to the creek this afternoon. His gravy was in a separate pan on the stovetop.

"This is a welcome sight after the day I've had," Clint said, shoveling food into his eager mouth. "Sheriff Hurst had a nerve, the way he was up there on the road to boss us all around like hired hands today. We're volunteers, I keep saying, not getting no pay for this job, and he better leave well enough alone." Clint followed this pronouncement with a huge spoonful of corn and beans, followed closely with half a biscuit. Lovey watched him. He had a greedy appetite. Even when he was drinking heavily, he ate well. She supposed that was one reason his body was so strong.

"Pass me some more of that gravy, Shug," Clint said. "It's the best you've ever made."

"I'll get it," Lovey said, taking the bowl from Melinda as she passed it and returning it to the table. Picking up Clint's plate and adding more chicken, Lovey returned to the stove to cover it with gravy. "This in the pan will be warmer.

"You're not eating, Lovey?" Clint watched her as she fluttered around the room.

"I will. You know I can't eat much after I've cooked." She took a small bite of chicken, chewing slowly around the broken jaw that still ached. Clint was almost finished with his plate and she hopped up again to bring the simple yellow cake over to the table and cut a slice for him. She had added brown sugar icing to it and knew it would be tasty. It was Clint's favorite and she was happy to oblige.

Chapter 79

L ovey stirred after a restless night and studied Clint there in the bed beside her. It was still dark outside and the room was cool. He lay unnaturally still in the pre-dawn light, his face white and stiff, and she knew he was gone without moving toward him or checking for breath. His head was thrown back and his mouth wide as if he had struggled for his last breath during the darkness of the night.

She had dreamed of so much more. She had once loved him so much her body hurt just to look at him. And when those strong arms of his had wrapped around her and he touched her, her ripe body had opened without question. It was as if her mind had no say at all. Then she had grown to hate him and that had caused her physical pain too, but in a different way. She hated her body when it betrayed her at his touch. Now it was over. She had known for a while that it would come to this terrible end.

Not knowing how long she lay and watched him, but not moving in the growing light through the window, her body had grown stiff when she heard the children stirring. She quickly rose, threw on an old blue robe, and went upstairs, but stood in the doorway quietly watching her girls. Melinda, almost thirteen, was so tall as to appear grown. She was mature and serious natured while Deloris was more nervous and fearful. Jackie seemed the happiest. At eight years old, she was still delighted with the world.

Melinda was reading at the small desk placed in front of the single window as the younger girls giggled over paper dolls on the bare floor, dressing them in paper clothing cut from old newsprint and Sears and Roebuck catalogs. "Girls, hurry and get dressed. Melinda, I need you and Deloris to run over to the Riley place and get Mr. Riley to come help me."

"What's wrong?" Melinda asked as she looked at her mother with worried blue eyes that seemed gray in the dim light. She lay aside the book as the younger girls became quiet in their play.

"Clint's dead." Lovey saw no reason to soften her words until Jackie started to cry. Then she regretted her sharp tone. Of course the little one had loved him as he was the only father she remembered. She pulled her close. "It'll be okay, honey." She patted her on the back and then lifted her and cradled her slender body in her arms, reaching to tuck a stray hair behind her ear as the child sobbed against her shoulder. "We'll be all right." She repeated the words as much for her own comfort as the child's.

The older girls ran out the door to do their mother's bidding without another word. Lovey paced the wooden floor with Jackie cuddled in her arms, the child's legs wrapped tightly around her mother's waist. Jackie snuffled more quietly against her mother and finally settled as Lovey sat down with her, worry and hope mingled together. She was alone but not afraid. She was a strong woman and would make her way in the world somehow. There would be no insurance money this time but something would come up to save her. It always did.

KATIE AND LOVEY
Christmas Day 1999

Chapter 80

This group was dangerous and would do as they said but Katie wouldn't hesitate to run if she got a chance – once she led them away from Lovey's. To her surprise, only her jeep sat in the drive and she walked toward it – assuming they would use it. Instead, Regina pushed her ahead and she followed the men along a path down to the river. Katie pulled gloves from her coat pockets and put them on. The freezing rain felt even colder along the river bank and her fingers were numb.

Katie was prodded toward the right as they arrived at the river's edge and the group walked a path along the shoreline to where a boat was tied up, secluded from the cabin road by a grove of cedar trees. The group led her aboard where a moaning young man lay on his back on the bench seat along one side of the top deck, his eyes fixed on the gray metal sky above without seeing. His eyes were glazed and sweat and rain water mixed and poured off his face. He shivered.

"What happened to him?" As she looked back to Regina for answers the men moved to the front of the boat, preparing it for a run. She leaned over the man, just a boy really. He couldn't be more than seventeen.

"He was shot in the leg last week. It's just a flesh wound and we got the bullet out okay but then his leg started swelling up and it got those red streaks. He started running a fever and shivering like this last night. I don't think he can hear us anymore." Regina came to stand by them and looked to the sky.

"Which leg? It must be badly infected." Katie patted down the boy's legs until she felt the swelling in his calf. As her hand came closer, he winced. She retreated and wrapped the blanket more tightly around his neck. "He needs a hat for his head – he's losing too much body heat."

"You got to save him, doc. He's my baby brother."

"Who shot him?"

"The fool was snooping around our new fields of operation and got caught from the home crew. He ran but not before he took a bullet. He ain't even involved in this. Just was in the wrong place at the wrong time."

"We have to get him out of this weather."

"Let's get going, boys." She turned to the front to see what held the others up from starting the boat and pushing off. The men looked down the river behind the boat, slack jawed and eyes wide.

Katie looked up and saw Lovey floating down the river, sitting ramrod straight in her little boat, a heavy quilt wrapped around her shoulders and a fur hat on her head. A large umbrella was gripped in one fist. She looked like a queen sitting in the little boat, rain falling all around her, kicking up ripples in the water.

"Damn," the tall man said. "She's a dang fool, ain't she? You hicks can go to hell and damnation when I get finished here," he mumbled.

The blond man pushed off with a long pole in time to move his boat to cut off Lovey's path down the river. He flung a rope over to her and she took it and held on as he pulled her alongside the larger boat. Lashing the two boats together, he stepped over the side and picked up the little woman and plopped her down at the feet of the hurt boy. The wind caught her umbrella and it went skipping across the river.

"You want to go with us, we can oblige ya, old woman." His face was red despite the cold rain, his anger evident in the purple bubbling up his thick neck. Katie saw a shiver race through Lovey but she held herself still as a statue and her stone-cold eyes meet the icy blue ones of the muscular blond man. He finally turned back toward the front of the boat, shaking his head.

Katie pushed the others aside, knelt in front of Lovey, and wrapped her arms around her friend. "Oh, Lovey. Why'd you follow us? I wanted you to be safe."

"I know sweetie, but I was worried about you too. The phone was dead, so I tried to start your car but I couldn't hot-wire it like I could the old models. Guess I've lost my touch. But I can't let this white trash hurt you." Lovey placed a large weathered hand on top of Katie's head.

"Who you calling trash, lady? I'll show you what I do with trash," the tall one threatened as he turned and threw the remains of his cigarette in the river. He stepped closer. Katie stood to face him, Lovey at her back.

The man stopped where he stood at a command from Regina but they all glared at one another, the quiet unnerving along with the storm lashing around them. So Regina was the head of this little gang, was she? Katie had suspected as much but almost couldn't believe it to be true. No wonder Bobby couldn't accept her suspicions.

Regina pulled her hood closer around her head. Her long hair streaked with blond highlights fell in curls as if she had just stepped from the salon, despite her wet coat.

Katie pushed in beside Lovey on the bench and stared hard at Regina. "I won't do anything for you if you hurt Lovey. Keep her safe and I'll do whatever you want."

"Fine with us," Regina said, again answering for all of them. "We can all work together."

She turned back to her men, nodding to them to helm the boat. "Get us as close to town as you can and we'll walk the rest of the way to the clinic."

The men yanked the rip cord and the boat roared to life. Katie felt hysteria bubbling up in her throat as they raced down the river without effort. Her mind searched for a solution.

Chapter 81

Katie huddled under the thick quilt with Lovey, but they both shivered. The boat raced through the water, throwing up a wake that only made it colder. They had wrapped the injured man as well as they could but he still lay in the open, rain falling in large drops and rolling off his delicate nose. Young and innocent himself, he had been pulled into the crime ring with his sister.

"How much farther do you think it is, Lovey?"

"Not sure but we're getting close. They'll have to put in under the bridge just below Caney Valley Road. It's the only place in town. Then it's a bit of a walk to get to Main Street."

"Are you alright? You look drained of blood and I can't tell if it's from the cold or not?" Katie put her finger on Lovey's pulse.

"Don't worry none about me, missy. We got bigger problems How we getting out of this fix. I think Bobby will come looking when you don't show up?"

"Maybe. We had a little spat last night so he might not."

"But, I…"

"What you two whispering about back there? Not planning to take a swim in the river to get away from us, are you?" Regina tittered at her own dark humor.

"No. I want to take your brother to the clinic. He needs help and I won't desert him but you must let Lovey go. Her pulse is low and thready. This excitement is too much for a woman her age to bear. Did you know she'll be one hundred years old next week?"

Regina left the front of the boat and stepped closer. "So, whoop to do. She's had a good long life, hasn't she?"

Lovey threw off the quilt and stood up in the boat. "Stop talking about me like I'm not even here, both of you. You always were a little shit, weren't you Regina. Some might say you 'went up Fool's Mountain and stayed too long', but I think you're just selfish and self-centered by nature."

Regina snickered. "I guess you would know all about that. You've got a history in these dark mountains too, old woman. From what I've heard, you weren't always so lily white yourself."

Lovey shook from head to toe, and Katie couldn't decide if it was from the cold rain or pure rage. She stood up beside her and took her arm, ready to protect her against Regina.

There were more houses coming up along the river bank so they must be getting closer to town.

"I think we're close, Regina. Help me look for the landing," the driver called back.

Lovey took a step forward, causing Regina to step back. When Regina turned to look for the boat dock, Lovey gave her a tiny little push. Regina tottered at the side of the boat for just a few seconds, trying to catch herself before she fell over the side.

Lovey roared with laughter as the young woman went under the water. When she surfaced, her hair was a straggly mop around her red face. The blond guy immediately jumped in to help her. The water wasn't deep here so there was no chance of drowning but they might catch pneumonia.

"Get ready to run, Katie. You need to get away while you can as soon as he docks the boat." Lovey stood close to Katie and urged her forward as the tall man steered the boat toward the dock.

"What about you? I can't leave you and you need me here with you. When we get to the clinic, I'll call for help then. I have a panic button and a camera in the office."

"You do?" Lovey nodded her head. "I knew you were a smart cookie."

"I put it in after I learned about the drug gangs operating here. Medical clinics are vulnerable to drug thieves." She pulled Lovey close and wrapped the quilt around them.

"Besides, I have to help Jeffrey. He needs immediate attention if he's to survive.

Chapter 82

Regina climbed up the riverbank with the help of her blond fellow. They both looked like a drowned mess that had been rolled in the mud and Katie tried not to smile. She pulled Lovey back to the bench where they had sat, trying to make them both appear meek and mild. Katie snuggled close.

The boat bumped against the decking as the driver hurried the landing. He jumped off to tie up the boat and then came back for them. He pulled them to their feet and prepared to march them off the boat. "Come on, you two. No more funny business. I can't guarantee Regina won't kill you for what you did, old woman. She doesn't like to be shown up like that." His voice was gruff but he smiled slightly, one crooked tooth visible.

Regina and the blond man stood shivering on the river bank as a group of men came out of the woods with guns raised. "Put up your hands. The jig is up." Katie would recognize that voice anywhere. Her heart soared with love for him.

Katie and Lovey raised their hands high as the officers rounded up the gang and hand-cuffed them. A van pulled up to load them and take them to jail.

"Take care of Jeffrey, Bobby. He's hurt." Regina shot daggers at the two women who stood alone as she was led away. "And tell the kid I love him. Sorry he didn't get his Christmas with me."

Bobby's deputy stepped forward with silver emergency blankets to wrap around Katie and Lovey. Bobby went aboard to check on the boy still lying in the rain. "Is he alright, Katie?"

"He will be but he needs to go to the hospital as soon as you can get him there. And maybe Lovey should go be checked out too. She's had an ordeal."

Bobby turned to radio for medical help. "Hush your mouth, child. This is the most fun I've had in ages."

Katie had to laugh at her. At her age she supposed the woman knew her own mind and body. She wouldn't push too hard.

Bobby walked back to where they stood under a grove of leafy trees. "So, you saw my note on the door, Bobby? I knew you would."

"But it looks like you started without me, Miss Lovey. Couldn't wait, huh?" He teased her. "Do I need to deputize you?"

Katie looked at both of them for an explanation of the events.

"I saw the boat early this morning and knew the group was up to something. Bobby said he would come and check it out as soon as his mother could get there to watch Mathew."

"I think I was already there snooping around when you left to follow Katie. When I came up to the cabin and nobody was home but Katie's jeep was there, I heard a splash and came running to the water. I knew something was wrong."

"Imagine my surprise when I saw Miss Lovey rolling down the river, pretty as you please. I came back up then and saw the note she had left me. I followed you all the way down the river on the bank back behind the trees as I radioed for help."

Katie leaned back against a wet tree. "I sure wish I had known that – it would have eased my mind a bit."

"Looked like you were in good hands with Lovey in control."

As the ambulances arrived and they loaded the young boy in one, Lovey agreed to go be checked out. "But I'm fine you know. I just want to give you two a minute to set things right." She grinned as the stretcher was wheeled away with her sitting up straight, a blanket covering her legs and another around her shoulders.

Bobby and Katie were finally alone in an alcove of large trees along the shore. Bobby put his arms around her and pulled her close, into the sheltered cocoon. His body heat warmed her and protected her from the strong wind and lighter rain that now fell. She stopped shivering. She lay her head against his strong shoulder and sighed.

"So, are you ready to love me, yet? Or should I rescue you a few more times."

Katie pulled away. "Oh no, you didn't rescue me."

"Really? I've been tracking that boat all morning for you."

"You were after that drug gang and I just happened to be part of the package."

"Maybe but I still saved you from those criminals."

"You didn't have to. I had a plan." Katie still argued until he pulled her against him again.

"I'm sure you did. I think you're a bit like Miss Lovey, strong and stubborn."

"Turns out I'm more like her than I knew but I'll tell you that story later. My plan would have totally worked." She snuggled against him. "I am glad you came when you did. After Lovey pushed Regina in the water, I thought we both might be dead before we even had a chance to get to the clinic."

"I'll always do everything I can to rescue you, Katie – whether you need it or not. Cause I love you, girl. And so does my son. What do you say about that?"

She looked up into his open honest face. "I love you too, Bobby."

A smile broke his face apart and his eyes misted. His mouth came down to cover hers and he held on to her as if he would never let her go. She felt safe. She was truly at home.